SHIFT OF RULE

SHIFTER LORDS

S.E. BABIN

CHAPTER

One

I sat at the top of the jacaranda tree watching Caelan's Keep. Two weeks had passed in total silence, neither of us reaching out to the other. Him because I'd accused him of terrible things. Me because I'm a coward.

I'd seen Garrett a couple of times because of Thalia. She stayed away from the store, rightfully assuming I wasn't ready to talk to her, but she had a coffee habit she couldn't break and frequented the Mer coffee shop.

Garrett had popped his head in once a few days ago, speared me with one of his trademark intense looks, barked out, "Stop being an idiot," then left. His words had pissed me off at first, but I missed Caelan, and, as much as I hated to admit it, he was right.

Thus, me sitting in a tree freezing my wings off in wren form, spying on my fiancé. If I could even call him that anymore.

I'd been in this tree for at least an hour trying to talk myself into flying down and knocking on the door. But what would I say? Sorry for being an asshole? Sorry I didn't trust you and totally flew off the handle and then doubled down?

Or, more fitting, *Hello, my name is Evie, and getting involved with me is gonna be a train wreck. Still want to ride?*

One of the side doors opened. I tucked my wings in and

ducked closer to the branch. My wren form was tiny, and there was no wind tonight, but the Keep was full of wolves with keen senses of smell.

As soon as the man stepped outside and took a step forward, I pegged him as Caelan.

My heartbeat picked up, a rapid hum inside my breast.

He stopped on the small stoop for a long moment, shoved his hands in the pockets of his ragged jeans, and headed straight for the tree I was in.

Shit.

He stopped a few feet away from the trunk, craned his neck up, and lifted his hand, palm up.

"Come inside," he said softly. "It's freezing out here."

I hesitated, wondering if I could wait him out and fly away as soon as he turned his back.

"Evie," Caelan said again. "I know you're there. Come inside."

I rose and flitted down, landing in the palm of his warm hand. He tucked me against his chest and jogged back inside the Keep. I shivered against his hand and waited.

He stayed quiet as he moved through the large house, his heartbeat strong and steady. My mind spun with everything I wanted to say, but every thought tangled up inside me.

It took a few minutes before he walked inside his private quarters, the one he used most often when the Keep was empty of guests. Caelan gently set me on the bed and turned away to pull the curtains closed.

"Shift," he demanded.

I didn't hesitate this time. Being in my fae form allowed me to keep my clothing, which was a huge relief. The last thing I wanted was to be naked and vulnerable in front of him right now.

He leaned against the door and studied me, those stormy eyes I loved so much ringed with gold. I opened my mouth to speak, and my mind went blank. All I could do was stare at him while tears flooded my eyes.

Caelan huffed and sank beside me, pulling me onto his lap. He tucked my head under his chin and held me tight.

"I know," he said, his voice a low rumble against my hair.

He smelled of pine and the earth, of all the things I loved. My fingers clutched his sweater so tightly my knuckles went white. He sent a rough hand through my hair, cupping the back of my head.

"I'm sorry," I croaked.

"We can't do this anymore."

I went still as death, knowing I'd screwed this up, knowing if I came here, it might mean the end…I'd finally gone and screwed up the best thing I had—

He let out a breath and pulled me closer, his breath warm against my cheek. "Evie, that's not what I mean. Letting you go would kill me, but we can't keep breaking apart and coming back together. It makes us weak. You have to trust in me against the forces trying to tear us apart. If you can't do that, we won't make it, and we shouldn't keep breaking each other's hearts."

I nodded. Easier said than done, but he was right. This time, it was me freaking out about everything. But he had lied to me and didn't seem exactly regretful about it.

As if he could sense the direction of my thoughts, he drew a deep breath. "I will never allow your father or anyone else to force me to keep a secret from you, ever again. I am so sorry for my complicity in what happened. I never meant to hurt you, Evie. Protecting my people and protecting you clashed—" He cut himself off and swallowed.

"And I made the wrong choice."

The declaration rang in the silence of the room.

"I love you so fucking much. I want you here with me every single day. When you walked out that door, my heart broke, but I knew I had to give you time, even though it went against every instinct I have not to go after you. I need you to trust me, Evie. You are the only one I want, the only one I need. You are more important to me than everything."

Caelan exhaled and fell silent. I turned in his arms and pressed a desperate kiss to his lips, pouring all my love and regret into the touch.

His hands slid through my hair. I straddled him, both of my palms pressed gently against his face.

"Forgive me," I murmured. "I'm so sorry, Caelan. Everything is coming at me from all sides, and I feel like I can't trust anyone."

"Me," he growled. "You can trust me."

I pressed my forehead against his. Caelan's hands slid up my shirt, his palms spanning my waist. "Trusting anyone is difficult. I'm trying. I'll do better."

He rose, lifting me effortlessly. I wrapped my legs around his waist. Caelan carried me into the bathroom, gently setting me on the edge of the tub. Without a word, he filled the tub with steaming hot water and poured something in from a decorative glass jar.

The smell of jasmine and roses wafted up as bubbles frothed in the water.

I grinned. "You like girly bubble baths?"

His eyes crinkled at the edges. "I like girly bubble baths with you. Simone bought me this a week ago and told me to get you back because I was 'being a massive, growly dickhead.' There's wine and good cheese in the fridge."

I laughed. "You don't have a tub caddy."

He jerked a thumb over his shoulder. "She bought one of those, too. It's in the closet."

Simone always thought of everything. I got up and put together a quick cheese board, chuckling at Simone's selections, plus the wine with the screw top. When I got back to the bathroom, Caelan had already placed the caddy over the top of the tub. He took everything out of my hands and put it on top, then reached for me, nimble fingers unbuttoning my top.

I shivered under his touch, remembering how much I'd craved him when I was having my pity party. But Caelan didn't touch me in the way I wanted. He was quick and thorough, and when I leaned forward to kiss him, he shook his head. "If we don't get in the tub now, we won't make it in there."

His eyes glowed, and I thought about pushing him, but when his eyes narrowed, I reached for him and helped him out of his sweater. And if my hands lingered a little too long over his pecs and abs, I was only a woman, right?

He hauled me against him, a large hand reaching to squeeze my rear end, before he scooped me up and stepped into the tub.

CHAPTER

Two

Cheese and crackers littered the floor and tub of Caelan's bathroom, but I couldn't be bothered to care. We'd lasted ten minutes before his fingers started wandering, and I was helpless against him.

The bed was about a foot away. Caelan and I were tangled together on the floor halfway between the tub and the bed.

"Devil woman," Caelan murmured against my ear.

I grinned. "I wasn't the one who got handsy first."

"Liar. You were handsy before my clothes were off."

"Yes," I said demurely, "but I controlled myself once we got into the tub."

His wicked chuckle vibrated my chest. I gently bit down on his pec muscle. Caelan's hands tightened on my hips. "Careful, unless you want another round."

I popped my head up and peered at him. "Your land needs tending to," I blurted.

Caelan blinked. "Um. Okay. Can we wait until I'm finished here?"

I nuzzled noses with him. "Yes, but I can feel its need. Fee and Poe help a little, but I'm tied to your land now. Wintertime leaves most of the land in slumber, but it still needs care."

Caelan brushed a kiss over my lips. "And you would know best. Alright. We'll go out later tonight and walk the property. Fee is missing you."

Regret panged inside me. "I missed her, too."

He took a deep inhale. "No matter what happens to us, you are always welcome on my land to see them and to care for the property."

I blinked at him. "Caelan. That's…extremely generous."

He cupped my chin. "No matter what happens, it will not be because I do not love you."

I sighed and let my head rest on his chest. "My father isn't answering my calls. He knows I'm onto him."

"Mine neither," he confirmed.

"Mom is trying to stay out of it, but she's furious with him."

"I don't think she's my biggest fan, either, but I'm glad to hear she doesn't like his meddling."

"Mom is no saint, but she's never gotten involved with my relationships. For all her faults, she believes I need to make my own mistakes in love and life."

"As any good parent would do." He rolled, trapping me under him. His eyes had grown serious. "There's something we should discuss."

"I'd rather be doing something else," I said.

His lips quirked. "We'll get to that in a minute."

Caelan nuzzled my neck and gently put his teeth on my collarbone, biting down enough to make me squirm. "Do you want children?"

I froze. "Um."

He licked my collarbone and bit down on my shoulder. "I'm asking because we haven't been careful."

My back arched. Caelan's hand slid up the side of my waist and cupped my breast before he toyed with my nipple. When his mouth replaced his fingers, a moan tore from my throat.

"Fae have trouble reproducing," I said breathlessly.

"So do shifters," he murmured.

His hand drifted down, nudging apart my thighs. "Do we continue on the path we're on, or should we take more care?"

"Birth control doesn't work on me." It made me crazy, but it didn't prevent me from ovulating. Fae were always hesitant to use any form of birth control because of low birth rates.

His fingers slid between my folds. I let out a gasp.

"I would find a child a blessing, Evie. But I would not presume to think you are of the same mind." He slid down my body, his thick hair brushing against my thighs. "This decision is yours. There might never be a child between us, but there is a chance, and you should be the one to say if you do not want one as much as I do."

My thoughts were scattered as Caelan played my body like a fine instrument. I'd never wanted children because of my childhood, but finding out the entire thing was a lie, and I was loved had changed some things.

Maybe I'd never have one. Maybe fae and shifters couldn't procreate, but the thought of having a child wasn't as terrifying as it once was.

He stilled at the apex of my thighs and waited.

"I like the path we're on," I said after a taut silence.

The wicked smile that curved his lips made me smile in return, but when his head dipped, and he put his mouth on me, my hands gripped the sheets tight, and a scream tore from my throat.

Two hours later, I was bundled up in one of Caelan's coats and a pair of sturdy boots Simone had loaned me. Joy Springs was experiencing a colder than normal winter, but we still had no snow on the ground. We had walked most of the property, Caelan waiting beside me as I tended to his land, lending bits and pieces of my power to the earth. A dark, purplish form high in the sky beelined for me, letting out a loud quark. Behind it came an orange and purple flash.

Fee and Poe. I held up my arms for both birds, waiting until they alighted on my forearms before I kissed both their feathery heads.

"Poe miss Evie," the raven said.

Fee hopped onto my shoulder and nuzzled my cheek.

"I missed both of you."

"Happy land," Poe said.

"Almost," I agreed. "There are a few more spots I need to check out."

I stroked Fee with the backs of my fingers. "How's Fee doing?"

The phoenix warbled happily in my ear.

"Happy, happy," Poe said. "Fly high. Magic good."

I blinked. "She's accessing her magic?"

Poe dipped his head. "Heal claw." He held up his small foot and waved it at me.

Caelan's eyes widened.

"Fee! That's awesome! You healed Poe?"

She bobbed her head up and down and warbled again.

"Good girl," I said, but worry filled me. Fee was a phoenix, a legendary bird capable of great magic. Her strongest power was healing, but until now, she'd been unable to use any magic.

"Poe, it's important that Fee stays within the boundaries of the Keep." I glanced at Caelan.

"If the Lord has any injured wolves, maybe he will allow Fee to practice."

Caelan nodded. "Of course. I will call for you if needed, Fee."

Poe croaked. "Fee practice. Fee powerful."

Exactly what I was afraid of. "Want to finish walking with me?"

Poe and Fee both bobbed their heads. "Alright then. Let's go."

We didn't take much longer, and by the time we finished, Caelan's land hummed, content in the back of my mind. I said my goodbyes to the raven and phoenix, watching in delight as they swooped across the skies.

"My mom still doesn't know I have Fee," I remarked on the way back to the house.

"I don't think you should tell her. Not yet anyway. Things are still new, and with all this stuff with your father, maybe you should put both of them on an information diet."

I glanced at him. "Information diet," I repeated, having never heard the term before. "I like that."

His idea was a good one. I'd been far too open with my father because he made me trust him. And I let him. I'd never known my father before recently, and he dazzled me with stories and his power. I saw similarities between us, and I let my guard down too soon.

This didn't discount all the times he'd helped me out, nor did it alter the fact that I was still heir to the fae throne.

Or maybe not with Thalia in the mix. Huh. Interesting.

"Caelan?"

He slung an arm over my shoulders and tugged me close.

"What if I'm not the fae heir anymore?"

Without a pause, he snorted. "That'd be a huge weight off your shoulders, wouldn't it?"

"Yeah," I said in all seriousness. "It would be."

CHAPTER

Three

One good thing about guilt is that I tend to pour all my efforts into work. I'd sat down with my team a few days after everything happened, and we'd come up with a promotions calendar and new designs for Valentine's Day. No one had found out about our relationship blip, so business was still booming. Now that V-Day was fast approaching, we expected to get slammed by forgetful partners desperate for bouquets, so we'd made twenty-five percent more than we expected to need.

Moira lounged on the couch, her long dark hair in a messy braid. She held a cup of tea in one hand and her e-reader in the other. Recently, she'd gotten into this niche romance thing. When I asked her a couple of weeks ago what she was reading, she said something about tentacles and swooned, and that was all I needed to hear before I switched topics.

She was dressed more casually than normal today. Wide-legged cotton pants, a tank, and a long cardigan completed her chic look, but the polka dot fuzzy socks toned down her elegant facade. A pair of lace-up boots sat near the couch end.

Tess was floating near Ash's shoulder, peering at something the dryad was bent over examining. He was patiently explaining something as he held up a leaf with a pair of angled tweezers. Over the past few months, her wardrobe had gone from drab to bright and sunny. Even though we were into February now, she was still wearing cheery and loud holiday sweaters topped with leggings and boots.

Ash looked like he always did. Handsome and well-dressed in browns and greens. His tousled chestnut hair was messy around his face as he focused on the greenery he held before him.

My cell pinged.

You're still marrying me.

A smile tugged my lips up. *Absolutely.*

How about three weeks from now? You, me, someone with the authority to sign off, and an enormous catered feast?

Sold.

The bell over the door rang. I turned and sucked in a breath as a new customer entered. A stunning woman stood just inside the door, tugging off her leather gloves. She was small and curvy, her long hair tumbling over her shoulders in a shiny sheath of amber brown. Her eyes were green and slightly turned up at the edges, reminding me of a cat. An adorable, perky nose, full lips, and high cheekbones coalesced into what seemed like the perfect physical package. She wore a chocolate brown turtleneck sweater and a pair of cream-colored pants, topped with shiny brown leather ankle boots. Gold jewelry, glittering with the occasional diamond and a bare left ring finger told me this woman was single.

Something twisted in my stomach because my instincts were telling me something else. This woman was also here for trouble.

Moira untangled herself and set her e-reader down. She gave me an odd look and smiled at the woman. "Welcome to Little Shop of Florals. How can I help you?"

The woman's gaze flicked up and down Moira's body, immediately dismissing her. "I am visiting a powerful ally and former..." She smirked. "Lover, though I expect to rekindle things very soon. I'm looking for a gift that is befitting a Shifter Lord."

She spoke with accented English, French. Of course, the stunning woman was French.

You could have heard a pin drop in the shop. Ash's tweezers clattered to the table. Tess thumped to the floor with an unusual lack of grace. I stood speechless, my fists clenching by my sides. Moira, as usual, was the first to recover. "You're here to see Lord Caelan?"

The woman nodded. "Yes. What do you have in stock right now?"

She glanced at an expensive golden watch on her left wrist. "I'm in a bit of a hurry if you don't mind."

Moira's eyes narrowed just a hair. "Of course." She motioned her over to the worktable. "If you'd like to have a seat, I'll bring out some of our most popular and some of our more unusual displays. Lord Caelan is an occasional patron of our shop and seems to have a preference for a more…violent sort of flower."

Moira's smile could have cut through diamonds.

Ash coughed.

My feet were still rooted to the floor. Why does the universe hate me so?

My phone pinged again. I reached down and read the screen.

I love you.

My fingers trembled. Trust. I have to trust him.

The woman sat down. Moira gave me a warning look before hurrying to the walk-in. I finally shook off the numbness and smiled. "Would you like a cup of coffee or tea?"

She turned to me. "You wouldn't happen to have any champagne?"

I shook my head. "Sorry. Fresh out." It was ten in the fucking morning, you wretched lush.

She sniffed. "Nothing, then."

My phone pinged again.

"I'll be right at the register if you need me, then."

The woman looked away and studied her freshly manicured fingernails.

I pulled my cell out again.

Do not murder her. And take a deep breath. You don't know where this is going yet.

She's beautiful, I wrote back to Moira.

So? Did you see her turtleneck? She's probably covered in warts.

A smile tugged at my lips.

The door opened. Moira came out holding two large displays, set them on the worktable, and went back in for more.

When she finished, the table was so full of flowers that the woman's face was concealed. Which helped a little, but I could still smell the deep musk of her perfume.

I turned away and let Moira help her, hoping she upcharged her by at least thirty percent.

When no other customers came inside, I hopped out of my seat and went to Ash's table. Tess was in the back, after she passed by the woman with a stare that could have frozen a vampire with fear.

"Hey," he said, his voice so low it was almost inaudible.

The woman wasn't human, but she wasn't a wolf either. Some kind of shifter, but I couldn't peg the type.

"You okay?"

I hadn't texted Caelan yet, and I wasn't sure I would. This was none of my business. Yet.

I gave him a reassuring smile. "I'm fine. I went to see him yesterday, and we're in a good place."

Ash's gaze flicked to the woman. "Alright. You'll let me know if that changes?"

I nodded. "I'm sure you'll know without me saying anything."

"That's what I'm afraid of."

Thankfully, the woman didn't stay long. She chose my least favorite of Moira's selections, one I knew Caelan would hate, and breezed out the door, her sleek hair rustling in the wind when she stepped outside.

No one spoke for a long moment.

"She's cheap," Moira said. "The bitch took the one with *carnations.*"

The horror in her voice broke the tension.

"Did you tell Caelan?" Ash asked.

I shook my head. "He'll find out soon enough."

Moira's lips thinned. "You can't catch a break."

I lifted a shoulder in a weary shrug. "Either the universe hates me or my father isn't done trying to break us up." Both were likely scenarios.

Ash shook his head. "I'm sorry, Evie."

"Not your fault. No one's fault." I slapped on a smile. "We'll see how it goes, I suppose."

All I could hope was that I could power through this disaster without losing my mind or my temper.

Simone burst into the office, her face white as a ghost.

"She's back!" she blurted, waving her hands around like a maniac. "Run. Leave. You can't see her!"

I set my pen down and stared. "Who's here?" I said calmly.

Someone needed to be calm. My usually unflappable Omega was beside herself. Her blonde hair was ruffled, her eyes were wide, and she was pacing back and forth like a military general.

"Rachel."

I stilled, the name sending an electric shock of horror through my body. "Rachel who?"

I needed clarification. The last name would decide whether I relaxed or if I shifted and went for a very long run.

Simone met my eyes, her lips pressed tight. "You know who."

My fists clenched, claws stretching out, ripping through the paper notebook I'd been writing in. "Why is she here?"

Simone sagged against the doorframe and pinched the space between her brows. "Hell if I know. One of our sentries spotted her pulling up the drive."

I squeezed my eyes shut. Rachel was the daughter of a powerful European lord, and what was supposed to be a youthful dalliance between us had turned into something furious and toxic. I'd fallen in love with her against my better judgment, and it took years for me to get her claws out of my heart.

If she were here now, she wouldn't be bringing good news with her.

The steady thump of Seymour's pot tore me away from my intrusive thoughts. I reached out for him, and the flytrap sailed through the air to land in my palm.

Simone snorted. "I do not know how he does that." She frowned. "You may need to change his pot soon. He's getting too big for it."

Seymour waved his traps in agreement.

I snuggled him against my chest. Not sure how it happened, but me and the sentient, sometimes aggressive flytrap had become buddies. "What do you think?" I asked. "You want racing flames down the side of the next one?"

He smacked me with one of his traps.

Simone smirked. "It seems our Seymour prefers a more elegant home."

"Millennial greige?" I asked.

If a plant could sigh, Seymour would have.

Simone pushed away from the door. "We have to greet her. Garrett isn't here right now, so I'll stand with you."

"Can't we just throw her out?"

My Omega's eyes glittered. "If you don't mind causing an international incident, sure."

I sighed and pushed my chair back, gently setting Seymour down as I stood. "You have to stay here for now. I don't want you to bite Rachel, okay?"

Seymour hopped off the desk, forcing me to catch him. "No," I said gently. "She's awful, but she's important. Plus, I don't want her to know about you."

I set him down once more. "We'll keep you as our secret weapon, okay?"

The flytrap thumped a few more times before he settled down.

I gave him a gentle pat on the head and motioned Simone out the door.

"Does Evie know?" she whispered.

My steps hitched. We'd just gotten back on track.

Simone winced. "Oh Caelan."

"I'll call her right after this meeting. Or whatever the hell this is," I grumbled.

Simone said nothing. Probably for the best. No matter what I did, I always seemed to screw things up. Logically, I knew it wasn't all me. Evie had an opaque, sometimes indestructible wall up, and I wasn't exactly great with boundaries.

Mostly because few people refused me.

And that was something I'd think about later.

Rachel's arrival, though? Curveball out of left field.

There was no reason for her to be here, and to show up without announcing a formal visit was shady.

Right before we stepped into the foyer, Simone grabbed my arm and leaned in close. "You are still single to the world and a Shifter Lord. Rachel has always been power hungry. Take care with your words and actions and do not get us into another Gianna situation."

She huffed a breath. "I do not want to get on Evie's bad side. She's terrifying."

I snorted and leaned away. "I'm well aware of her temper. You do not need to worry."

Simone gave me a long look before she nodded. She was around during the Rachel years, and trust me, I did not come out of that mess looking like a knight in shining armor. More like a mercenary who'd somehow managed to escape a nuclear bomb.

I squared my shoulders and opened the door.

Rachel sat on the blue fainting couch, one leg over her knee. Her hands were crossed on her lap, and she wore a faintly amused expression. A server had given her refreshments, which she hadn't touched.

Seeing her again was a punch to my solar plexus, and not in a good way. She was as beautiful as she was the day I'd finally broken away from her, and she oozed elegance and wealth. Her hair was a sheet of silk tumbling over her shoulders, and her green eyes were just as calculating as they used to be, maybe even more.

Her painted lips curved into a carefully crafted smile. "Hello, Caelan," she purred.

Simone stepped in behind me. Rachel's gaze flicked to my Omega's and back to me, her smile less warm than it was just a moment ago.

My Omega stepped up and offered her hand. "Simone," she said. "We've met before."

Rachel shook her hand in that limp way of one with too much self-importance. "You were Caelan's little friend."

The emphasis on the last two words missed their mark because Simone was familiar with all of Rachel's tactics.

"I am now his Omega." Simone's smile brightened. "If you're having trouble controlling your emotions while you're here, Caelan will call on me for assistance."

Rachel's eyes narrowed. Bullseye.

She'd always had a control problem, one overlooked and excused by her powerful parents.

"But feel free to call on me yourself, if you're able to." Simone stepped away and poured herself a cup of tea from the tray on the other table. She raised the kettle at me, but I shook my head.

I wanted Rachel out of here and sharing a drink with her wasn't on my list today. "Rachel," I said without preamble. "Why are you here?"

Her lips turned into a pout. "What kind of welcome is that?"

"The welcome I reserve for unwelcome guests who don't call in advance."

Her eyes flickered, the amusement in them guttering. "Being Lord does not seem to appeal to you," she said after a long silence.

"Being Lord is fine." I leaned against the opposite couch. "It allows me to deal with nuisances any way I see fit."

Rachel sucked in a shocked breath.

Simone gave me a warning look, but I didn't back down. "State your business, Rachel. A Lord does not schedule around your whim."

She blinked in surprise, her hands trembling as she reached for her teacup. I knew for a fact she hated tea, and she was using the cup as a crutch so she could get her emotions under control.

When I first walked in, she smelled of satisfaction and pleasure. Now, her scent had turned a little sour and fearful. She needed something from me and wasn't pleased I'd called her out. Rachel liked arriving at things her way and didn't like to be reminded she was at anyone's mercy.

I was happy to remind her. Seeing her again stirred no fond memories. We had none together. Only mutual destruction. Once, I'd wanted her more than anything in the world. She wanted everything else. Power, fame, money, status, all the things I'd never cared for much, those were the things Rachel worked toward.

I was Lord because I was too powerful to be anything else. Rarely did I access those powers, preferring to save them for when they might be necessary, but I could access them at any time. Rachel had no idea how close she walked the line between death and freedom.

I could crush her with a moment's notice, and a small part of me wished to. Wiping her off the face of the earth would save a lot of people in her orbit heartache and destruction. Rachel was a user, a creature so self-absorbed she didn't care who she took down on her way to the top.

I'd become Lord to stop people like her, and yet, here she was sitting on my couch and drinking my tea. The irony of it left a bitter taste in my mouth. Walking away from her was the hardest thing I'd ever done.

I never thought she'd darken my doorstep. Yet here she was.

I crossed my arms over my chest and waited for her to lie to me.

"My father sent me here with a warning of rogue shifters trying to infiltrate packs all over Europe. He's convinced some of those rogues are coming from America."

I knew all about the rogues and knew my Pack had none. "Try again."

Anger rolled over Rachel's eyes. "It's true."

I lifted a shoulder in an unconcerned shrug. "Perhaps, but it isn't the complete reason you showed up. A message like that could have been sent via email or phone call."

Rachel huffed. "You know my father hates modern technology."

Another tactic of hers. Trying to humanize her family, so I'd soften my stance. "Your father has been using email for the past thirty years and you know it. He's also been in several of our last video conferences. This is your last chance to be honest. If you lie to me one more time, I'll throw you out myself."

Her green gaze landed on Simone. "Can you ask your Omega to step out?"

"No," I said shortly.

Rachel blinked, unused to being refused. "Do you trust me so little?"

"Yes." I flicked an impatient hand.

Rachel rose in a liquid move and slunk over to where I stood. She reached out a slender hand tipped with burgundy manicured nails and was about to press her palm against my chest, when I snatched her wrist and held it two inches away.

"No."

She clicked her tongue. "Scared, Caelan?"

I let the gold shine through my eyes, a slow grin curving my lips. "Not at all. More like taken."

Her nostrils flared. "Who?" she demanded.

At that moment, one of the part-time butlers came through the door carrying a massive floral display, seasonally appropriate, but filled with carnations.

I almost smiled even as dread filled me. Evie would have judged Rachel for this order. Knowing the shifter before me, she'd already told Evie who she was and where she was going.

I'd have to do more than call her when this was over.

"I apologize for the interruption," the man said. "Your guest was so kind as to bring this as a gift."

Simone let out a little choking noise, recognizing Evie's work.

"You've already met her," I said.

Rachel's eyes narrowed. The butler set the display on the table and backed out of the room, his eyes down. I couldn't blame him. There was a lot of tension in this room.

Most of it coming from my pissed off ex-lover.

She let out a bark of laughter a second later. "That tall, lanky vampire?" Rachel snorted and pulled her hand away. "She doesn't seem like your type."

Funny how she assumed Moira was the more dangerous of the two. "Not the vampire. The other dark-haired one."

Rachel stared at me for a long moment. "The stupid one?"

One moment, I was standing there staring down at her. The next, my hand was wrapped around Rachel's throat, one second from snapping her neck.

I leaned in close and quietly said, "Speak that way about my fiancée ever again, and they'll never find your body."

Rachel stank with fear. She swallowed and gave me a short nod. "Fine."

I released her and stepped back. "State your business and leave."

Her eyes flashed with anger. "I'm afraid my father has requested I stay for a while." She offered a thin smile. "You should have received an email from him already. If not, before the end of the day. I'm sure you won't mind hosting me for a while."

Simone's lips tightened. Her request was a tricky one. If I

wanted to avoid offending her father, I'd be forced to put her up in one of the extra rooms in the Keep befitting her station.

But if I wanted to avoid being impaled on the end of a sharp tree limb when Evie got wind of this, I'd refuse.

I'd chosen wrong the last time, but this one was Shifter business. I couldn't afford to start a war with the European Lords. Fuck.

"For now, Simone will show you to temporary quarters. Do not get too comfortable."

Her full lips parted in a satisfied smile. "I look forward to catching up."

I very much did not.

CHAPTER
Five

My father sat on my front porch when I got home from work that evening.

I walked up the steps and opened the door, juggling my keys and a few bags of groceries. Cernunnos took two of the bags and followed me inside.

"Set them on the island, please."

I tossed my purse onto the table by the door and went straight to the kitchen. Dinner would be a simple, comforting affair. I rarely made this because it was fatty and cheesy, and I tried to eat as naturally as possible, but it was colder than usual outside and some of the restaurants had closed early.

"Hope you like enchiladas and mac and cheese." I started unpacking the groceries.

Cernunnos gave me an odd look. "Together?"

"It's better than it sounds."

I was still furious at him, but I could share my meal. He was my father, and I couldn't just write him off. I wanted answers, though.

I chopped a shallot and set it aside for a can of enchilada sauce. As I cooked, my father took a seat at the island and watched me intently.

"Do you ever cook for yourself?" I asked.

He blinked in surprise. "Erm. No. I have people for that."

I snorted. "Don't you worry they'll try to poison you?"

Cernunnos frowned. "I wasn't until just now."

Royalty. So smart and yet so clueless. "You probably have poison sniffers you don't know about."

"My chefs have been with me for years. I don't worry about it too much. Why do you enjoy cooking?"

"Well, first of all, I don't have 'hire a private chef money.'"

My father rolled his eyes. "You do."

My hand stilled in the act of stirring the cream into the enchilada sauce. I'd forgotten about this supposed account he had for me. "You were serious about that."

"Evangeline." His tone was chiding. "You are my daughter. Of course I'm serious about providing for you. I will send Birch over later with the pertinent details."

"I have money." My voice sounded a little more petulant than I wanted it to be.

"Never said you didn't." He smiled. "But you now have private chef money."

"I like cooking. There's something therapeutic about taking something in its rawest form and transforming it into something else, something delicious that provides comfort and sustenance."

My father's face softened. "Spoke like a true Floromancer. Life begins as a seed and produces some incredible things, does it not?"

I thought of the massive jacaranda tree still blooming in Caelan's yard. "It certainly does." Once the pasta water was on, I softened the onions and added the ground beef, seasoning the mixture as I thought about when to chew my father out for his actions.

The conversation could wait until after dinner.

Dad and I made small talk as I made him a bowl. I'd discovered the recipe several years back, gave it a hesitant try, and ended up loving everything about the dish. Seasoned ground beef with a little sauteed shallot mixed into a heavily seasoned enchilada, cream, and cheese mixture, and poured over the top of elbow pasta sounded weird but tasted like heaven.

We carried over our bowls and drinks and settled into the living room. The house was a little cool, so I pulled a blanket over my lap.

Dad took a bite and grunted in surprise. "This is delicious."

"Thanks. It's one of my go-to comfort meals."

"I can see why. Maybe I'll pass the recipe to my chef." A sly grin curved his lips. "I tire of greens for every dish. This would give the poor man apoplexy."

"Can you source ground beef in fae?"

"I can source anything I wish to."

"Ah yes," I said dryly. "With all your private chef money."

Dad laughed. The sound warmed me, almost making me forget I was pissed at him. We ate in companionable silence after that, and when the meal was finished, and I'd poured us another glass of wine, I curved my hands around my glass and studied him.

He sighed. "Have at me, Evangeline. Your disapproval shimmers through the air like fairy lights."

I stared at him over my glass, thinking of all the questions I wanted to ask, all the things I wanted to say to him, but none of it mattered except for the most important one. "Why?"

Surprise flickered over my father's face. He'd expected something else. An emotional outburst, maybe? I was way too tired for those.

He leaned back in his seat and steepled his fingers together. "I'm afraid I must ask the reason for your anger."

I rolled my eyes. "You're stalling. Trying to come up with an answer that won't make me kick you out of my house? You know exactly what you did and why I'm pissed off."

"You're the future queen of every fae walking the worlds."

"And that means you get to dictate my life?'

My father's face went blank. "It means you are required to

choose a suitable match, one who holds as much power as you do. One who will keep our bloodline—"

The glass snapped in my hand, wine flooding down my fingers and onto my lap. "If you say pure, you and I are finished."

Rage brought the Chimera roaring to the surface. My breath became shallow, my heart beating furiously in my chest.

My father tilted his head. "Rest easy, Evangeline. You are not completely fae, remember. I was going to say 'compatible.'" He gestured toward the window. "Our bloodlines are tied to the natural world, though your mother is also tied to death. But your bloodline is more complicated. No fae blood has ever been tainted by the Chimera."

He winced at his word choice before I could judge him. "'Tainted' is the wrong word choice. What I'm saying is your Chimera blood should be impossible, and yet, we know it is not. You and the person you choose—"

I cut him off. "Caelan. I choose Caelan."

A muscle in his cheek twitched. "Will be compatible no matter what. But you are not thinking far enough into the future. It's possible your children will experience...defects."

I stared. "Excuse me?"

"A Chimera isn't a true shifter. Their blood is pure magic. A true shifter has one animal form and is half beast, half human. Some shifters have magic due to dilutions of their bloodlines, i.e., an ancestor marrying a witch or other paranormal species, but most only have their innate shifting magic and enhanced senses and physical prowess." My father leaned forward. "I'm explaining so you understand the potential ramifications of breeding with a shifter."

I squeezed my eyes shut so I wouldn't stab him with a flower stem. "Breeding?"

He waved a hand. "You've been with the humans for far too long. Procreation, then, if the word prickles you. If you have a child with a shifter, your blood might make something... monstrous. Something neither of you can control."

"I don't want to control my children." But the words sounded mulish to me. Children required maybe not control, but discipline when they were young. Especially those who held magic in their blood.

"You must. You are borne from two powerful bloodlines, Evangeline. With the Chimera thrown into the mix, you must realize how dangerous procreation can be with another shifter."

"Is this why you sent someone from Caelan's past back into his life?"

The pause told me everything I needed to know.

"Sometimes a challenge is necessary to examine the mettle of a man," he said cryptically.

"Or you could just stay the hell out of our business."

"You're the heir. Everything you do is my business."

I glared at him. "Speaking of being the heir, that's not quite true, is it?"

My father sighed and studied his fingernails. "Thalia is defective."

I sucked in a breath. *"Dad."*

"There's no use sugarcoating things. A seer can never hold the throne. Someone like Thalia serves best by being at the ruler's side."

"So you can use her to hold onto your throne."

"Again, my dear, you are thinking like a citizen and not like a queen."

I bit down angry words. I'd never sacrifice my sister's life to increase my power base, so he was right. I was still thinking like a citizen rather than a queen. A true ruler should be a citizen and should think like the people do. Otherwise, what was the point?

Cernunnos stood. "I can see how angry you are."

Past the point of anger, actually. I was a screaming teakettle of rage. "Call off your dogs, Father."

"Ooh, we're at Father now. Not Dad?"

"A father donates genetic material. A dad anticipates each of his children's needs and acts accordingly. They nurture and nudge. A father sends an old lover to tempt his daughter's fiancé. A dad might think of a decision as a mistake, but he'd deal with it."

"You are poised to take over a kingdom of bloodthirsty monsters, Evangeline. You don't need a dad right now. You need a father."

Thunder rumbled in the room, and he was gone.

I sagged against the back of the couch. Children had never been at the forefront of my mind. I never thought I'd find anyone I could trust enough with my secrets. But things were different now, weren't they?

Yes, but could I in good conscience give birth to a monster, one who'd never stand a chance in the world of the living? Could I chance it, even knowing it might never happen?

I picked up a pillow and threw it at the door. Life was a lot simpler when my day consisted of making fun of people who went too carnation-heavy in their bouquets. Now I had enemies on all sides and was worried about world-ending spawn birthed from my loins.

I needed a drink.

CHAPTER
Six

The first indication something wasn't quite right with Moira came when a puff of smoke appeared from the tips of her fingers. It was almost faster than the eye could catch, but I happened to be standing over her shoulder, watching as she attempted to match a moody dahlia color palette to the woman's wallpaper.

We had the occasional wealthy client who had to have everything just so, and we did our best to accommodate them, but the wallpaper was a new one. Moira attempted to hide her fingers but gave up when she caught my raised brow.

"Is that a new thing?"

She sighed. "Over the last few months."

I counted back in my head. "How many are a few?"

She'd been resistant and avoiding a conversation about her burgeoning powers and refused to acknowledge anything had changed. I didn't press too much, knowing if I did, she'd clam up for even longer.

The smoke was an interesting development, though.

"Can you control it?"

She shrugged a slim shoulder. "It only happens in moments of high stress or emotion."

"You're stressed about something?"

Moira slumped. "It's nothing."

I gestured at her fingers. "The smoke says otherwise."

"It has nothing to do with you or anyone else. This is my burden to bear."

My eyes narrowed. "All three of you have been with me on this crazy ride for months now, and none of you had to be. You, most of all, have shared all this bullshit."

Moira's eyes softened. "So now it's your turn to share my bullshit?"

"Exactly." I flicked my fingers at her. "Now spill it before we get busy."

Moira let out a little laugh, rose, and locked the shop door.

My eyebrows went up.

"Things start out manageable," she said. "I've summoned plants—"

"Cool."

She gave me a withering look. "Not cool. They weren't from earth."

I blinked.

"Sometimes I get rocks, sometimes weapons." She sighed. "I have no idea what's going on, but I can't seem to stop whatever is happening."

She held her fingers out and twisted her wrist. "Whatever this is feels...large." Her brow furrowed.

"Can you stop?"

She shook her head. "I've been fighting it all morning. Whatever this is wants to come through."

A frisson of nerves zipped through me. "Should we go outside?"

"It's never too big," she tried to assure me. "Mostly inanimate except for the plants."

Thunder cracked through the shop. Darkness crawled along the ceiling, shadowy veins creeping down the walls.

"Um," I said eloquently.

A swirling portal opened above our heads. Before I could swear and dive out of the way, something fell through and landed on the ground with a bone-jarring thud.

Thunder cracked one more time before the darkness zipped back up the walls and disappeared with a disturbing pop of sound.

Moira stared at the ground, horror written all over her face.

A naked man lay unconscious on the store floor.

Ash pushed through the doors from the back and stopped abruptly, blinking in surprise at what Moira had summoned.

"Errr," he said. "Do we need to call the police?"

Moira's mouth worked, but no sound came out.

"No police," I said. "Moira brought him here."

Ash's brows flew together. "Naked?"

"Summoned somehow," I shook my head. "He looks human."

Ash let out a breath, put down the flower arrangement he'd been holding, and crouched beside the prone man. He placed two fingers over the stranger's pulse. "Alive. Thready heartbeat."

"Interdimensional travel will do that to you," I said dryly.

Moira let out a panicked squeal. "What did I do? Ohmygods, ohmygods."

I put a hand on her shoulder. "Breathe. As soon as he wakes up, we'll figure this out."

She closed her eyes and took in a deep breath.

"Good." Internally, I was freaking out, but someone had to be calm because there was a freaking naked dude on our floor, and we had customers starting to mill outside the door. They couldn't see in very well, but the Joy Springs rumor mill was alive and well if someone spotted the guy.

"Help me," I said to Ash. "I'll take his feet, you take his shoulders. Let's get him inside the office. Moira, stand in front of the door and wait until you hear us call out the 'all okay' before you open it up to customers, okay?"

She stared at me.

"Okay?" I asked again.

Moira blinked. "Um. Yes. Sure. Got it."

I sighed and picked up the man's tanned legs, averting my eyes at the rest of him. Ash smirked. "You don't want to turn him over first?"

"Absolutely not."

Ash reached down and scooped him up under the shoulders. The position made carrying the stranger more difficult, but I did not want a penis flopping around in my shop. It was bad enough that a penis was *exposed* in my flower shop.

I grunted as we lifted him from the floor. He was heavier than I thought. "Straight back to the office," I said. "And hurry."

Shadows fell into the store as some curious customers tried to peer in only to see Moira frantically waving her arms around to distract them. "Open in just a couple of minutes. Sorry! We had a bad spill and needed some cleanup."

We rounded the corner and slipped out of sight.

Once we had him situated and covered with a blanket, Ash called out to Moira. I stared down at the unexpected company.

"Moira summoned him, you said?" Ash ran a hand through his chestnut hair when he shut the door. "She's never done something like that before, has she?"

"Never."

"He's not human."

"I think he might be fae or some type of nature being. His magic has a fae feel to it."

Ash nodded. "Not a dryad. I'd know."

The man was leanly built and chiseled. His face was almost unearthly beautiful, tanned, and perfectly sculpted. Perfect patrician nose, long amber lashes, and messy hair that held several different shades of blond and light brown. His skin shone with a golden glow.

Everywhere.

Oy vey.

"Someone should stay in here with him so he won't freak out when he wakes up."

"I'll do it," I offered. In a strength test, I'd beat Ash every time. He had his own share of gifts, but mine had changed over the years.

Plus, shapeshifter. I could subdue him if I needed to.

"Call if you need assistance." He grimaced. "Should we close early?"

I sank into my seat and closed my eyes. "Let's try not to. People are starting to whisper about financial trouble."

Ash rolled his eyes. "Dating a Lord is good for business until it's not."

"Truer words have never been spoken."

A grim smile touched his lips before he slipped out the door, leaving me with a handsome stranger I had no idea what to do with.

My life had a way of keeping me on my toes these days, and I wasn't sure I liked it.

I MUST HAVE DOZED off for a while, curled in my chair. Silence had fallen, the kind of quiet that raises the hair on the back of your neck. The kind of quiet the darkness preferred.

I pulled magic to me.

"I wouldn't do that if I were you," a deep, masculine voice said.

My eyes opened. Golden naked guy had my blanket wrapped around him and knotted low on his hips. If he wasn't holding magic at the end of his fingertips and staring at me with my death in his eyes, my attention might have lingered a little longer on his six-pack because he was *pretty*. His hair was mussed, and his eyes glowed with a strange violet light, their depths swirling with flashes of pink.

Definitely fae.

I held up my hands. "You're in my flower shop. My friend accidentally summoned you."

He blinked. "Summoned? I am no *demon*."

"Yes, well, a hole opened in the ceiling, and you fell through, so…"

His eyes narrowed. "You are lying."

"Swear to the gods, I'm not. We're just as freaked out as you are." I touched my hand to my chest. "I'm Evie. Ash and Moira are outside in the shop area. There's a banshee who works with us, but she isn't here today. If you tell us where you're from, we can help you get back."

The magic in his hands sparked and died. He sank onto the couch and let out a long breath. "You truly didn't intend to bring me here?"

"Nope. And neither did Moira. We have no idea who you are."

His lips twitched. Silence stretched between us. "You may call me Lou."

My brows lifted. "Lou?" When I thought of the name Lou, I thought of 1950s Vegas and mob dealings, not someone who looked like a supermodel Olympic swimmer.

"That's my name, Lady Evie."

I snorted and reached for my cell. "I'm no Lady, sir."

Ash knocked on the door less than thirty seconds after I shot him a text. He held a small bag in his hands. "Brought this for our guest."

Lou stared at the bag with suspicion.

"Clothes," Ash clarified. "Clean and mine. I thought you might want to wear something other than Evie's blanket."

Lou reached out for the bag. "Thanks."

Ash nodded. "The shop closes in ten minutes. We should all chat afterward." His gaze rested on Lou. "Would you like some tea or coffee?"

He shook his head. "No, thank you. I should get home before people notice I'm gone." Lou grimaced. "Though I have no idea where I am."

"Joy Springs," Ash supplied. "A small town in Texas run by our local Shifter Lord."

Lou's brow furrowed. "Your what?"

His accent had the crisp sound of the United Kingdom, but most regions had their own Shifter Lords. "Where are you from?" I asked.

Those strange eyes rested on my face. "I can see from your face you know that I am fae. And I can tell by the magic humming from your body you are one of us, though your magic has a strange flavor reminiscent of our missing gate and something else I can't put my finger on."

I stiffened. While it wasn't exactly a secret that I was the one who'd destroyed the World tree, very few realized I could function as a gate between the fae and human worlds. The power wasn't one I knew how to use exactly, but I could send people where they needed to go if I concentrated hard enough.

Since he'd confessed to being fae, I could send him back right now if I wanted to, but this was Moira's screw up, and I wanted her to see if she could learn to control the magic flowing through her. If she couldn't figure out how to send him back, I'd have to step in, and trust Lou wouldn't blab about my ability to anyone who asked.

Funny how trust was the one thing that usually got me into a whole lot of trouble, but it also happened to get me out of quite a few scrapes, too. "I am the product of mixed genetics," I said with a thin smile.

Lou chuckled. "Aren't we all, my dear?"

Ash gave me a warning look. "Ten minutes. Then we'll talk."

When he left the room, I crossed my arms over my chest. "Are you going to cause any trouble?"

Lou laughed, a bright, merry sound. "We are strangers! Why would I want to cause trouble for you?"

He sounded innocent. Too innocent.

"Because you're fae," I grumbled.

Lou laid a hand over his heart. "I am wounded."

"Go put some clothes on."

Lou grinned, a touch of heat in his smile. "Does my nakedness disturb you, Evie?"

I pressed a thumb to the middle of my brow. Men. They were all the same.

"Eight minutes," I snarled as I pointed to the small restroom tucked into the back of the office.

The fae laughed out loud but carried the bag into the bathroom.

I'd forgotten all about Caelan for a while. Turns out, dropping a naked fae from thin air was a good distraction from one's troubles.

But now, I wondered if Lou might be another addition to our trouble.

It seemed like our errant fae didn't want to return home. This was his first time "earthside" as he said, and he quite liked the look of the shop and the outside.

We sat around the small seating area in the shop, gaping at him.

"Let me get this straight," Moira said slowly. "You popped out of thin air into a strange place with no clothes, no money, and no identification, and now you want to stay a while?"

Lou shrugged. "It has been far too long since I've had an adventure. And this..." he swept his hand out, "is more of an adventure than I'd ever hoped to find."

Ash let out an exasperated breath. "Why haven't you come here before now?"

"I never had a reason to, I suppose. It's easy to never leave home unless you have to. Home is so cozy and warm. But now that I'm here, I find I want to see more."

"You have no money!"

Lou laughed. "I am fae. We always have money."

"If the Shifter Lord catches you passing sticks and leaves off as currency, you will find yourself in more trouble than you can imagine," Moira murmured.

"I will be long gone before then," Lou assured us.

"And the shop owners you've duped?" I asked.

He shrugged. "They should expect no better from the fae."

Ash's expression darkened. "And fae like you are the reason why. Many of those shop owners you seek to cheat are fae or descended from your people."

Lou's eyes flicked to me. "And her people." And back to Ash. "And yours, though the dryads do not love being grouped in with some of the fae."

"Regardless," Moira said. "Stealing is wrong."

"You stole me from my garden," Lou said, his lips twitching.

"That was an accident!" Moira huffed and crossed her arms over his chest.

Lou held his hands up in surrender. "Fine. I promise not to dupe or steal while I am here." He laid a hand against his heart. "I swear it upon my honor."

"We have no idea who you are," Moira grumbled. "So how do we know you have any honor?"

I put a hand on Moira's arm. Saying something like that to certain fae would be a mortal slap to their honor. Thankfully Lou only stared at Moira, an amused tilt to his lips.

"You'll just have to trust me then, won't you?"

I did not like this. Not even a little bit. But what could I do? And who was I to begrudge a fae who'd never been here the opportunity to sightsee?

"Fine. Three days."

"Seven," Lou fired back.

I barked a laugh. "Not a chance."

"Six then."

"Three. Any more and you'll need to report to the Shifter Lord.

I'll notify him of your presence. Do not be surprised if he goes looking for you."

Lou's eyes narrowed. "Five."

"You want to report to him yourself?" I shrugged. "Fine. I'm still telling him you're here, though."

"Done. Five days hence I will return to your shop for transport home." He rose. "I will return your clothes at that time, Ash. Thank you for your unusual hospitality."

"That's it?" Moira blurted. "You're not angry or upset that I brought you here?"

"At first, sure," Lou said. "Until I began to see this as an opportunity."

"But I can send you home right now," Moira argued.

The tremor in her voice told me she wasn't so sure she could.

"I'm sure you can," Lou said, his eyes sparkling. "Since I'm here, I'd like to see what this big wide world is all about."

"Alright then. Five days. No more."

Lou grinned. "I'll find your Shifter Lord faster than he'll find me."

And with those ominous words, Lou snapped his fingers and disappeared.

"I don't have a good feeling about this," Ash said, echoing my own thoughts.

"How much harm can he do?" Moira said.

Ash and I both sent her matching incredulous looks.

Moira groaned and put her hands over her face. "I know. I'll call Hazel tonight and see if she can help."

Ash nudged her over and sat beside her. "Fae magic hit you a few months ago. During Evie's transformation at Caelan's."

The words were not a question. Ash must have seen what happened.

There was no way to forget that night. I'd transformed into the true Chimera form, the mythical beast with dragon wings, and killed Finn and Rhona. Magic had been flying all over the place that night.

Moira nodded miserably. "I thought it was fine. And it was for a while. But odd things started happening a couple of weeks later."

"And they're getting worse," I added.

"Yes," she said with a sigh. "This power isn't going away, and I have no idea what to do." She waved a hand in the direction where Lou had disappeared. "And I certainly can't keep doing that! Who knows what I'll bring through next time."

"All that means is we need someone who can help you learn to control the magic. I was in the same boat not too long ago." Things weren't perfect with my magic, but they were way better. For the most part, I had a handle on things, but I still needed guidance.

Enter Barrett. Handsome, annoying, and adept with Chimera magic, as he was one. We had yet to have our first official training session since both of us were still trying to clean up the mess with the swans and figure out where they were holding a male Chimera.

To Barrett's credit, he was far busier with that than I was, but I did pass on information after picking Caelan's brain about where they might have stashed the missing Chimera, and I ensured I was aware of my surroundings at all times. Nadia might be out of the picture, but the swans wouldn't stop until they saved their people.

Unfortunately, they saw me and my intact womb as their savior.

"Evie?" Ash's brow furrowed. "We lost you for a minute."

I shook the dark thoughts away. "Sorry. I was thinking about Barrett."

Moira grunted. "How's that going?"

"Very little progress on that front," I said with a laugh. "But let's get back to you. Barrett can't help, but this town is full of people who can. I can ask my father, too."

Ash tilted his head. "You don't seem enthused about that, either."

"He's being…difficult right now."

"Typical dad stuff?" Moira asked.

If typical dad stuff was bringing an old lover around to tempt your current one and trying to force you into a crown you didn't want, sure. "I wish. I'm heading over to the diner later this evening to take care of the plants. I'll ask for recommendations."

Moira stared down at her hands. "I wish I could get rid of whatever this is."

Ash slung an arm over her shoulders. "Maybe you'll learn how to start pulling really cool things from other dimensions. Like alien rabbits."

"Or something just like chocolate! You could start a craze and become a billionaire."

Her lips tugged into a smile. "Sure. I'll share my wealth with you."

"Sold," Ash said. He pressed a kiss to Moira's temple. "Try not to worry. If Evie can get the Chimera under control, you can stop pulling men from thin air."

"Thanks for the vote of confidence," Moira said dryly. With a long sigh, she stood and straightened her sweater. "I'm going home. It's been a long day."

I stood and reached for a hug. "I'll text you later."

Before she pulled away, I gave her a little squeeze. "Don't worry. Lou just wants a little time to explore. Who knows? Maybe he'll discover Sirena's gelato, and she'll distract him for the next four days."

Ash grinned and pulled out his phone. "Great idea. I'm texting her now."

The first real smile in hours reached Moira's eyes. "I'll see you tomorrow."

When she was out the door, and it was only Ash and I left, he slumped against the couch. "Lou's going to be a problem, isn't he?"

I nodded. "I suspect so. Caelan won't want an unknown fae

running around Joy Springs unsupervised. I'll talk to him this evening."

"I'll reach out to my people as well. Dryads see everything."

"Let me know if you hear anything. I'll do the same."

With that agreement, we worked quickly to close up the shop. As I was driving to Caelan's a little while later, I couldn't help but feel a strange sense of doom creeping over me.

Disturbed, I shook it off before adjusting the mirror to fluff my hair before heading inside the Keep.

CHAPTER
Eight

CAELAN

Simone had shown Rachel to the guest quarters farthest away from my own quarters. Parts of the Keep were maze-like, so that should keep her busy for a while. When Simone returned, she collapsed into the seat across from my desk.

Seymour thumped over and launched himself into her lap. Simone snorted and stroked the top of his trap. "Never thought this monster could be more like a dog than a vicious, venomous pain in the ass, but he's turned out to be pretty cute."

Seymour bumped her with his head.

"Who needs a dog when you can poison your enemies via plants?"

She laughed but sobered. "Rachel is going to be nothing but trouble."

"I'm more aware than you know," I murmured. Getting her thorns out of me was one of the most difficult things I'd ever done.

"Evie won't like this."

"She understands political relations more than she wants to admit. Her father has been busy training her as well."

Simone rolled her eyes. "Yes, but she's still a woman and your fiancée. No matter how much she understands, she won't like it."

My jaw clenched. My Omega was right, but I was in a tricky situation. "I can't risk alienating Europe. I'm already on thin ice with the other Lords and am walking a tightrope with fae relations as well."

Simone gave me a look. "You chose wrong once before. If you keep putting politics above Evie, you'll lose her."

I threw my hands up. "I'm well aware. There has to be a balance, and so far, I've yet to find one. Evie keeps refusing her crown, but when she finally steps up to her heritage, she will be in the same boat I am."

My Omega laughed. "I don't think there's a force in any of the worlds that can make Evie do something she doesn't want to do."

I rubbed my hands over my face. "Then what would you have me do?"

Simone shrugged. "Start by figuring out the real reason Rachel is here. Make sure Evie knows your hands are somewhat tied, at least for now. Do not meet with Rachel without someone else to bear witness. She can and will complicate your life more than you even realize if she gets her hooks into you."

"I'll call her father tomorrow." The European Lord wasn't an unreasonable man, but he'd never liked me all that much. Perhaps that would encourage Rachel to leave as soon as possible.

Simone's phone chimed. She looked down and chuckled. "Speaking of Evie. She's outside."

My heart leapt in my chest for two reasons. First, because every time I saw her felt like the first time. Second, because she was absolutely going to chew my ass over Rachel staying here.

My Omega saw my expression and let out a merry laugh.

"Shut it," I growled.

She stood and gently set Seymour down, giving him a final stroke over his traps. "This is what you get for loving an independent girl."

I sighed and picked up Seymour before following behind her. "Evie has had enough of everyone's shit to last her three lifetimes, but the hits just keep coming."

Evie wore casual clothes—jeans and a puffy jacket. Her dark hair was loose around her shoulder, and her nose was pink with cold. She grinned when she saw me.

I snagged her around the waist and pulled her inside. Her breathy laugh made me want to hug her tighter.

Evie waved at Simone when I set her down. "Hey! I'm glad you're both here. There's something we need to chat about."

Simone's eyebrows rose. "You met Rachel earlier."

Evie rolled her eyes. "I did. She said she was on her way to see Caelan."

I winced.

One of her eyebrows rose. "I take it she was true to her word?"

At the worst moment, Rachel poked her head around the corner. "Oh, hello." Her perfect brow wrinkled. "You're the florist, right?"

She goddamned well knew Evie was far more than just a florist. But Evie didn't even stutter. "Florist and Caelan's fiancée." A thin smile. "Since you're still here, I assume you're taking advantage of Caelan's hospitality. The Keep really is a wonderful place. I spend lots of my free time here."

Rachel blinked.

Pride filled me. *That's right. Your mean girl charms don't work on real women.*

I brought Evie in closer, holding her tight to my side. "Dinner is in a few minutes. Can you stay?"

Evie nodded. "We can talk after dinner." She glanced at Rachel. "In private."

Two high spots of color appeared on Rachel's cheeks. Evie smiled and brushed past her, tugging my hand to follow.

And I did. Like a happy little puppy.

Dinner was an awkward affair. Rachel tried to snag the chair closest to me, only to receive a not-so-subtle hip check from Simone. Evie rolled her eyes and sat next to me, twisting the knife by scooting her chair a little closer.

Rachel's nostrils flared as she took her seat on the opposite side of the table, next to Simone.

"Garrett is coming," Simone said once we were all situated.

I hid my smile.

"Thalia will be with him," she added with a twinkle in her eye.

Evie stiffened but relaxed a moment later. Thalia's relationship to Evie threw a wrench in our relationship due to my keeping Cernunnos's secret. The Fae King hadn't wanted Evie to know for whatever reason, but she'd found out and was pissed I hadn't told her.

We were both right, and we were both wrong. Fortunately, we'd worked it out.

Only for Rachel to abruptly show up out of the blue. I swear, it felt like I couldn't win these days.

Evie reached over and took my hand under the table. My shoulders dropped from my ears.

We were still okay.

The first two courses were eaten in relative silence, Rachel casting odd glances Evie's way every so often as if she couldn't quite figure her out—the same way most people looked at Evie when they first met her. Simone wore an amused expression, but her eyes glittered with ill-concealed violence. She wanted a piece of Rachel, and the other shifter was completely clueless, too vain and entitled to realize she danced on the edge of violence.

Most shifters never attained the level of cluelessness Rachel currently exhibited, given that Packs were often savage and dangerous places if they had the wrong kind of Alpha leading them. If a shifter wanted to survive in a Pack like that, they never let their guard down.

A few still existed in the U.S., but most of the Lords put cruel Alphas down. But even if an Alpha was fair and just, it was never a good idea to get too relaxed. Dominance challenges happened every day.

By not being aware of the danger Simone presented, Rachel was edging toward a violent line. But Evie had no such compunctions. Simone would wait and act with the behavior expected from one of Caelan's Pack members. Evie would throttle Rachel with a vine the first chance she got.

A smile played upon my lips.

The doors opened then, announcing the presence of my Enforcer. Garrett was leanly muscled, his body a weapon—the better to hunt down our enemies—but his mind was even sharper. Looking at him without knowing him, you might see the scars flecking his hands and arms, the way his eyes never missed a thing, but you might miss the gleam of intelligence in his amber eyes.

And those gleaming eyes had just landed on Rachel and narrowed with suspicion.

Simone must not have told him the reason why she'd summoned him to dinner.

His lips tightened for a brief second before he turned to me and dipped his head in acknowledgment. "Lord."

"Second." I gestured to the seat next to me. "Just in time."

Garrett sat and acknowledged Simone with another nod. When he spotted Evie, his eyes lingered. "Thalia sends her regards. She's working this evening and cannot attend."

Rachel hadn't taken her eyes off Garrett from the moment he walked in the door. "You've grown up," she murmured.

Simone sighed.

Evie sipped her wine, her eyes resting on Rachel's face.

A server appeared as if by thin air and filled Garrett's glass. "I was immune to your charms then, just as I am now," Garrett said.

Rachel's nostrils flared.

"Strike two," Evie murmured and smiled

Rachel's nostrils flared, a thin golden sheen ringing the irises of her eyes.

"To what do we owe the pleasure of your visit?" Garrett asked after he'd taken a sip of his wine.

Rachel demurred. "My father wishes for me to explore the world more."

"I wouldn't think he would ship you to a Lord's house knowing how busy their respective territories are. Caelan does not have time to babysit guests."

Simone choked on a laugh.

Rachel sucked in a breath. "I do not require babysitting, Second. And you should mind your tongue."

A slow, savage grin crossed Garrett's face. "You are in the house of the Texas Lord. If anyone needs to watch their mouth, it's you." He set his wine glass down and leaned forward. "Now why don't you tell us why you're really here."

An hour later and we were still no closer to finding out the real reason Rachel had randomly shown up at my door. She had succeeded in annoying every single one of the servers, and Simone was glaring daggers. Rachel would be lucky if she got out of the room without someone plunging a knife in her back.

Evie seemed completely at ease, which was unusual for her. I couldn't sense a single thread of tension emanating from her. For all intents and purposes, she seemed completely unbothered by my new guest.

I wasn't sure how I felt about this. Did she not see Rachel as a threat? If not, I'd be relieved. The only threat Rachel posed was to herself. She and I were over and had been for years. Rachel was a complication, but not one I couldn't handle.

Simone toyed with the napkin in her life. "When are you scheduled to return home?"

Her voice was suspiciously sweet.

Rachel's eyes glinted. "I don't have a return date as of yet. Father wants me to take in the sights."

"The sights?" Garrett snorted. "We're in Joy Springs. Our population is small and our goods are artisan, but this is not a world-class destination. We have no amusement parks, no malls, and none of the big city charm people look for when they're researching places to vacation. We're a one-day destination at most, a quaint, small town where you might get some of the best jam you've ever tasted, but with zero night life."

Simone nodded and tipped her glass in a salute. "Exactly. We really could use a few bars around here. Instead, everything closes by nine, most by eight. If you're looking for fun, Rachel, you're in the wrong place."

Rachel rolled her eyes. "Once I leave Joy Springs, I'll be on my way to Austin. But I have no plans to hurry through my visit here." Her eyes landed on Caelan as a wicked smile tipped her lips up. "I'm sure I can find at least one thing here to distract me until I'm ready to leave."

Evie stiffened. My hand tightened on her thigh. "It sounds easy for you," she murmured.

Rachel smiled. "Oh? What's easy?"

Evie's azure eyes glittered. "Your willingness to open your legs for any male who gives you a hint of attention."

Garrett barked a laugh and tried to turn it into a cough.

Rachel's eyes blazed with fury. "Are you calling me a whore?"

Evie laughed, a sharp crack of sound. "There are two men here this evening and you've all but bared your chest to both of them in the space of half an hour. You'd think you'd be a little more circumspect in mixed company."

Rachel bared her teeth. "And you'd think our Lord would have better taste than trying to wed a mongrel."

Fury roared through me. "Enough!" I pointed at Rachel. "Leave the table. Now."

Rachel pressed her victim button and reacted the same way she had every single time someone reprimanded her for her behavior. Her lower lip wobbled, and tears swam in her bright eyes. "Caelan, I meant no harm by my words. I was only responding to her insults."

Evie snorted.

"Your response to my fiancée was to fire back and insult both of us. I am well equipped to choose my own bride, no matter what you might think of her blood."

"Evie is royalty," Simone said quietly.

Evie's attention snapped to my Omega, her eyes burning with anger.

Simone gave her a sympathetic look and shrugged in apology. "She should know who you are so she knows how to behave around you."

Evie shook her head. "Someone like her will never check her behavior because no one has ever held her accountable for a single thing in her life."

Rachel opened her mouth.

"Do not say a word," I commanded, sending Simone a withering glare. "Evie is royalty and holds high standing in my home. Even if she did not hold the position she does in the fae court, she would still be welcome in my Keep. Who I date or do not date is none of your concern, and if you bring it up one more time, I will personally have you escorted off my land, your father be damned."

Rachel dropped her eyes but not before I saw two pink spots of fury appear high on her cheekbones. "Of course. My apologies, Caelan."

I waited for the other shoe to drop, but she kept her mouth shut, seemingly cowed.

If she really was, this was only temporary. I squeezed Evie's hand one more time and rose, tugging her up to stand beside me. Rachel's lips tightened when I slid my arm around her waist. "I trust you can find your own way back to your quarters," I said to her. "If not, Simone or Garrett can show you the way."

Garrett bared his teeth, and Simone stared at Rachel, death glimmering in her eyes.

Evie huffed a laugh.

Rachel did not respond, only stared with a sullen expression.

"Good." I nodded and led Evie away from the dining area.

CHAPTER

Nine

The urge to strangle Rachel with a pothos vine stayed with me for the entire walk to Caelan's study. His soft laugh told me he knew exactly how I was feeling.

This felt different than Gianna. The swan shifter hadn't wanted Caelan. She only wanted his power. This woman…I think she wanted both, and that was enough to send a burning thread of fear into my heart.

When the doors shut and Caelan pulled me against his chest, I melted into him and sighed. "She's awful."

"I'm well aware," he murmured.

The rhythmic thump of ceramic on wood made me smile. I pulled away from him and held my arms out, waiting for Seymour to launch himself from the edge of the desk.

His traps opened wide as he sailed through the air. I laughed and caught him, hugging him close when he landed in the circle of my arms. "Hey."

Seymour bumped me with his main trap and made an odd clicking noise.

I grinned and held him out at arm's length, studying the way his roots tumbled over the edge of his pot. "Hmm. You need a bigger pot again."

Seymour waved his traps at me.

"Maybe Caelan will let you come home with me. You can hang out in the greenhouse while I work."

"I'm sure we can arrange a visit," he rumbled.

Caelan reached over and plucked Seymour from my hands. "It's getting late. You need to go to bed. Evie and I have a lot to talk about."

That clicking noise turned annoyed.

Caelan chuckled and carried him over to a spot by the window. There was a mister, some fertilizer and—

"A cat bed?" I laughed.

Caelan's smile turned sheepish. "He likes it."

"And a blanket?"

Caelan tipped Seymour's pot on its side and covered the flytrap with a blue flowered blanket.

I covered my mouth with my hand so he couldn't see me grinning.

He bent down and murmured a few words to Seymour before he straightened.

"Aren't you worried about the dirt in his pot spilling?"

"I keep extra in the cabinets and fill him up when he needs some."

I might explode with the cuteness of it all. "He doesn't need to lie down."

The sight of him tucking Seymour in for the night was so adorable I wanted to lean over and squeeze his cheeks.

"He likes it," Caelan grumbled. The first time he did it, I thought the pot tipped over by accident, so I lifted him back up, only for him to thump right over again. The next time I reached for him, he growled at me."

I'd created Seymour out of anger and fury at Caelan's behavior and ended up creating something never seen before. The Red Dragon flytrap had somehow become sentient and was evolving into not quite a pet, but something. A companion, maybe.

Once Seymour was settled in, his traps turned away from us and facing the window, Caelan gestured toward one of the sofas. After I kicked off my shoes and sat, he settled beside me, pulling my legs onto his lap.

I leaned against the edge and sighed.

"She won't be here long," he rumbled. "I'll ensure it."

"Why is she here in the first place?"

His expression darkened. "She won't come out and say. Rogue shifters are becoming an issue across the world, and she claims she's here because of them, but she's lying."

Caelan shook his head. "Whatever the reason, I don't think it bodes well."

I agreed. Caelan's fingers dug into the arch of my foot, sending a delicious ache through my body. "She wants you."

The Shifter Lord sighed. "Evie—"

"I trust you," I said hurriedly. "I know we've had our issues, but I can't help but think this situation is different from Gianna. She's here because she has her sights set on you, for whatever reason. And with the history between you, she sees you as an easy catch." I eyed him. "I don't know everything that went on between you, but if there's anything I need to worry about, I hope you tell me now. I'd like to avoid flying off the handle again."

I gave him a somewhat sheepish smile. He was wrong to keep Thalia's heritage from me, but I should have also understood how much pressure he was under from my father. Caelan couldn't think only of himself or me. He was a Shifter Lord, responsible for thousands of shifters all across a swath of the country. And with Donovan's territory still in dispute…

"Rachel is a viper," he said to my relief. "I'd rather cut off my arm than be involved with her again."

"Then I think you should assign someone to keep a careful eye on her. Can you get her out of the Keep without an incident?"

He sighed. "Protocol is allowing her here for five days. Then I can move her to local lodging."

Five days could be a lifetime with a toxic presence living in close quarters. Rachel could do a lot of damage in less than a week if left to her own devices. "Maybe you should make yourself scarce during that time."

A flash of teeth. "Are you inviting me to stay over?"

My blood thrummed. "Always."

Caelan's deep chuckle made me grin. "I can't leave for the entire five days. Things are still unsettled with the Lords."

After the events of a few weeks ago, Caelan had finally exploded. I didn't know everything that had gone on, but I hadn't seen a Lord around since then, and none of them had contacted me or tried to force my hand in any way. The breathing room was a long time coming, but Caelan's actions had led to a rift between him and the other Lords.

He'd been totally justified in standing up for me, but it had cost him. "Are they coming in?"

Caelan nodded. "Rowan is coming in late tomorrow. Soren is due in the morning."

I clicked my tongue. "He didn't tell me he was coming!"

Everyone knew I had a soft spot for the handsome Lord. Rowan's powers were similar to mine, and we'd clicked over our shared love of all things plant. He'd given me some wonderful cuttings of apple trees and gorgeous flowers, and I'd gifted him with a few things he'd never seen before. There was a long-standing invite for me to visit his property, but I hadn't yet taken him up on it because of everything I had going on here.

"He wanted it to be a surprise." The growl in his voice made me smile.

I eyed him. "Don't be jealous. You know Rowan and I are only friends."

"That's because of the boundaries you've set. If you gave Rowan an opening, he'd drive a semi right through it."

I wasn't so sure of that. There was something between us, but it wasn't the roaring bonfire Caelan and I had. "I hope he brings me more cuttings."

Caelan snorted. "I'm sure the pretty Lord will bring lots of gifts for you."

I grinned before remembering why I'd come tonight. "We had an unexpected visitor today."

His eyebrows rose. "Oh? Do I want to know?"

"I'm not sure. Back when Rhona and Finn and my mother showed up on your property, you remember the amount of magic flying around?"

Caelan grimaced. "How could I forget?"

"Some of that magic hit Moira and has coalesced in unusual ways."

His attention sharpened. "What kind of unusual ways?"

I rubbed a hand over my face. "A portal opened up in my shop and a fae fell through the roof."

Caelan blinked like an owl. "I'm sorry. What?"

In a world of magic and shifters and Chimeras, I dealt with unusual things every single day. But the portal was an unusual occurrence. Topped off with Moira being able to flick a wrist and boom, naked fae dude getting yoinked through space was a little bit unbelievable in the scheme of things.

"Do you need a moment to form a picture in your brain?"

Caelan tweaked my toe and snorted. "Sometimes these words come out of your mouth that shouldn't make sense, and yet, I do not doubt that your strange vampire friend summoned a fae who fell through a portal in your shop."

"I bet I could kick total ass if we ever decided to play two truths and a lie," I said off-handedly.

Caelan let out a long breath. "No doubt. Who was he?"

"Said his name was Lou."

"Lou?' he repeated. "Like an Italian Lou?"

"He didn't look Italian. He was very pretty and had fae magic clinging to him."

Caelan's eyes narrowed. "Pretty?"

I waved a hand. "Pretty in the way that all the fae are. Too perfect."

"Go on." A ring of gold shone through Caelan's irises.

"He asked to stay for five days."

"This just gets better and better," he muttered. "Did you tell him he was required to check in?"

"I did. He said he would find you. Whatever that meant."

I could almost see the wheels turning in his mind. "Did he seem powerful?"

"Hard to say. Some fae can hide their power signatures." I was one of them. My tattoos had been repaired and hid the truth of what I was, and for some reason, they seemed to affect my fae power signature as well. Not a bad thing, considering whose daughter I was, but if other fae could hide their power in a similar way as I could, Lou could be anyone.

"Do you think he's here to harm anyone?"

I slowly shook my head. "He seems more curious than anything." It was the truth, though curiosity in the fae and gods had caused more harm to humans than any other force in the world.

I could only hope his curiosity stayed with food and drinks and women rather than meddling in any of the other hundreds of things that could make life go sideways for us all.

I t was too damn cold for gelato, but only a fool passed up a dessert made by a siren. I tasted no magic in the confection, but sometimes sweet treats held their own innate magic, no fairy dust required.

Moira and I sat on a bench by the food truck area, bundled up in coats, hats, scarfs, our gloved hands clutching our cups.

She'd chosen the rocky road, but I'd gone for the salted caramel walnut. La Sirena Gelato sat a few feet away, the siren owned truck painted a soothing blue. Celestial themed doodles were hand painted on top of sea foam swirls, and a constantly changing menu was tacked to the side. We'd chosen mundane flavors this evening, neither of us willing to risk the sometimes-unexpected effects of some of Sirena's magic.

"Have you seen Lou?" I asked her.

Moira stabbed her gelato with the colorful spoon she held. "Neither hide nor hair."

"No news is good news."

Moira slid me a glance. "Seriously? You of all people can't believe that."

I didn't. I'd found over the years no news meant whatever it was would creep up and bite you hard on the ass when you least expected it.

"We can at least try to keep a positive attitude," I said glumly.

Moira snickered. "I haven't heard a thing. Everything seems normal."

A shiver of unease rolled down my spine. "Good!"

My voice sounded chirpy and upbeat, but Moira knew me well enough to know I was just as nervous as she was.

"Are you ready to chat with her?" I asked after a moment of silence.

We hadn't come here for just the gelato. Sirena was an ancient being filled to the brim with knowledge about old magic. When we'd gone up to the food truck, one of her new assistants had helped us, but the siren had pinned us to our spot with a look and held her finger up.

"Soon," she said ominously. "Do not leave."

We both knew better than to disregard Sirena's instructions. She might appear to be the benevolent owner of a gelato truck, but she was ancient and could probably kick our asses with one hand tied behind her back if she set her mind to it.

Well...maybe not me anymore, but she could probably give me a run for my money.

Moira set her cup down and rubbed her hands over her jacketed arms. "She'll come out when she's ready. I'm half convinced she's making us sweat on purpose."

"Who's sweating?" It was fucking cold out here today.

"On the inside," Moira grumbled. "Sirena is scary as hell."

"It keeps all the sailors under control," a voice said from behind us.

Moira squeaked in fright.

The siren laughed and came around to face us. With a wave of her hand, sparkles appeared, and a small, pink chair covered in what had to be diamond dust surfaced from thin air.

She brushed her flowing skirts away and sat down. The siren was so beautiful she could cause a traffic jam. With night-black hair, sea-foam green eyes, and a body filled with dangerous curves, one might dismiss her for a gorgeous nymph at their own peril. Sirena was stunning, but she was also graced with a deadly intelligence and years of experience with all the power players in the magical space.

And for some odd reason, she liked us both—as much as someone like her could like anyone. Sirens were a little understood race. Everyone knew their voices were the source of their power, but how it worked was a closely held secret. If she wanted, she could lure someone to their death with her voice. But if she ever deigned to sing, Sirena could lure the entire town into walking off a cliff. People wisely stayed on her good side, us included.

"You've been naughty," Sirena said, her full lips curving as she studied Moira.

"Accidentally," Moira grumbled.

"Doesn't matter to me. But you've unleashed a power neither of you expected." Her green eyes flashed. "And for that, you will experience great sorrow."

I stilled. "Sorrow?" I echoed.

Sirena didn't look at me, though. All her attention was on Moira. "Tell me, vampire who is not just a vampire, could you feel what you grasped when you held it?"

Moira's brow furrowed. "I'm not sure what you mean."

Sirena's eyes narrowed. "When your hand opened and that power brushed your skin, did you know what you were pulling through?"

Moira slowly shook her head. She swallowed hard. "No. I—I felt something, but I couldn't stop the power from grabbing it—him."

Moira's shoulders slumped. "I can't seem to control what I touch and...whatever this is just pulls it through."

Sirena sat back in her soft pink, diamond crusted chair and studied Moira for a long moment before clicking her tongue. "You've been touched by the fae." She took Moira's hand in her own and ran her fingers over the vampire's palm. "Normally, a human will brush off such exposure through time, but your magic…" Sirena shook her head. "You already had a touch of the fae in you. Something in your magic craved this power and reached out for it. Whatever happened, it's permanent now."

Sirena let go of her hand, and Moira curled her fingers into a fist. "Can I learn how to control whatever this is?"

"Of course," Sirena said. "But it will take time and effort and extreme will. This magic is greedy. It craves."

When they fell silent, I asked the question that had been bothering me since everything had happened. "Who did Moira bring through?"

An unamused laugh came from Sirena's throat. "Who?" She shook her head. "Who is not the question you should be asking. What is the right question?" Her eyes glowed sea-foam green. "What have you unleashed on Joy Springs?"

My stomach clenched.

Sirena's lips pulled into a grim smile. "You are here to ask me to help you, no?"

Moira nodded. "Or send me to someone who can."

"No need for that. I will help. For a price."

I stifled my sigh. Good neighbors weren't really a thing in fae culture. No fae did a clean favor. They always involved a price, whether or not one could pay. Sirena's eyes slid to me, amusement sparkling in their depths.

"One day, I will require your assistance. Moira and you, shapeshifter."

I froze. How could she know the secrets simmering in my blood?

Her lips quirked. "When that day comes, you will ask no questions and come to aid me."

Moira's eyes narrowed. "I won't do anything illegal."

"No one asked you to," Sirena said.

"Yet," I snapped.

Sirena rolled her eyes. "You forget Joy Springs has much

different laws than the human world. I will agree that it will be nothing illegal under our laws."

"And no killing," Moira added.

"Now that, I cannot agree too."

I scoffed. "You can't honestly expect us to agree to murder."

"No one said that either, stupid girl."

I opened my mouth to argue.

Sirena held up a hand. "If you have to kill, be assured it will be someone or something who richly deserves it. Now, will you agree to those terms?"

I could see Moira's thoughts all over her face. Not like I have a choice.

"I will agree," I said finally. Moira needed the help.

"Fine," Moira said, with much less grace than me.

Sirena laughed and clapped her hands. "Good. Come to me in three days' time. Meet here at seven p.m. I will show you what you are, and I will show you how to control your new gifts."

With that, the siren stood. "Now, before I take my leave, I have one more question for you."

Moira and I stared at her expectantly.

Sirena's irises went full-on cerulean blue. Her voice changed and strange magic swirled around her curvaceous form. "Have you seen your banshee lately?"

Before the thought could penetrate, Sirena disappeared in a splash of cold water, leaving Moira and I gaping at each other on the bench.

"Shit," Moira breathed. "I haven't seen Tess in at least twenty-four hours."

My brain scrambled as I tried to piece a timeline together. "She was at work when Lou fell through the roof, right?"

Moira nodded. "But we didn't see her at all. Lou came through and Tess was gone." Her brow furrowed. "Did you see her leave that evening?"

I shook my head.

Moira cursed and pulled her cell out. "I'm texting Ash."

It took less than a minute for the dryad to respond. Moira closed her eyes. "He hasn't seen her either. Ash thought you let Tess go early. He texted her earlier today and she never responded."

"Shit," I breathed. "Do you think Lou has her?"

"Let's hope not," she said ominously.

Both of us rose from the bench at the same time. Tess wasn't an easy target, but depending on who Lou really was, it might not matter.

CHAPTER
Eleven

CAELAN

Few shifters wore perfume or cologne. Most paranormal beings had an enhanced sense of smell and could scent shifters much faster than the average human. Wearing any sort of perfumed body products threw any chances of stealth right out the window.

Rachel was either profoundly stupid or she wanted me to know she was here. I stopped at the entrance to my bedroom and waited for her to reveal herself.

Seconds later, she walked out from the bathroom area, wearing a blue satin robe loosely tied around her waist. One of the shoulders had fallen, no doubt on purpose, showcasing an expanse of pale, creamy skin. She wore her hair loose and tumbling over her shoulder in a wave of amber. Her green eyes shone in the low light.

Rachel slunk toward me, a seductive smile curving her full lips, her bare feet making no sound on the floor. I held my hand up.

"Do. Not."

The power in my voice halted her in her tracks. She'd never been a powerful shifter. Content to know her beauty was usually enough to assure her place in a Pack hierarchy, Rachel rarely had to ask for anything she wanted because most shifters were chomping at the bit to lay her desires at her feet.

But I was no ordinary shifter. "If Evie were here, she would kill you," I said mildly.

Rachel scoffed. "As if a puny woman like her could harm me."

My soft laugh made her eyes narrow. Her languid posture tensed.

"You honestly think your fiancée could do any damage?" Her laugh was amused, but tentative. She knew I knew something she didn't, and it was making her nervous.

Good. "You've always underestimated everyone." Even me, once upon a time. I'd done everything to prove myself to her, thrown myself at her feet just so she'd turn those gemstone-colored eyes to me, and she'd thrown it back on my face.

The only eyes I wanted upon me now belonged to a blue-eyed hurricane—a woman with a tender heart and a vicious mouth.

Rachel trailed a finger over the mahogany of the dresser. "She's cast a spell on you. The Caelan I know would never have settled for someone so plain."

"The Rachel I used to know would never have deigned to be someone's last choice."

Rachel sucked in a breath. "I've never known you to be so cruel." Tears shimmered in her eyes.

"Get out of my bedroom. This will be my one and only warning." I released my hold, and Rachel waited a long moment, her eyes narrowing as she thought about testing my boundaries.

When rationality finally won, Rachel breezed past me, but not before trailing a hand across my hip on her way out.

I waited until the door closed behind her before letting out a breath and sinking onto the edge of my bed.

She was going to be a problem. I'd call her father tomorrow to figure out the real reason she was here. Until then, I rose and locked my bedroom door.

If I wasn't meeting with the Lords first thing in the morning, I'd stay with Evie tonight.

My phone pinged with a message. *See you tomorrow night?*

I smiled. *I'll be at your house by nine.*

Night, Caelan.

Night, darling.

I set my phone on my nightstand and buried my head in my hands.

"He's not coming?"

I shook my head. "Not tonight. He'll be occupied most of the day tomorrow, too."

"More time for us to find Tess," Moira said quietly.

Ash planned to join us a little later, but he couldn't stay long. Tomorrow, if we hadn't yet found Tess, he'd open the shop and pretend like everything was normal.

Tonight, Moira and I were exploring Joy Springs, trying to trail our errant fae. We'd gone back to the shop and thoroughly vacuumed the small spot he'd landed using a brand-new handheld vac. Modern problems required modern solutions.

Moira held the tote bag with the vacuum. We walked into the Thistle and Thread and waved at Marnie, one of the two hedge-witches who owned the place. The scents of warm bread and hearty soup teased our noses as we headed to a table toward the very back.

"The usual?" Moira asked.

I nodded gratefully, taking the bag from her outstretched hand before she headed toward the register. The cafe rarely changed unless the sisters had put up decorations, but we were clean into

February now and there wasn't a hint of Valentine's Day anywhere in the place.

Instead, the sisters had decorated with small, twinkling fairy lights strung across the ceiling in deep loops and numerous vining plants and ferns. It lent the place the air of an outdoor garden. I smiled and exhaled, reaching up to curl my finger around one of the ferns that had swept one of its fronds down to brush my hair.

As my powers continued to grow, the plants had begun acting oddly toward me, sometimes reaching out without me reaching for them first. I sent a small thread of magic out, enveloping the frond in my power. The fronds shivered and a small sound like a sigh came from the top of the pot.

This was what my powers were meant to do. Most things around us held some form of sentience, even if we didn't understand what they said. Houses made of wood creaked and groaned, the sounds giving voice to the untold drama of our mundane and sometimes not so mundane lives. The soil whispered its secrets to the trees, and the rain washed away the worst of our sins.

Life was everywhere. All we had to do was open ourselves enough to listen.

Moira returned holding a tray with two cappuccinos. "On the house," she said, gently sitting one in front of me before she reached for hers. I took the tray and set it aside.

"Marnie and Twila will be over once they shoo the rest of the customers out. Shouldn't be long. They said they haven't been that busy this evening."

"Think they can help?"

Moira shrugged. We'd chosen the sisters because we knew them well enough to trust they'd keep their mouth shut, and they had powerful magic. They were hedgewitches, skilled in herbal lore and homecrafting, but it didn't mean they didn't have some tricks up their sleeves. And tracking spells weren't all that difficult. Moira could have done one if we weren't concerned about what she might pull out of thin air if she tried one. For now, her magic was tightly leashed, but both of us were still nervous of what might happen if she relaxed her guard.

Marnie brought over two plates not too long afterward. One had a Salisbury steak piled high with mashed potatoes and roasted broccoli. The other held what looked like chicken pot pie with a side of braised carrots.

"Mmm," I said, rubbing my hands together greedily.

Marnie smiled. "Want another cappuccino?"

"Please," Moira and I said at the same time.

Her blue eyes twinkled merrily. "Coming right up, dears."

She took the empty tray and hurried away.

Moira and I didn't speak for a while, too busy shoveling in sustenance for the potentially long night ahead.

AN HOUR AND A HALF LATER, Marnie and Twila had pulled up chairs and stared dubiously down at the vacuum cleaner.

Twila rubbed a hand over her mouth. "Well, I guess that's one way to do it."

Marnie snorted. "No one ever realizes how much hair and skin a single person drops per day."

"We sweep the shop every day," Moira grumbled.

"Doesn't matter," Twila announced. "The body is constantly exfoliating itself."

"Gross." Moira sat back with a sigh. "He's blondish. Does that help?"

"Isn't Tess blonde?" Marnie asked.

"She's more silvery. His was more of a golden color."

The pile of dirt and debris said nothing, waiting for us to dig through and try to decipher which part of it was Lou and which part was our...exfoliation.

"We should have brought gloves," I said with a sigh.

"Don't fret," Marnie said. "We'll start looking for the blonde hairs first. But before we do, we can sort out the flotsam from the jetsam."

Twila nodded and lifted her hands. Her eyes flashed purple with magic before she closed them and murmured some words in a strange language. As she chanted, power rose in the air, and the vacuum debris began to rise and separate, bits and pieces floating like space junk.

Moira stared at it with a slightly horrified expression.

I thought it was a cool trick and wondered how I could use it in my business.

"Bowl," Twila barked.

Marnie fished in the canvas bag she'd brought to the table and pulled out four tiny misshapen ceramic bowls that she sat directly underneath the floating debris.

With a deft flick of her hand, Twila guided each into their respective bowls and dropped her magic.

"Cool trick," I said.

Twila was the taller and quieter one of the sister duo. She spoke only when she had something to say, and I found I should always listen when she deigned to speak.

"The living material is in the red bowl."

I grimaced.

"The blue bowl contains dirt and dust and a little bit of plant debris. The orange holds small fragments of magic given form. And the green bowl is..." Her voice trailed off. "Miscellaneous."

Moira blinked. "You don't know what it is?"

Twila shrugged. "Not what we need. That's all I know for now. At least for tracking. Maybe it's important. Maybe it's not. No way to know until we begin."

I leaned over and peered down at the green bowl. "Looks like dirt to me."

Thalia gave me a sharp look. "Dirt is where powerful things grow, Evie."

Unsettled, I sat back in my chair. Moira pushed her coffee

away. "Now we have to dig through the…" She waved her hand at the bowl of hair and other bits. "Living material?"

"Do you have tweezers?" I asked.

Marnie rolled her eyes. "Don't think the major players of this town don't know what you two have been up to. You've seen far worse things than a bowl full of hair and nail clippings."

Moira and I exchanged a glance.

"Fine," she growled as she took the bowl and tipped the contents out onto a white napkin.

I dug through my purse and pulled out a pencil.

Moira saw it and exclaimed, "Cheater!"

"You're just jealous you didn't think of it first," I crowed.

"You got another one?"

I shoved my purse at her.

After a fruitless search, Moira finally pulled out a toothpick. Both of us scooted our chairs closer and started going through the pile.

Thirteen

"**P**eople are disgusting," I announced half an hour later.

"If you think this is bad, imagine all the things people knowingly do," Marnie said ominously.

Moira's nose wrinkled. "I do not want to know."

I frowned at my pencil. "I'm not putting this back in my purse. It's seen some things."

We were left with three tiny piles of hair. Some we couldn't identify at all. Some was Tess's, some was mine, and two short strands were blond enough to give us hope that they belonged to Lou.

"Where's yours?" I asked.

Moira shrugged. "I don't grow hair," she said.

I gaped at her. "Anywhere?"

"I have what I had when my immortality switched on. That's all."

"Oh man. You can never get laser hair removal, can you?"

Moira flashed a grin, the first one I'd seen since this mess started. "I'd shaved the morning of. Fortunately."

"Imagine if you'd let the bush go free. You'd have to hope the 70s came back into style. Forever cursed by style trends."

"*Ladies*," Marnie drawled disapprovingly. "We have more important things to focus on."

Twila cleared her throat, but I didn't miss the sparkle in her eye.

"I can cut it," Moira quickly added. "But it's back within 24 hours."

"There is a God," I said.

Marnie snorted. "Trouble magnets."

She swiped the rest of the bowls and moved them. Twila picked up the rest of the sorted debris and floated it to another table, then focused on what was left.

"If this works, it will lead you to this person's current location."

"But if it's not his, we'll find someone else, I assume."

"Yes. Depending on who it is, they may sense they're being tracked, but there's no way to know until you arrive." Marnie's gaze flicked to Moira. "Do you know how powerful this being is?"

We both shook our heads.

"Very well." She raised her hands over the pile and closed her eyes. "Let us begin."

We left with a small silken bag holding a blue glowing ball and a promise to fulfill a favor of their choosing at an undetermined time. As loath as I was to hand out favors without strict parameters, we didn't have much of a choice.

"Maybe we should have narrowed the tracking spell to Tess," Moira said quietly as we piled into my car and pulled into traffic.

"If this doesn't work, we will. I want to know if he has her first. Plus, I want to see what he's up to. Tess can handle herself." I believed the words, and Tess had shown me how powerful she was before, but I still couldn't shake my sense of unease. Why would Lou want a banshee he'd never seen before?

Or had he seen her?

Or, even worse, was this all a weird fluke and he'd shown up on purpose under the guise of a magic blip.

That last theory sounded bonkers, but strange things had happened over the last few months, strange enough to make me believe just about anything.

The bag held a steady glow as we drove, brightening when we were on the right track, dimming when we'd either passed a turn or gone too far down a street. For twenty minutes we drove around in what felt like circles until the bag pulsed twice and warmed just as we passed a small, nondescript house behind the busiest area of Joy Springs.

Lights blazed from the porch and inside the house and music pumped through the streets. Someone was hosting a party, a big one from the number of cars in the driveway and crowded along both sides of the street.

We slowed the vehicle to a crawl and passed by, Moira craning her head to scan all the people milling around. "I recognize a few people, but there's no one we know well. Most are locals."

"Lou's made some new friends, it appears."

Moira leaned back and crossed her arms over her chest. "Well, I don't like it."

"We don't have to like it. We just need to find our banshee."

"Pull around and park a couple of blocks away. Maybe we can talk to some people and find out if Tess is here before Lou spots us."

As plans went, it wasn't a bad one, but I had a bad feeling Tess wasn't here unless Lou was holding her somewhere, away from other people. A locked room, maybe a basement.

The question was, why would he do something like that and what did he want from Tess?

If he even had her at all.

We drove a couple of blocks down and parked on the street, making sure we locked our doors before starting down the street.

Our breath made steam clouds in the frigid air. When we arrived at the house, a few people waved and smiled. Moira got out way more than I did, so the odds were they recognized her before me.

Moira headed over, shoving her hands in her coat pockets. I followed behind and let her charm them.

The first was a handsome young man with light brown eyes covered with wire spectacles and messy hair. He looked like a young scholar at a party he was being held hostage at. "Moira." He held out a hand. "I'm surprised to see you here."

They shook as Moira gave a self-deprecating laugh. "Tess finally managed to drag me out of the house. You haven't seen her around, have you? I might be a little early."

The man's brow furrowed. "Tess?" He slowly shook his head. "I'm sorry. I haven't been inside yet, so she might be in there. She hasn't been outside yet."

"I'll check inside in a few minutes. I see a few other people I know."

The man glanced at me. When Moira didn't introduce us, he rolled his eyes and stuck his hand out again. "Martin," he said. "I run a bookshop downtown. You're the florist, right?"

"That's right." We shook, and I was surprised to feel callouses on the palm of his hand. Martin was more than a bookseller, wasn't he?

"I don't think I've ever seen you outside the shop."

It took everything I had not to bristle. Yes, I was not very social. No, it was not polite to point it out. "What can I say," I said with a sheepish smile, "it's hard to deny the comforts of home."

To my surprise, Martin's eyes lit up. "I agree! One of my friends dragged me out tonight. He said there's a new guy in town that has access to some rare tomes I might be interested in."

He rolled his eyes. "Unfortunately, I have yet to see my friend or the tomes, so I'm not sure I'll be here much longer."

Moira was fidgeting and jerking her head toward the door. "Me neither. I won't stay too long once we find Tess." I thumbed at Moira. "She's the real party animal among us."

Moira rolled her eyes. "Well, let's find her so we can get this old lady home." She looped her arm through mine and tugged. "Nice to see you again, Martin."

"You, too," he said, but his eyes lingered on me as she dragged me away.

"Martin has the hots for you," Moira said with an amused hiss when we were far enough away to keep him from hearing our conversation.

"Martin would be a fool to act on that," I said quietly. "Caelan wouldn't take kindly to anyone flirting with me."

Moira glanced at me. "Are you okay with his influence on you?"

I blinked. "What does that mean?"

Moira shook her head. "He has eyes everywhere. If someone steps an inch over the line, he's going to know about it."

"I have no plans to step over the line."

Moira snorted. "I know you won't, but you're a hot little commodity, and once word gets out about who your daddy is, you're going to have man meat beating down your door."

"If you remember, that has already happened."

Moira's grin held a sharp edge. "Yes, and have you noticed how abruptly that stopped?"

My steps halted. "What do you mean by that?"

She tugged me forward again. "You're a smart girl. It'll come to you."

We stepped into the house, me slightly behind Moira. The vampire stopped abruptly, and I bumped into her back with an *oof*.

"My gods," Moira murmured.

I peeked over her shoulder and was stunned into silence. All I could do was stand there for a long moment gawking before I leaned away and poked my head outside, my gaze taking in the dimension of the porch which wrapped around the house.

Then I leaned back inside and shook my head. "Fae magic," I said quietly.

"Powerful fae magic," she agreed.

Who or what had come through that portal? I shut the door behind us with a soft click. The music pounding from outside wasn't the same as inside. This music was softer, sultrier, holding a hypnotic beat that made me want to sway my hips.

And wasn't that curious?

Moira found my hand and squeezed. "Glamour magic," she hissed. "Be careful."

She didn't let go, and I didn't protest. A press of bodies surrounded us, most unbothered by our presence, others who didn't even notice we were there.

Some had their eyes closed and danced in place, their mouths open in ecstasy. Whatever was happening to them disturbed me on a cellular level.

I might be a fae, but I hated glamour magic. Such power could make you feel anything. Horror or excitement, pleasure or pain, it didn't matter. You could walk through a living dream and become a king or queen, a tyrant or a savior. Rich or poor, a movie star or a pauper, anything was possible.

I only wanted to be myself, Evie. Nothing else. As far-fetched as it sounded, after my ride in the World Tree, I'd stopped wanting anything other than what was best for me. My friends and family loved me, and I loved them. Those were what made me rich, not gold coins spilling into my palms from a trickster's hands.

Unfortunately, my father had all but stopped our training sessions lately, perhaps to punish me for being difficult, as he liked to say. I knew some of what I could do, but most of it pertained to the natural world, nothing that could help me if I let the magic sweep me under.

We walked through the press of bodies, some human, some fae, a shifter here and there which would make Caelan extremely unhappy if he found out about it, and some tinges of unfamiliar magic—neither fae nor shifter nor witch or water creature.

My gaze swept the room, looking for anything I could focus on.

"There," I said quietly, pulling Moira toward a familiar muscular figure dressed in familiar armor.

Neit's eyes widened when he spotted me. He stepped forward, pulling Moira and I into a dark corner.

"What are you doing here?" he hissed.

Like most fae, Neit was a stone-cold fox, but his face held more character than the unearthly, almost unreal beauty much of the other fae possessed. He was dark-haired and dark-eyed, though those eyes burned with cold violet power.

Moira pressed in closer, her body almost smashed against mine. She looked around the room with a furrowed brow, and I got the impression she liked it here less than I did.

"We're searching for Tess. She disappeared when our new guest popped in for a visit."

Neit's eyes narrowed. The god of war wasn't a friend, exactly, but he was Mom's ex-boyfriend or current boyfriend or...something, so he'd not exactly intervened for me before, but he had shown up and helped as much as he could on occasion. It didn't mean I trusted him, but he was familiar and he'd never actively tried to murder me. Right now, Neit was the most trustworthy thing in this room.

"Let me guess. Did you two have anything to do with this new guest who decided to visit?"

Moira looked at her feet. Neit's long suffering sigh almost made me laugh, but I stifled my amusement.

He let out a string of blistering curses. "Do you know who you've let in?" he hissed, scraping a palm over his five o'clock shadow.

"Someone not good, I presume?" I gave him a hopeful smile.

Neit closed his eyes and sighed. "What did he tell you?"

"He said his name was Lou." I shrugged. "That was pretty much it, as far as identity wise. He said this was his first visit and he wanted to explore the town before he went home."

"Lou," Neit said, staring at me like I'd sprouted a third eye. "And are you familiar with Lou?"

Moira shook her head. "It's an odd name for a fae. You don't often find fae with Italian names like that."

Neit took a beat before his jaw dropped. An epic sigh broke from him. "I swear to the gods. Does your mother know what happened?"

"Mom hasn't been around too much." Cliona and I were still on unfamiliar ground. We were trying to have a relationship, but there were a lot of hard truths to get through first. Mom visited when she could, but she'd canceled more often than not these days, and when I asked why, all she would tell me was there was unrest in the realms.

Whatever the hell that meant.

I always felt unrestful these days.

"That's because she's fending off challenges on all sides." He shook his head. "You could visit her, you know."

I blinked. "She hasn't invited me."

Neit's lip curled. "You're just as hard-headed as she is," he murmured before shaking his head. "Regardless, let's get back to the current epic fuck up you're dealing with."

Moira froze. "Fuck up?"

"Yes," Neit growled. "Your Lou might sound Italian, but it's not. You invited *Lugh* in. L-U-G-H," he spelled. "As in the trickster god." A faint smile. "Surprise."

I stood there for a moment, racking my brain for lore. But Lugh wasn't a figure Mom spoke about too much. "I'm afraid I don't follow. Is he harmful?"

Neit leaned against the wall and watched me with those dark eyes. "Ever heard of Loki?"

"Who hasn't?" Moira said.

"Think Loki but four times as powerful. Lugh is not a bad guy, as much as any of us are, but it takes a lot to amuse him. And when he gets bored…" His voice trailed off as he raised his hand and swept it to encompass the room. "Do not go into any of the empty bedrooms. They are all portals. Don't touch the walls and do not accept any food or drink."

Moira winced as she reached out for a cocktail from a server passing by.

Neit swept the drink from her hand. "No sustenance. At all. Even if someone promises you it's safe." His teeth flashed. "We are all liars, Evie. Remember this while you are in this house tonight."

"We won't be here for long," Moira said. "As soon as we find Tess, we plan to leave."

Neit's eyes narrowed. His irises flashed with bright violet light before he shook his head. "Your banshee is not here. Nor has she been here in the last few days."

Moira and I glanced at each other. "Back to the drawing board?" she asked.

"You can call your mother," Neit suggested. "She can track all her banshees." He smiled. "Except for those who step into your shop."

And wasn't that a source of annoyance for my mother? Because I thought she was dangerous to me and my friends, I'd blocked her from accessing my shop and my house. Even after she'd proven she wasn't quite the villain I'd thought she was, I hadn't lightened my protections.

None of that would help Tess now, though.

"Maybe I will," I said. "Though it would help if she carried a cell phone."

Neit rolled his eyes and pushed away from the wall. "Go see your mother, child. She misses you."

I blinked. "Uh."

Neit's eyes swirled. "Remember. Eat and drink nothing. You'd do well to leave before Lugh finds you here."

Moira snorted. "We were the ones who let him stay."

A faint smile appeared on Neit's lips. "If that's what you think, my dear, Lugh's visit should prove extremely interesting."

He winked and walked away, his form fading into mist before our eyes.

"Should we get the hell out of here?" I whispered.

"No need," boomed a jovial voice. "The party is just beginning!"

Lugh stood before us, his arm draped over a nubile young woman wearing a foggy smile.

Shit.

CHAPTER
Fourteen

I nudged Moira and straightened. "Looks like you're settling in well," I said.

He spread his arms. "It's a brand-new world out there, and I am a starving man." His smile held an edge of malice. "I have you both to thank for this."

A flash of crimson rolled over Moira's eyes. Lugh tsked. "There's no need for anger, my dear. I've done nothing alarming or concerning."

"Where is Tess?" Moira growled.

To Lugh's credit, his brow furrowed. Confusion flashed over his face. "Tess?"

I jumped in before Moira said something unforgivable. "Our friend is missing. We were concerned she might be here."

"There's no need for concern," Lugh said. "I'm sure she'll turn up somewhere."

Someone called his name, and he turned away from us, his arm once again heavy around the shoulder of the woman who accompanied him. He shouted something unintelligible back and turned to us once more. "I apologize," he said, his teeth too white against the tan of his skin. "There's plenty to eat and drink and much more revelry to be had if you'd like to stay."

Moira stepped forward. I gripped her arm firmly in warning. "We'll mill around for a little while, then leave you be."

Moira's skin heated under my fingers as she bristled with fury.

"If you happen to see our friend, please let us know."

Lugh nodded, eyes lingering on Moira. "Happy to. Enjoy yourselves."

Without another word, he turned and escorted the stumbling woman away.

"I hate him," she seethed. "He has Tess. I can feel it."

But I wasn't so sure. "Neit has no reason to lie to us. If he said she hasn't been here, then I believe him."

"He's fae," she hissed.

I frowned. "So am I, Moira."

My friend closed her eyes and let out a breath. "Sorry." She held up a hand. "I'm sorry. I'm just worried."

When she opened her eyes, they were clear, the worry wiped away and replaced with resolve.

"Then let's poke around here for a bit and see if we can find anything out to help us find her."

Moira nodded. "Let's go."

And with that, we were off to interrogate the inebriated fae.

A FEW HOURS later I was back home in my pajamas, sitting on my back porch drinking hot chocolate. Stars twinkled and winked above me, the moon hidden on the other side of the world. I always marveled at the stars and wondered how they could exist with other fae realms above and below us. Did the night sky look the same in their realms as ours, or was there an entirely new solar system to explore?

The only time I ever visited another realm at night was when my father dragged me to that fae ball to show me off, but there hadn't been time for exploration. I'd marveled at the sparkle and elegance of the other fae beings surrounding us, not thinking about stepping outside to see the wonders of the outdoors.

The next time I went, I'd stay long enough to satisfy my curiosity.

My fingers curled around the mug, steam rising above the liquid. Fragrant and heady, with just a hint of spice, the recipe was passed down to my husband's family and eventually to me. As much as I'd tried to distance myself, this recipe was one I could never let go of. It was too delicious and too comforting, and there'd been little of that during those years.

The wards tingled against my skin. I smiled over the rim of my cup as one of the Lords appeared.

"Hello, Rowan."

The handsome Lord grinned. "Hello, Evie." He shoved his hands in his pockets and walked up the back steps. "Any more of that left?"

I held out my mug. "Take this. I'll get another."

Rowan took the mug and lifted it in a salute. "Thanks."

I hurried inside to get another mug. When I walked back outside, Rowan had made himself at home on the outdoor sofa.

"You didn't tell me you were coming."

His eyes twinkled. "I wanted to surprise you, but I can tell Caelan spilled the beans."

"Guilty."

He sighed and sipped his cocoa. "This is delicious."

"Thanks. I simmer a chipotle pepper with the milk."

"That's what I taste!"

We fell into a comfortable silence for a while. "How are things?" he asked after a while.

"Heating up," I said with a sigh.

One of his eyebrows rose. "Oh? Anything I should be concerned about?"

I waved my hand at him. "Nah. Moira accidentally let a trickster god loose, and Caelan has an old lover staying with him."

Rowan blinked. "An old lover?"

I knew he'd be more concerned about that one than the errant god. "Rachel."

Rowan's eyes widened. "Seriously?"

"You know her?" I sat up straight, interested in any information he could give me.

To my disappointment, he shook his head. "I've only heard of her. And what I heard wasn't good."

"Caelan said he has to keep her here five days before he can dump her in a hotel."

"Mmm. True. But he can make things difficult for her." He smiled. "And so can you if you're so inclined."

I sighed and curled my feet underneath my thighs. "She's lying about why she's here."

"Unsurprising. She's the spoiled and entitled daughter of one of the European Lords. As far as I know, she's unmarried." He said the last word with emphasis, and one of his eyebrows rose.

"Oh," he said. "You think she's here scoping out Caelan as marriage material." His teeth flashed in a grin. "What do you think about that?"

I think I'd like to rip out her spleen through her belly button, but I said, "I think Caelan is old enough to choose who he wants to be with."

But Rowan was too smart to take my words at face value. "You want to scratch her eyes out, don't you?"

"He'll make the right decision," I said quietly.

"If he doesn't, he's a fool," Rowan answered.

I leaned forward. "What's in the bag?"

He chuckled and nudged the canvas forward with his foot. "Who says there's anything inside for you?"

"Because a Lord has lowly peons to carry their bags for them. And the only peon I see here is you."

Rowan laughed and clutched his heart in mock pain. "Peons aren't smart enough to bring great presents. Perhaps there's only dry dirt and worms in there."

My eyes narrowed. "Depends on the worms. Earthworms or grubs?"

Rowan grinned and picked up the bag. "Let's see, shall we?"

I scooted my chair closer and peered down into the bag, but it was too dark to see what was inside.

Rowan reached in and pulled out a rolled-up paper towel. "First is a new hybrid of fruit tree I've been working on. The blossoms are larger and the fruit a touch sweeter."

"Oranges?" I guessed.

"Half," he agreed. "The other is a lemon." At my look, he laughed. "But it's not a Meyer. Those are cross bred with mandarins. This one is bred with a clementine."

Meyer lemons were delicious, but I never thought they were a one-on-one sub for a true lemon. I reached for the cuttings Rowan held out and unrolled them.

"We can plant them tomorrow if you like."

"Yes, please. I have a few things in the greenhouse for you."

His expression lit up. "Excellent!"

We chatted for a little while longer. When Rowan's hot chocolate was finished, he rose and stretched. "It's getting late. Caelan will get mad if he catches me here past midnight."

I clicked my tongue. Rowan winked and set his mug down on the small table. "Meet at seven tomorrow?"

"It's a date. Caelan will be over later, so don't be surprised."

He rolled his eyes. "I'll see him before you do, so I'll let him know I'll be here."

I waved as he walked down the steps. "Be careful going home."

His eyes glowed golden in the darkness. "I'll do my best."

As he disappeared into the forest behind my house, I sighed and picked up our mugs. Tomorrow, I planned to visit my mother to see if she could tell me where Tess was. If she could help, I'd grab the banshee tomorrow and be back in time for Rowan's visit.

Famous last words.

CHAPTER
Fifteen

om was way easier to visit than she used to be, and from the way she waved at me from the top of one of the mounds surrounding her property, she was expecting me to visit.

I put my hands on my hips and peered up at her. "Neit told you?"

Mom nodded and jumped down from her perch, landing gracefully. "I wasn't sure you'd show up today, but I had a feeling. What he didn't say was why." She pulled me in for an embrace, her sweet scent enveloping me.

Mom stepped away and studied me, her azure eyes, *my* eyes, taking in my face. "You seem worried." She looped her arm through mine and led me away. "I made some soup. Are you hungry?"

I nodded, surprised by the domesticity. Mom could cook and she had a few times before during my childhood, but she often left it to the household help to feed me, her thoughts usually somewhere else.

She led me inside her dwelling and toward the kitchen. I pulled out a scarred wooden chair and sat down while Mom bustled around, filling a glass of lemonade for me before she set a bowl of hot vegetable soup before me.

Following that was a slice of freshly baked bread that she spread with soft, slightly salted butter. I waited while she served herself before taking a bite.

The soup flavors hit my tongue and exploded. I could cook, but this recipe was out of this world.

"Mom!" I said when I could speak. "This is amazing!"

A tinge of pink colored her cheeks. "Well, thank you. I do enjoy cooking, but it's only recently that I've had the time."

"And the bread is amazing, too. Mind sharing your recipes?"

Mom stared at me for a long moment. "Of course I will, Evie." She reached over and touched my arm. "I'd be honored to share with you." A hesitant smile, one I'd never seen her make, touched her lips.

"I'd make this all the time," I promised. "It's delicious."

Mom's lips trembled, but she played it off and forced a smile. "I'm glad to hear it."

We ate in silence for a while, and when we were done, Mom stood and poured herself a tea and started a cup of coffee for me. She'd bought one of the pod machines, and I knew she didn't drink coffee.

A knot inside my heart loosened. She'd bought it for me.

When the coffee was ready, she poured me a cup and fixed her tea before bringing both to the table.

"Now," she said, once she'd settled into her seat. "Tell me what you need."

I didn't beat around the bush. "Tess is missing. We thought Lugh might—"

Mom's attention sharpened. "Lugh?"

I nodded. "Long story. We thought Lugh might have her, but Neit said he didn't sense Tess's presence anywhere where Lugh was staying."

Her mouth pursed. "Why would Lugh have anything to do with your banshee?"

"She's not my banshee," I said gently.

Mom sighed. "I know. It's only a term. I call Moira your vampire and your Lord your wolf." She waved my concern away. "I'm well aware Tess is powerful enough to resist any attempts to claim her."

Mom sounded so disgruntled over that I almost smiled. Instead, I told her the story of how Lugh had come to Joy Springs, and when I finished, Mom's face had gone from slightly amused to grim. "He's bad news, Evie."

"I'm starting to understand that."

Mom stirred a little sugar into her tea. "He's not bad, not exactly. None of us are complete villains, despite what others might think."

I tried not to resemble that remark. Over the last several months, I'd learned exactly how deep prejudices could go.

"But Lugh," Mom continued, "is perpetually bored. Nothing much holds his attention anymore. Ennui catches up to him faster than any other immortal I've ever known. Banshees do not exist where Lugh is from. Death is merely an ending, not a precursor to something new. If he spotted her, he very well might have taken her. Neit might not have sensed her because Lugh never held her there."

Our eyes met. "Would you like me to see if I can track her?"

I bit down the question I was dying to ask. What will it cost me?

But Mom wasn't stupid. A sad smile touched her lips. "You do not have to worry about asking me for anything. Not anymore. The game I played to keep you safe is long over. Those who do not know who you are to me, and your father will know soon enough. Word is already spreading."

Sympathy touched her eyes. "For that, my dear, I can never apologize enough."

I wanted to ask about her cryptic words, but Tess was more important.

Mom rose and took her tea. "Come," she commanded.

I grabbed my coffee and followed her deep into the back of her house. Magic rose around us as we walked, the smell of flowers intensifying the deeper we went. Finally, she stopped at a scarred wooden door with a large, ornate doorknob.

Mom turned the knob and pushed the door open. Death magic rolled over my shoulders, cold and clammy, fingers of mist touching my neck and hair. I shivered and paused at the threshold.

"This is your heritage too, Evie," Mom said quietly. "Enter and do not be afraid. The dead cannot harm the living." A faint smile. "Usually."

"Gee, Mom. That last qualifier makes me feel so much better."

To my surprise, Mom laughed. "You are safe with me," she clarified.

I stepped into the room. Even though Mom hadn't touched the door, it slammed behind her, the boom of sound making me jerk in fear.

I looked around the room with wonder. The wood was dark and shiny, a deep blue woven rug taking up a large expanse. Two burgundy chairs sat on either side of a bookshelf stuffed to the brim. Tomes and journals filled with random scraps of paper lay scattered in random order on every shelf. In the middle of the room sat a round table with a leather-bound book atop the surface. Two fat, squat candles sat on either side. On the right sat a small silver bowl holding a charcoal brick and the remnants of something burned, incense if I had to guess. There was a small bowl of soil toward the top, a feather to its left, another charcoal brick filled with a fragrant powder below it, and another silver bowl filled with water above that.

An altar.

Mom tied her hair back and picked up a bundle of sage, lighting it with nothing more than a thought. When the sage caught fire and the flame went out, releasing a pungent but pleasant scent with its smoke, she motioned me over and used a large feather to flick smoke over my hair, face, and body, doing the same for herself when she finished.

I watched as Mom took the formal steps of ritual before she returned to the place at the table. She pulled up a chair and sat down.

"It will take a few minutes," she said.

"Try to be as quiet and still as possible, and do not disrupt the energy, no matter what you might see or hear."

I nodded, more curious than anything. Mom had always kept her rituals private from me. I'd never seen her use this side of her power for anything other than control. I'd received gifts from both my parents, but I'd never held any dominion over the dead or my mother's banshees.

Tess had once told me she liked my energy. Maybe some of my mother's power clung to me, but it wasn't enough to hold any power over the afterlife. I was glad of it. The powers I had were enough to deal with, and I'd barely touched the surface of any of them.

When I thought about that, I felt overwhelmed. How was it that I could have the ability to shift into anything I desired and not be using those powers every single day of my life? I'd embraced myself and my gifts, but sitting here now, watching my ageless mother commune with death, I wondered if I truly had.

My Floromancy felt like an extension of one of my limbs. My Chimera powers felt like an afterthought sometimes. I spent far too long being afraid of them than using the magic to my advantage.

I itched to fidget as I thought about it, uncomfortable in the assessment of myself. Maybe I should call Barrett back and ask him to come over. He'd offered, but the swans had thrown a wrench into everything.

Mom's eyes widened, a silver film covering her irises. I sucked in a breath and froze, wondering if I should intervene, until her words came back to me.

No matter what I saw, do not interrupt.

But it was hard. Mom went still as stone, her eyes clouded with the film of death.

The room had fallen silent except for the crackling noise of the burning incense. Fragrant smoke filled the area, the scent at odds with the scene before me.

Death was not a power I coveted. I preferred the warmth and fiery power of life. Death was a release. Life was holding on to everything for as long as you could and fighting like hell to stay on the ride no matter how hard things got.

Death was letting go, and let's face it, I'd never been good at that.

Mom sucked in a ragged breath and opened her mouth, a wail tearing from her throat. It wasn't quite the same as a banshee wail, but it was similar enough to make my eyes water and my teeth grit.

A second later, the room fell into silence once more.

Mom gasped and opened her eyes, the film clearing away like it had never existed.

"I know where she is," she croaked.

Mom wasn't sure if Lugh had taken Tess or not. She said there was no way to tell, but what she did know was that Tess was no longer on Earth. She'd gone to the fae realms, and she was alive.

That's all Mom could tell, but it was enough. Relief filled me, and I sank against the chair.

"You could go, you know," Mom said, staring at me over the rim of her mug. "The fae lands have no borders with you. As the bridge, you can go anywhere. No king or queen can keep you out."

I grimaced. "I know nothing about those lands. Even here, I've never ventured further than your barrow mounds."

Mom shrugged. "Every realm holds danger, Evie. My lands are relatively safe on the marked roads and villages. But you belong here just as much as I do, and my people will sense your blood. There are few who would dare attack you here."

"But not in the other realms."

Mom shrugged. "I have no control over the other places in our lands. Most rulers do not allow the savage things of the wilds to infiltrate their cities and towns, though."

I studied her. "You're saying stick to the main roads and stay out of the forests."

"In many ways, our lands are similar to yours. Stay out of the dark alleys and trust no one with a sharp smile."

"I'd be a fool to go alone."

"Your vampire friend's power grows every day. She or one of your preferred Lords might be a good companion." She paused for a beat. "Or perhaps…I would be a good companion."

I tilted my head. "You'd want to come with me?"

"We've never had a true adventure together, daughter. You've been too busy hating me."

"Mom," I growled. "You gave me no reason not to hate you."

"Perhaps," she said. "Youth sees what it wants to, but games of the immortals dig far under the surface and grow roots longer than you or I can see."

"Pretty words," I grumbled. "You can't just call Tess back?"

Mom shook her head. "Not in the fae lands. Earth is one place. Our lands are not. They exist atop each other, every realm unique in its own way."

A thought occurred to me. "Are the stars the same?"

Mom frowned. "Pardon?"

"The night stars. Are they different in each realm?"

Her eyes crinkled at the edges. "Yes. Quite different. Consider each realm a different planet in a separate solar system. Earth and Mars have the same solar system, with different atmospheres. Tir Tairngire, where Tess has gone, has a breathable atmosphere for all fae, but it is in an entirely different space than my land."

"Is it dangerous?"

Mom shrugged. "As lands go, it's one of the better ones. The humans call it the Land of Promise. They believe if they reach the place, all their dreams have the potential to come true."

"Have you been there?"

Mom shook her head. "No, though your Father has traveled extensively to all the fae realms. He may be a better person to accompany you than I am."

She gave me a side-eye. I groaned. "He spoke to you?"

"Enough for me to know you two have had a falling out. Is there anything I can help with?"

"Can you make a fae king stop meddling?" I grumbled.

Mom laughed, a bright, amused sound. "Meddling is his very favorite thing to do! I could sooner stop the sun from shining."

"That's what I thought." I sighed and set my mug down. "Can you feel if Tess is in any distress?"

Mom shook her head. "She's too far away to be sure, but the cord binding us together is firm and strong. I do not believe she's in distress." She frowned. "Are you sure she hasn't gone willingly?"

"She'd leave a note." Wouldn't she? I wasn't sure about anything these days. Tess had always been independent. She showed up for work on time and never called in sick, not that any of us ever caught a cold, and she rarely used her vacation days. But as far as what she did in her downtime, I couldn't say. For a while, she and Ash spent much of their time together, but once they broke up, Tess had pulled away seemingly from all of us.

Mom's eyebrows lifted. "Are you sure she'd have left you a message of some kind?"

I groaned. "A few months ago, I would have been positive."

"Maybe you can find her and make sure she's not in distress. If she wants to stay, she can."

"I don't want her to feel like I'm checking up on her. She's an adult."

Mom rose and gestured for me to follow. As we walked back down the hall, the magic swept away from us, gently blowing my hair away from my neck. Soon enough, we were back in Mom's kitchen.

"Even adults need friends," Mom finally said. "I think for everyone's peace of mind, you should at least try to reach out to her. Then you can see if she needs assistance."

I still had a bad feeling about this, but I couldn't link Lugh to her disappearance.

"What realm is Lugh from?"

Mom took the mug from my hand and set the dishes in the sink. "No one really knows, but he tends to move through the realms more than many of us. The man has always been restless."

"Good to know."

Mom leaned against the sink and crossed her arms. "You still aren't convinced Tess left of her own free will, are you?"

"She's never left before and never showed any inclination to go anywhere, especially not the fae lands. It's out of character."

"Your instincts have treated you well over the years, Evie. If you feel Lugh is involved, you should trust those instincts. Call upon me when you're ready to go. I will accompany you and… smooth the way if we run into any trouble on our way to find her."

Mom held my gaze as I struggled to find the words. Our relationship had changed so much over the last few months that I had no idea how to act. Treating her like a normal mom didn't feel right but treating her like I used to felt worse.

But what I could do? I could let her have this. "Sure. I'll give you a call. Let me dig around a little more at home first. How about I call you tomorrow?"

Mom's posture loosened. Her eyes gleamed with a suspicious wetness. "That—" she swallowed and tried again. "I'll look forward to your call then."

I gave her a quick hug and left her standing in the kitchen.

Never thought I'd see the day when I trusted my mother to have my back in a dangerous situation.

The world felt topsy-turvy.

CHAPTER

Seventeen

Rachel was sitting in my driveway when I made it home that evening. My steps slowed and stilled until I stood at the edge staring at the woman testing my wards to see if she could get through.

I cleared my throat.

Rachel whirled around. "Oh!" She laid a hand over her throat. "You scared me!"

Her words were a little breathless, her expression was innocent, but there was a gleam in her eyes I didn't like. "Can I help you?"

I made no move to come closer.

Rachel's brow furrowed. "Can we talk inside?"

"Nope," I said cheerily.

She huffed. "It's freezing out tonight."

"You're a shifter. The cold should be nothing to you."

Rachel rolled her eyes. "That's some ward you got up. Having some trouble?"

I crossed my arms over my chest and watched her. "I don't know. Am I?"

I didn't like the way she was looking at me. People who weren't naturally friendly had trouble faking it. Rachel was smiling at me, but she was using too many teeth, and the expression didn't reach her eyes.

When she didn't answer, I nodded. "Does Caelan know you're here?"

"Why would he care if I was here? I'm new in town. Maybe I want a friend."

"Do you always try to break the wards of your friends?"

She gasped. "I'm not trying to break your wards! I've never seen any quite like this, so I was curious about them. My father is always interested in ward work."

I stayed silent and watchful. When I didn't respond, Rachel sighed and leaned against the hood of her car. "You aren't very nice, you know."

"You don't know me, and you haven't been very nice to me. Now you're on my property, and I caught you messing with my wards. Tell me what you want and leave."

A sheen of color rolled over Rachel's irises. "You've got a sharp tongue for someone who has no claws."

I almost laughed. Claws were in plentiful supply on this property, but I wouldn't show them unless she forced my hand. "Do I need claws this evening? If you're here to make a friend, you're doing a poor job at convincing me."

"So suspicious." Rachel rolled her eyes and pushed off her vehicle. She walked toward me stopping a couple of feet away. "I'm having a party at the Keep and wanted to invite you."

"Caelan would have told me. There was no need for you to come by. A phone call would have sufficed if he didn't have time to message me."

Rachel smiled. "I'm afraid he is quite busy."

The way she said it meant to wound, but I wasn't in the mood for games. "Yes, he is," I agreed. "Being a Shifter Lord requires devotion and time. He can't afford distractions right now."

"Very true," Rachel agreed. "Which is the other reason I'm here."

Oh, this should be good. "You're leaving?" I asked. "Not surprising. Caelan has very little time for company these days."

Her eyes flashed with fury. "I'm not going anywhere," she seethed.

"I don't think it's up to you."

A familiar ping on the ward announced Rowan's presence at the back of my property. There was no use signaling for him to stay where he was. He would have heard our voices by now, and the man could rarely resist poking his nose into everyone's business.

He came around the side of the house quiet as a cat. I kept my eyes on Rachel.

"Caelan rarely gets caught up with gutter trash like you, but every once in a while, he lets his guard slip. Not surprised someone like you took advantage of his vulnerability."

A golden sheen rolled over Rowan's eyes at the words. He crept closer and closer.

"Gutter trash?" I snorted. "That's not even worth responding to. If you think Caelan is vulnerable, you haven't learned a single thing during your time apart."

I sighed and shoved my hands in my jacket pockets. "I don't have time to fight with you. There is no fight. I don't care if you like me or not. I don't care if you want to rip my throat out. I don't even care if you want Caelan for your own. I'm too tired to get down in the mud you're rolling in, and I'm certainly not in the mood to get dirty."

I opened myself to my power and felt the earth respond. Vines snaked from the ground and wrapped themself around my calves, twining up my thighs. A phantom wind blew my hair away from my face, and a crimson sheen rolled over my irises. "Leave now before I get annoyed."

Rachel's eyes widened. She took a step back and bumped right into Rowan's broad chest. She squeaked and spun around, her eyes widening when she saw who stood behind her.

"Rachel, I presume." Rowan tilted his head, his golden eyes

casting a sheen over her pale skin. "Your Lord won't take kindly to your behavior this evening."

The shifter stood frozen, her mouth working as she scrambled to find some excuse for her behavior. An annoying thread of empathy filled me, but as I was about to say something, Rowan shot me an amused look as if he knew what I was about to do.

"If I were you, I'd listen to Evie's warning. I'm not the one you should be afraid of."

Rachel frowned, her attention returning to me. "A little bit of Floromancy isn't enough to make me tremble in my boots."

For the last minute or so, a vine had been creeping up Rachel's leg. More than done with her shenanigans, I issued a mental command. Seconds later, Rachel was jerked off her feet. She slammed into the ground with a wild screech.

Rowan leaned over her, his hazel eyes sparkling. "You've never met a Floromancer like Evie."

We grinned at each other. With a flick of my finger, the vine lifted her up and tossed her off my property. The quiet evening shattered with the sound of a high-pitched scream of "AIEEEEEEE!"

Rowan lost it. He threw back his head and burst out laughing which made me laugh, until both of us were standing bent over in the driveway wheezing for air.

An HOUR LATER, we were in the greenhouse sorting through the seedlings and cuttings I'd set aside for him.

"How was today?" I asked as Rowan studied a new strain of petunia I'd been working on.

"Same bullshit, different day." He pulled the sketch over and peered down. "You really created a triple bloom petunia?"

"Sure did. It performs like the waving variety, so it produces a ton of flowers that mount and vine, but the blooms themselves are in triplicate."

Rowan shook his head and straightened. "You could be filthy rich, Evie."

"No desire for it. I do it for the thrill."

He snorted. "What a pair we are. You thinking about selling the seedlings?"

"Not sure yet. I doubt it. Humans still don't know all the things that go bump in the night actually exist, and these bad boys aren't made with only science. If I do sell them, I may have to force residents into signing an agreement not to move the plants outside of Joy Springs."

He grimaced. "Hard to enforce."

"I'll sic Caelan on them if they violate it."

Rowan chuckled and pulled the next seedling over and studied that one just as intently.

"Tess is missing," I said after a few beats of silence.

Rowan's head jerked up. "Elaborate."

I told him everything I found out. When I got to the part about my mother, he pushed the seedlings and sketches away. "Things have changed between you two."

"They have." I sighed and pulled a flat of basil seedlings over. I brushed my fingers over the tops and let magic trickle from the tips. "My father is being a real shit lately."

Rowan's attention sharpened. "How so?"

"He didn't come right out and admit it, but I suspect he dropped Rachel onto Caelan's lap."

His low whistle made me sigh. "Daddy doesn't approve of Caelan for a husband?"

"I don't think Daddy would approve of anyone other than a pretty fae male, so the blood will run true."

Rowan's eyes narrowed. "He doesn't want shifter blood in his line?"

I'd been wanting to tell him what I was for a long time now, but I still couldn't bring myself to utter the words. Trust wasn't the issue.

I was afraid.

Not of Rowan, but what he'd think of me, how he might change the way he looked at me. Change our friendship.

I liked the way things were, even if I were holding back one of the most important parts of myself.

"Evie?" Rowan coaxed. "Lost you there for a moment."

I shook those thoughts off. "No. Cernunnos wants to keep the bloodline as pure as possible. He considers additional shifter blood a dilution."

His eyes flashed gold. "And you're sure it's the shifter blood and not Caelan?"

I chuckled. "I can't tell if my dad likes anyone to be honest. Maybe I should ask him to be more specific."

"Mixing bloodlines can be a volatile practice." Rowan pulled the next flat, this one full of herbs, over to him. "But it's necessary to breed outside the lines to ensure the future health of our species."

"A healthy outlook," I mused.

The wards tingled over my skin. "Caelan's here."

Rowan nodded. "Let me finish looking this over, and I'll take my toys and leave."

"There's no need for you to rush off."

Caelan stepped inside the greenhouse and nodded to Rowan. I smiled and jerked my head toward the table. "Come help me pot these. Then I'll feed you."

He flashed a smile and came up behind me to drop a kiss against the back of my neck.

Rowan let out an aggrieved sigh. "Can't you two at least wait five minutes for me to clean this up?"

"Nope," Caelan said cheerfully.

He tugged a pair of gloves on and reached for some of the larger pots. "I heard something interesting tonight," he mused as he popped one of the oregano seedlings from the tray.

Rowan and I exchanged looks. He gave me a sympathetic wince and dropped his gaze. "Oh?" I said.

Caelan snorted. "Garrett reported seeing a woman being flung through the air from the vicinity of your property. He noted the woman looked a lot like the Keep's visiting guest."

"Huh," I said. "I wonder who it was."

Rowan huffed a laugh. Caelan sent him a withering look. "When you two get together, there's always trouble."

Rowan held his hands up. "I got here after things had already escalated."

At Caelan's disbelieving look, I snickered. "He's telling the truth. I tossed her while Rowan was here, but he had nothing to do with it."

"Would you like to share why you chose to toss her?"

"She was being a bitch."

Rowan couldn't hold his laugh in that time.

Caelan sighed. "Evie."

"She came onto my property, tried to get through my wards, then insulted me numerous times. Rachel deserved much more than I gave her."

Caelan pushed the tray away and leaned against the potting bench. "She's at the Keep Healer."

"But alive," I emphasized. "Maybe a few broken bones will keep her from showing up here again."

"If her father hears about it, we might have trouble."

"Then I'll throw him off my property, too," I grumbled.

Caelan's eyes flashed gold. "Evie, you have to get better about your temper."

Rowan's hands stilled. His brow furrowed, and I saw his inhale. He opened his mouth, but I interrupted him, shooting him a warning look. There was no need for him and Caelan to have issues over something that involved me.

"And what about her?" I asked quietly.

"What about her?" Caelan snapped.

"She trespassed on my property, attempted to interfere with my warding, then implied I was gutter trash."

Caelan stared at me for a long moment. "There were other

ways of dealing with her than using your magic to toss her half a mile."

I crossed my arms over my chest. "But none were as fun as that one was."

He didn't smile. A moment ago, I'd been annoyed, but now I was full-blown angry. "Why is it that I can get harassed from all sides and yet, when I react, it suddenly becomes all my fault?"

His jaw tightened. "I'm not blaming you."

"Oh? Just my temper?"

Rowan repacked the plants and seedlings I'd gifted him and nodded at me, a warning in his eyes.

See you later, he mouthed, before slinking out the door.

"You have to admit you have an impressive temper."

"A temper that never comes out unless someone, nine times out of ten connected to you, decides to do something to violate my boundaries."

"So, it's my fault now?"

"It sure as shit is not my fault!"

"Are you saying you are not responsible for what you might do when someone...annoys you?"

I laughed, though there was no amusement in the sound. "We've had this fight a dozen times. I will not apologize for defending myself or my property. You are the one who invited that dreadful woman into your home. Why are you here getting onto me for reacting to her antagonizing me?"

"Because I am a LORD!" he roared. "Because there is decorum when dealing with shifters! Because I cannot afford to take a wife who reacts with adolescent mischief when someone pisses her off!"

The words peppered against me like thrown stones, each sentence making me flinch.

When he finished, his eyes widened. He reached a hand out for me. "Evie."

I stepped away, tears burning the back of my eyes. "Get out."

"I—I didn't mean that. I'm frustrated and aggravated, and I'm—"

"I do not care. Get out of my house before I react with *adolescent mischief.*"

Caelan closed his eyes for a moment. When he opened them, a ring of gold swallowed his irises. "Evie. Please. We can sort this out. We've already agreed that we needed to do better."

"That was before I realized my fiancé is someone who will not stand up for me when I need him the most. I understand politics, Caelan. What I do not understand is bending over backward to soothe the ego of someone who is actively trying to ruin our relationship. She is the one who made the error in judgment. The only thing I am guilty of is reacting. But I won't lie down and let a bully kick me. Politics or no politics, I have a spine. But I'm no longer sure you do."

Color flushed the tops of Caelan's cheekbones. Rage flickered in his eyes. "Evie," he warned.

"This is your last warning," I said softly. The ground rumbled underneath my feet. "Leave now."

A phantom wind rose, brushing my hair away from my neck.

Caelan's upper lip curled into a snarl. "Is this how you want it to be?"

An otherworldly note turned my voice deeper. "I'm not the one who chose this."

Caelan took a step back and turned on his heel, slamming the door behind him as he exited.

I waited for him to come back in, to apologize, to say something to end this unbearable silence, but he didn't. The wards tingled one more time as he passed through, and I wondered…

I wondered if maybe I wasn't cut out for affairs of the heart.

CHAPTER
Eighteen

To add insult to injury, my father showed up half an hour later, as if he knew what had just happened. He didn't bother knocking this time but did me the favor of warning me by sending the scent of wild magic through my kitchen before appearing on my couch.

I was holding the coffee pot when he appeared and debated chucking the thing at his head.

"I wouldn't," he said mildly.

He was dressed in the guise of a thirty-something athletic human male. White t-shirt, dark joggers, athletic shoes with ankle socks.

"You remembered the shoes today." I poured us both a mug of coffee and brought it over.

He frowned at his feet. "Shoes are the most foolish invention humans have ever come up with. Our feet are meant to touch bare earth. Such keeps our hearts rooted to the world."

"Pollution and litter have sort of ruined that for us."

Dad picked up his coffee and was about to sip it when he paused and held the mug closer to his nose to take a sniff.

"Irish cream," I answered the question in his eyes. "A healthy dose."

"Rough day?" He sipped and made a curious noise. "This is interesting."

"It's delicious," I corrected.

Dad's lips quirked in a smile. "I heard you visited your mother."

I sighed. "When are you going to stop spying on me?"

He lifted a shoulder. "I cannot help when my people spot you outside of your home."

"And report back to you everything I said and did?"

"Your mother has more than adequate privacy around her home to prevent that."

"Serves you right," I muttered. "Why are you here?"

"Can't a father see his daughter without such questions?"

My eyebrows went up.

"Honestly, Evie. Have you always been this...ornery?"

"Caelan just stomped out of here. You should ask him."

His eyes flashed. "Your Lord is angry?"

"You know the answer to that since you're the one who threw that brunette homewrecker in his path."

My father set his mug down. "Are you so sure I'm guilty of such?"

There was an odd note in his voice. "Are you saying you aren't the one who sent Rachel to him?"

"I'm not saying anything. While I might not approve of your Lord, I do want the best for you."

"Which is not him."

A thin smile. "I'm here to continue your training. Regardless of whether you're angry with me, you are still my daughter and my heir."

When I opened my mouth to protest, Cernunnos raised his hand. "On top of that, you deserve to know the depths of your power. There are rumblings around the world about your heritage. Word is getting out about who you are. You will need to know the scope of what you can do so you can field...challengers off."

I took a long sip of my coffee. "Challengers?" I echoed.

"Our kind are bloodthirsty, Evie. I'm surprised you haven't already had issues."

"Nothing more than normal." I eyed him. "Though I hear you're the one responsible for curbing the inordinate number of suitors I've had lately."

"None of those men could have held the crown alongside you."

The words were said so casually, but his eyes held a deadly gleam.

"Just like Caelan could not."

He lifted a shoulder. "You need someone who will always have your back."

I snorted. "I knew you were spying! No one has timing that immaculate!"

He laughed. "I wasn't spying. I just happened to venture onto your land and overheard the fallout." His eyes twinkled. "You really tossed the woman off your land?"

"Yes," I grumbled. "She deserved it."

"I'm sure she did." He drained the rest of his coffee and sat the mug down. "Though I'm curious about Caelan's opinion about your temper. Do you feel the Lord is right?"

I rolled my eyes. "Of course not. I'm not saying I don't have a temper. I'm merely saying it only comes out when someone pushes me too far."

"Like Caelan?"

A begrudging smile tilted my lips. The first time Caelan really pissed me off, I embarrassed him at one of his parties with an automaton I made that taunted him with the story of a wolf being outsmarted by a fox.

He was livid and destroyed my shop.

To be honest, that was the most fun I'd ever had in my life.

"To be fair, he deserved it, too."

"Then you have your answer." He leaned forward. "You do not go out looking for fights, Evie. That's the most important part of being a leader. But when a fight comes to you, you do not hesitate. You are decisive, sometimes vicious, and you never regret how you chose to respond. Those are the traits of a queen."

I still hadn't decided whether I planned to take up my crown. My life here was a good one, even with my sometimes-rocky relationship with Caelan. Moira, Ash, and Tess were my family, and I couldn't imagine leaving them to rule over a people I had little experience with.

I changed the subject. "Have you seen Tess?"

My father's eyebrows rose. "Your banshee? I do not speak with her one-on-one. Is she missing?"

I told him where she was.

My father looked disturbed. "Strange place for a banshee to visit. Are you planning to retrieve her?"

"If she's there of her own volition, I don't want her to think I don't trust her. But I don't know if she is, so I plan to find her."

"I'm also here about Lugh."

I groaned. "He asked for five days."

"You should have sent him home the second he fell through whatever portal your vampire friend opened."

"We're well aware of that now."

"You don't think it's curious your banshee friend disappeared when Lugh appeared?"

"It's very curious," I agreed. "But I have it on good authority that Lugh isn't stashing her where he's staying. Nor has he ever held her there." I slid a glance his way. "Are you keeping something from me about her?"

"Banshees are not meant to be in those lands. You must retrieve her soon."

"Cryptic," I said, my brow furrowing. "Can you elaborate?"

He gave me a thin smile and rose. "Come. Let us go outside and test your mettle. Perhaps you can burn off a little of that temper."

I chucked a paper coaster at his head, but my father blinked from the couch to the door, grinning at me before he stepped out.

Nineteen

THE MEDDLER

"What were you *thinking*?" the male hissed.

Rachel rolled her eyes. "She's unbearable. Did you honestly think I'd be able to befriend that awful woman?"

"I knew I should have used someone else for this."

Rachel pouted. "Please." She fanned herself with a delicate hand, hiding her wince. That bitch throwing her had resulted in some lingering injuries. She'd be fine tomorrow but tonight was proving unpleasant. "I'm the only one who has so much history with the Lord. Things might have gotten off on the wrong foot, but he'll visit me tonight. He can't help himself."

His eyes narrowed. "I suppose you're right. Few shifters can resist their urge to nurture wounded females."

"Exactly. Caelan's healer wrote up a full report." She fluttered her eyelashes. "I might have embellished my injuries a tad."

He smirked. "I suppose we'll see what happens."

"He's always been resistant in matters of the heart." She lowered her voice and leaned in. "Though I heard he and that bitch had a fight tonight. He'll be vulnerable, and I am not without my charms."

The male didn't seem as convinced of her charms as she was,

but he nodded and pulled something glowing from the breast pocket of his suit. He'd started visiting her a few months ago, under the guise of business with her father, but Rachel noticed he'd always try to catch her alone.

At first, she'd been flattered by his attention until she realized he wasn't there for romance. He'd come for something far more sinister.

Rachel was happy to oblige him, considering how Caelan ended things between them. The massive paycheck she was slated to receive at the end didn't hurt her willingness either.

"What is that?" Rachel leaned forward and sniffed, recoiling at the scent. There was something wrong about the liquid, something she didn't like.

"If you expect failure, you will use this. Put it in his food or drink. But do not use it if things are going to plan—only as a last resort."

"What is it?" she asked again.

"Harmless," the male said, but there was a gleam in his eyes Rachel didn't like. "It will make him more susceptible to suggestion, that's all."

"Temporarily?"

He shrugged. "It will wear off. Eventually. But I fully expect you to charm him without using the bottle. I've been slowly softening him up for you."

At her look of alarm, he chuckled. "Nothing obvious. Caelan won't notice. It's just enough for him to drop his guard a little."

He dropped the bottle into her outstretched palm, and Rachel recoiled. "It smells. Caelan is too smart not to notice."

"Once it's mixed, it's tasteless and odorless."

Rachel rolled the bottle in her fingers, holding it up to the light. The color was pretty, reminiscent of that bitch's eyes, a clear azure blue. Silver sparkles danced inside the bottle, flecks that seemed to move of their own volition.

She set it on her nightstand and wiped her hands on her

pajama pants. "I doubt I'll need to use it, but it's there if I need a boost."

He stepped up to her, power rolling from his muscular frame. Rachel swallowed hard and resisted the urge to lean away. If she wasn't so set on Caelan, she might have tested the waters to see if he was interested in something more. Few males as powerful as this one ever came to Europe. Her father didn't allow powers like him entrance into his country.

Standing before him, Rachel finally realized why. Despite her reservations, Rachel leaned forward and tugged the man's tie. "If things don't work out between Caelan and I, perhaps—"

He knocked her hand away, his eyes narrowing. A spark of power rolled over his irises. "Do not test me on this. I do not sample the merchandise before the deal is done."

Rachel smirked. That wasn't a no. "I've only been here for a little while. Caelan has always had a strong will. His unique relationship to Evie might prove to be his downfall. She is difficult and angry, and from his scent I can tell Caelan is irritated more often than not." She clicked her tongue. "I'll win your Lord away from her. Mark my words."

"See that you do," he growled. Without another word, he turned and exited her room.

She waited until the sounds of his footsteps faded before she let out a long breath. Dangerous waters she was treading in. But the payoff for herself and for the other Lords would be worth it.

All she had to do was get under Caelan's guard. Once she did, the path to his heart was wide open.

She should know. She'd traveled it once before.

Still no sign of Tess and no word from her, either. Ash had gone over to her apartment last night using the key she'd never taken back and searched for any sign she might have left willingly. Or unwillingly.

He came back empty-handed. No signs of struggle, but no packed suitcase either. She'd left her clothes, her toiletries, and her favorite shoes and blanket behind. We all knew Tess rarely went anywhere without that blanket. She even brought it to the store sometimes and curled up on the couch with tea during slowdowns.

There might not be signs of her being taken against her will, but the things she'd left behind proved suspicious.

"Mom said she'd come with us," I said to Moira the next morning as we both cringed at the state of the pink roses our temporary supplier had sent. Half the petals were drooping, and they hadn't de-thorned most of the stems, causing us to do twice the amount of work we normally had to do.

Moira's dark eyebrows lifted. "You'd trust her to have our backs?"

"I'm not sure who I trust anymore," I said honestly. "Dad was at the house last night helping me figure out the magic he'd passed to me, and things seemed normal. Mom fed me soup the other day and didn't poison me. The world is topsy-turvy right now, Moira. I'm not sure what to make of things. Honestly," I grumbled, "things feel apocalyptic."

Moira snorted. "Two trustworthy fae in the same family? The odds are against you." But her lips twitched and she slung an arm over my shoulders. "They're your parents, and you're amazing. Obviously, they love you. Maybe let them show it when they can."

I eyed her over a particularly droopy rose. "By letting my mother have our backs in a strange, dangerous land?"

"She can have *your* back," Moira said. "I'll watch both of ours just to make sure she doesn't try anything funny." She rubbed her hands over her arms and shivered. "Cliona is scary as hell. If she has our back, we're golden, but if she doesn't…"

If she doesn't, we're screwed. I tried for chirpy. "Mom has never let me die before, and that's when I thought she hated me, so I'm choosing to think positive."

Moira shook her head but smiled. "Let's hope. Want to leave right after work?"

"Meet me at my house?"

"Six?"

"Done." Moira picked up a dried petal and threw it at me. "Now, let's get through these pink monstrosities so we can make something cooler."

I WAS PUTTING the final touches on the last table centerpiece when the bell over the door jingled. Hiding my smile at Moira's almost inaudible groan, I looked up to see Thalia walking in.

Garrett was nowhere to be found, so he was either outside or things had changed in a big way. Caelan's Enforcer and my sister were attached at the hip these days, and you rarely saw her without him anymore.

She stopped at the entrance, her gaze sweeping the store until it landed on me. We stared at each other for a long moment.

"Thalia!" Moira said, giving me an annoyed look. She was on Team Thalia, only because she was my sister and I had so little reliable family around. The seer had done nothing to violate my trust except keep her paternity secret, but I still felt that sense of betrayal lingering in my stomach every time I saw her or thought about her.

And yet, here she was in the flesh, the hesitant look on her face making me squirm with guilt.

Moira took her by the elbow and ushered her deeper into the store. "Tea? Coffee? Water?"

"Nothing for me, thanks." She shrugged off her brown jacket and folded it over her arm.

Thalia was a small woman, fine-boned and petite. Now that I knew who she was, I acknowledged we resembled each other, though no one who saw us together would guess we were sisters right away. Where my eyes were bright blue, Thalia's were hazel, amber flecked with green and she had high cheekbones and full lips. She was pretty in a girl next doorway, but Thalia was a powerful seer, and her magic packed a punch.

Her dark hair, so similar to mine, was plaited in her trademark braid and slung over her shoulder. She held a brightly colored patchworked bag which clashed with her outfit. Thalia normally favored skirts, but the weather wasn't conducive to her normal style. Today she wore a pair of corduroy boot cut pants with shiny patent leather boots and a fuzzy white sweater. Several strands of thin beaded gemstone necklaces graced her neck, and she wore a pair of elaborately twisted silver earrings.

"Hey, Evie," she said in a hesitant voice.

"Thalia." There was a seat right across from me at my worktable. Not offering it was rude, but Moira didn't give me the chance to decide. She led the seer over and pulled the chair out, then brushed away leaf and petal litter from the table's surface.

Thalia put her bag on the ground.

"Sure you don't want something to drink?" Moira asked.

Thalia shook her head. "I'm here to see Evie. I won't take up much of your time."

"Where's Garrett?" I asked.

"Outside. Waiting for me in the car."

"He can come inside if he wants," Moira said.

"I told him I'd be no longer than five minutes." She chewed on the edge of her lips and twisted her fingers together. "I'm here with a warning."

Brushing off a warning from a seer was foolhardy. I couldn't afford to let my pride get in the way of our safety. Setting the tools down, I crossed my arms and stared.

"Alright then. What is it?"

Thalia swallowed.

"Evie," Moira snapped. "May I speak with you for a moment?"

"No."

Moira snorted and reached for my elbow, yanking me unceremoniously from the chair.

"Excuse me," she said to Thalia, her voice so sweet it could be bottled and sold as a Canadian export.

My sister watched with wide eyes as Moira dragged me to the walk-in fridge and shoved me inside.

"What is wrong with you?" she hissed as soon as the door shut behind us.

I knew I was being a huge brat, but I didn't particularly care.

Moira's eyes widened. "Oh my gods. Evie! You know you're being an asshole and you're doubling down on it!" She laughed out loud. "Never thought I'd see the day when you acted like a petulant teenager."

I crossed my arms over my chest and glared at her.

Amusement sparkled in Moira's eyes. "As much as I want to gloat about this, Thalia is your sister. She had as much control over her birth as you did over what happened in Scotland."

I stiffened, anger blooming in my chest. "It's not the same," I snapped.

"No," Moira agreed, "but Thalia had nothing to do with her conception, just like you had nothing to do with Finn's actions. Those things happened to you, not because of you."

"Conception is a far different scenario than Scotland."

"Sure," Moira agreed. "But again, Thalia couldn't help being born, just like you couldn't help becoming a Chimera. She could have stayed away, but she didn't. You don't have to decide immediately if you want to braid each other's hair and have sleepovers together, but taking it out on her is a dick move, and you know it."

I huffed a breath. "I know," I admitted.

"Good. I'm glad you know you're being a huge brat. Acceptance is the first step in the brat recovery process."

I rolled my eyes. "Shut up."

"Are you ready to suck your hurt feelings up and go speak to your sister like the adult you are? You're a big sister. You should act like one."

"I liked it much better when I was the one lecturing all of you."

"Yes," Moira said, shuffling me out of the fridge. "We're all well aware, but we've been especially well-behaved lately."

When I returned to my seat, Thalia was still twisting her fingers together.

"I'm sorry," she blurted. "I shouldn't have come." Thalia rose from her seat.

"No." I shook my head. "I'm being rude. Please," I said, gesturing for her to sit back down. "I'm sorry. Things are just… weird for me right now."

"I know," Thalia said. "Having a sister is already weird. Having a secret sister is way worse." She dropped her eyes. "And I'm sorry I didn't tell you."

"You seemed a little gleeful about it, to be honest."

Thalia snorted. "Not about you. Knowing our father was about to get an earful was the highlight of my year, though."

A smile tugged at my lips. Soon, Thalia and I were grinning at each other.

We chatted for a little while before she got to the reason she'd stopped by. Thalia reached for her handbag and pulled out a small notebook decorated with ink doodles. "I had Garrett write down what I said this time."

She flipped through a few pages and skimmed down the page. "Some of this sounds insane, so I'll go over the highlights."

Thalia pointed to a scribbled passage in her notebook. "Beware the promised land," she read. "Not all is as it appears."

I went still.

"Beware the mouth with teeth but know the bark is worse than the bite. Remember who you are, but it's more important to remember who you can be. Do not be afraid. Great change is coming." Thalia frowned. "The last one seems odd but..." she trailed off and shook her head. "The rowan tree is dying. You must go and tend to the land where it grows."

Some of that made sense. Some of it sounded like nonsense. "I'm due to travel to a place called the promised land soon. I'll keep your warnings in mind."

Thalia's smile was sheepish. "I can't often decipher the things I say, and I usually don't remember them anyway." She slung her bag over her shoulder and stood. "Some seer I am," she said dryly. "But at least I have Garrett around to help. At least for a little while."

"A little while?" I questioned. "Are you going somewhere?"

"Dad hasn't said much, but he was not pleased about you finding out how we were related. He tends to move me when too many people know who I am."

"That doesn't make sense. I'm his daughter, too, and he's never tried to make me go anywhere."

Thalia's fingers tightened on the strap of her bag. "That's because you're you, and I'm me. I have zero offensive or defensive magic. Being a seer leaves me completely vulnerable." She shook her head and headed toward the door. "I'm sure your Lord wants his Enforcer back, too. Garrett doesn't enjoy babysitting me, and I know he's ready to get back to his regular duties."

I'm not sure why I did it, but I reached for her hand and squeezed gently. "I think you're mistaken about Garrett, and I've heard nothing about moving you anywhere." I paused. "Which leads to another question. Do you like it here? If you don't want to stay, I won't interfere, but if you like Joy Springs, I can speak to our father."

Hope flared over her face like the sun, there and gone in a heartbeat. "He never listens to anyone," she grumbled. "Though I appreciate you asking."

"I have my ways," I assured her.

She pulled away and stopped at the door. "Thanks, Evie. I—I appreciate your kindness today."

There was nothing I could say because I felt like shit. I'd been an ass to her and couldn't make up for that. All I could do was try harder in the future. Moira was right. The circumstances of her birth were not her fault and holding it against her said more about me than her.

Guilt racked me the rest of the day.

Twenty-One

Being the bridge to all the fae realms came in handy, though I still carried the seed Mom had given me for ease of traveling directly to her. We arrived by seven, and Mom was already outside waiting for us. She carried a small travel bag and was dressed more casually than I'd ever seen.

"Jeans?" I gaped at her.

"Wow," Moira said. "Who knew you had all that junk in your trunk?"

"Moira!" I hissed.

Mom gave Moira a dark look. "You brought your pet vampire, I see."

Moira's grin was a touch too toothy. "She sure did. I made sure to sharpen my canines, too. Just in case I got hungry."

The evening air was cool and humid. Tiny fae flitted around, their skin giving off a soft bioluminescent glow, reminding me of fireflies. They brushed through Mom's hair, several braiding strands of her hair. Sometimes I forgot my mother was a goddess who claimed her own realm, and that she was beloved by her people.

I tilted my head up and gasped at the wide canopy of glimmering stars above our head. Mom was right. They were different here. Gloriously so. Mom's land had no real light pollution. Her home was lit by magic, soft, warm lighting throughout. On the outside of the mounds, there were small candle flames, lighting the paths enough to see by.

Back home, I could see the stars well if I ventured far enough into my land, but even with my acreage, there were still too many towns around. I'd have to venture fifty or so miles away before I could even dream of catching a view like this one.

Moira reached out and grabbed my hand. Her lips were parted as she tilted her head and caught what I was looking at. "Wow," she breathed.

Mom's smile was indulgent. "I believe you might be the first vampire who's witnessed our skies. Stay close to Evie. She is the bridge and you will be safe with her." Mom sniffed, her eyes widening slightly. "You have fae blood," she said softly. "How have I never caught that before?"

Moira's cheeks colored. "A distant ancestor, I believe. You've only seen me at the shop and Evie's home. Her home always carries a heavy scent of flowers. Perhaps that's why."

But Mom's eyes lingered on Moira for longer than was comfortable before she gave a short nod. "Well. I'm sure that's it." She ran her gaze down both our bodies and back up. "You're dressed well for travel. Comfortable shoes, I hope?"

Moira and I nodded.

"Good." Mom pulled a map out from her bag and handed it over. The map wasn't anything spectacular and consisted of a small, ink drawn tree, showing the different realms and their levels. "Tir Tairngire," she said, "is the second level. All you have to do is take our hands and focus on the place."

I frowned down at the map. "How can I focus on a place I've never seen?"

Mom took my hand. "Close your eyes."

Her cool fingers slid through mine. Soft magic, reminding me a little of Tess's knocked at my mind. I opened a tiny crack of my mind and a picture pushed in of a place that had green rolling hills and azure, blue seas. Birds with wildly colored wings swept through the air and trilled their songs. The air had a sweet, fresh tang to it, and I inhaled, even though I knew it was an illusion.

When I opened my eyes, the image faded away.

"Ready?" Mom asked.

I blinked away the tears in my eyes, surprised by my reaction. The fae lands held no real appeal to me, or they hadn't until recently, but the place we were about to go to was something right out of a storybook.

I reached for Moira's hand. "Yes,"

A tingle of magic rolled over my skin as I recalled the place in my mind's eye.

WE LANDED in a field of silky grass. Strangely, it was daylight. I blinked in surprise and let go of Mom and Moira.

"Time is different here," Mom observed. "Such is common between the realms."

"How much time will have passed when we return home?"

Mom shook her head. "There's no way to tell. I hope you've made arrangements for your business."

"Ash knows if he doesn't hear from us by midnight to open the store the next morning." I'd need to give them all a bonus soon because they'd been picking up an extraordinary amount of slack lately.

"Good." Mom pointed toward the west. "Your banshee resides over there."

And with that, we were off.

THALIA'S WORDS kept playing on repeat through my brain. *Beware the promised lands.* Tir Tairngire literally meant Land of Promise. I knew as well as anyone that looks could be deceiving, but this place seemed like paradise. The temperature was comfortable, borderline cool. No bugs bit or pinched. There were no thorns on any of the plants or flowers growing wild in the grass. No poisonous air. No birds swooped down to attack us from the crystal blue skies. Nothing zoomed out from the woods to harm us.

I could walk through this place for the rest of my life and be content.

Usually when I felt like this, something or someone would crawl out from the woodwork and screw it up for me. But the wind stayed gentle, and the sway of grass against our calves made my shoulders drop, the stress over the last few weeks fading away.

I took my first deep inhale that I could remember and slowly released my breath.

Mom glanced over her shoulder. "Better?"

"This place feels like I smoked the best weed known to man," Moira mused.

Mom's lips twitched. "You found weed that worked with your metabolism?"

"I grew it," Moira said absentmindedly.

"You grew super weed?" I asked, my eyes wide as I watched her.

Moira grinned. "You aren't the only good gardener out there, you know."

"I'm a Floromancer, and I never even thought about growing weed like that." To be fair, I never thought about growing weed at all. "Have you sold any?"

"Weed is still illegal in most states." Her prim tone made me roll my eyes.

"Like you give a damn about that."

Mom's eyes bounced back and forth between us. "Would you consider selling some to your best friend's mother?"

Moira and I stopped walking.

"Mom!" I said with a gasp.

Moira blinked in surprise and started laughing.

"Being a goddess is stressful," Mom said. "And as you both know, they don't make substances for people like us." She moved her hand back and forth. "And if they do, they're extremely addictive and dangerous. I assume your new pot strain is not?"

Moira fished around in her purse and pulled out a perfectly rolled joint.

"I am in an alternate universe," I muttered.

"May I?" Mom asked.

"You can have this one. I have another in my purse."

"Moira! What the hell?"

"It helps me not summon interdimensional beings," she said with a shrug. "I started experimenting some time back, and it's not perfect, but in my defense, I had never pulled a god out of thin air until I took a weed break."

"I'm going to need weed if you two don't knock it off."

Mom lifted the joint and sniffed it, the thing hovering under her noise like a white mustache.

"Don't you dare light that thing up," I snapped.

Mom's grin held a wicked edge. I'd never seen her smile like that, and the blooming smile I returned might have been the first real one I'd ever given her.

I waved both of them off. "Be careful with that stuff, and do not show it to Thalia!"

My sister looked like she'd smoke all the weed in the world if she could.

"You've seen Thalia?" Mom asked as she tucked the joint into an inner pocket of her bag.

I told Mom about her warning. Mom frowned. "This place is one of the least dangerous realms, but we should heed her words all the same. I do not know what the other means, though I think it might refer to your other Lord."

"He's not my Lord," I grumbled.

"Perception is everything. Even if you do not consider him yours, it's worth paying close attention, looking for any danger coming his way and, perhaps, sending him a warning if you haven't already."

I hadn't. Finding Tess had taken up all the space in my over-worked brain.

We fell silent as we continued walking across the field, and it wasn't long until we came upon a stone path. Mom stepped off the grass and waited for us. When we were on the road, Mom adjusted her bag but didn't move.

"Mom?"

"Wait a moment," she said quietly.

The ground rumbled underneath our feet. "The curious things started watching us halfway through. I'm glad you brought me."

"Things?" A ripple in the grass caught my eye. Moira stilled next to me as she caught the same.

A few seconds later, a chitinous body rose above the swaying grass. It had no eyes, only a perfectly round mouth edged with serrated teeth.

"What the fuck?" I whispered.

Moira's hand reached out and gripped my arm. "And here I was worried about ticks." She shuddered.

The thing resembled a caterpillar, if said caterpillar was three feet wide, wore armor, and had teeth straight out of a slasher movie.

"What is that thing?" I asked.

Mom shook her head. "I've never seen its like, but you visit enough, you'll find many unexplainable things in the fae lands."

"Gods, I hope not," Moira muttered.

"We are not walking through grass like that again." I rubbed my hands over my arms.

Mom shot me an amused look. "Next time, when you look at the map, try to pick a road or town as a landing spot."

I stared for a long moment before a low curse tore from my throat. Hadn't even thought about that!

She patted me on the shoulder. "I was with you. Few things will mess with one of their old gods, no matter what realm they're from."

"What about the old gods' kids?"

Mom's lips twitched. "Only if their mettle has been tested."

My eyes narrowed. "What does that mean?"

"You are new to our lands. There is much to learn if you wish to accept your place as Cernunnos' heir."

She started off down the road. I jerked a thumb over my shoulder. "If I did, could I start my reign off by killing all of those things?"

Moira snorted.

"Hardly," Mom said. "As the humans say, all of God's creatures, blah, blah, blah."

"Yeah, well, I'd kill all the mosquitoes too if I could."

Mom slid a glance my way. "You could, you know."

"Really? I could take all of them out like a giant bug zapper?"

She lifted a shoulder. "Sure. If you want to wipe out the food supply while you're at it."

Moira's brow furrowed. "That's the bees, right?"

It took a moment for my brain to click into on mode. "Mosquitoes are pollinators."

"Those little fuckers," Moira mused. "They know we want to murder them all, so they made sure they served a purpose."

"Mosquitos are critical for pollinating cacao. Can you imagine a world without chocolate?"

Moira's gasp made Mom laugh. "Orchids, too," she added. "Even ticks serve a larger purpose in the world."

"I changed my mind. I vote to destroy ticks and live with the consequences," Moira announced.

We walked for quite a while debating which species was worse and almost didn't notice when the road began to curve to the left. As we went around the bend, small stone houses appeared. "Tess is somewhere in this village," Mom murmured. "Be on your guard."

I'd brought no weapons and didn't look like much of a threat. None of us did. Mom pulsed with power, but many fae did that. Maybe when you lived here, you didn't notice stuff like someone else being at the power level of the freaking sun anymore.

"How's my hair?" Moira whispered.

I wheezed a laugh. Mom gave us a pointed look. "Remember, you are not in the human lands. There is a decorum that must be followed."

Moira nodded solemnly and put her hand over her heart. "I hope it's second breakfast."

I elbowed her. "Just don't say anything, okay?"

"But how will everyone know about my dating life?"

Mom flicked her fingers over her shoulder. A zap of white light hit Moira in the shoulder. The vampire hissed. "Shit! What was that?"

"There's more where that came from if you don't get it together," Mom murmured.

Moira sighed and mimed a zipping motion over her lips.

A few minutes later, we stepped foot into the fae village.

CHAPTER

Twenty~Two

Absolutely nothing happened. I thought maybe Tess might be in the middle of the town square, being crowned queen or something, with the way everything was playing out these days, but there was no sign of the banshee. Fae milled around the shops, dressed in a bright array of shimmering fabrics. Some of the females wore dresses with swirly skirts, and others made do with sensible pants and leather moccasins.

The men dressed in more drab colors, earth tones in shades of brown and green. No one pretended not to be staring at us, but no one made a move to approach.

"Do they know who you are?" I whispered to Mom.

"Maybe, though it's also likely they don't. I do not travel outside my own realm much, unless it's to see you."

Her azure gaze swept the air, not lingering on anything until it settled on a nondescript house closer to the edge of the path, slightly offset by another, larger shop.

"I believe she's in there, but we should look around first, pretend to be tourists so no one has the chance to warn the inhabitants of the house."

I looked at Mom. "Why would we be worried about anyone warning her?"

"We have no idea who Tess might be with."

That shut me up. Mom didn't say Tess was in distress, but she didn't look worried, and that made my nerves calm down a little. She pushed into a small shop. Instead of a bell over the door, a high tinkling charm went off close to the register.

A small man with grey hair and spectacles perched on the end of his nose greeted us. "Welcome to Penn's," he said in a surprisingly deep voice. "We have the finest selections of writing tools in the entire realm, all handmade in my workshop above the store."

Moira's eyes glowed as she took in the array of leatherbound journals, ink pens with elaborate feathers attached, hand carved pencils, and inks in a dazzling array of shades. Mom wandered off, looking every inch the interested tourist, and I stood there for a beat too long looking like I'd left my wits back on the sidewalk.

Moira finally pulled me by the shirt. "Come," she said a little too loudly. "Look at these gorgeous pens!"

I followed her dumbly. Moira gave me a withering look. "Are you alright?"

I blinked. "I'm fine." But was I? Physically, I felt fine, but mentally I felt overwhelmed. All of these other worlds had always been at my fingertips, and I'd missed out on knowing them due to…many things. Being stubborn. Other people lying to me. The period in my life where I'd stuck my head in the sand and refused to come out.

The people here were not exactly people, but they were my people. Weren't they?

Moira gave me a sympathetic smile. "For me this is Disneyland, but for you…" Her voice trailed off. "You must have a lot of mixed feelings."

I nodded. "I do. This is overwhelming."

"Once we find Tess, we can leave if you want to." Her eyes narrowed. "Or find a 24-hour fae rave and see where the night takes us."

Her lighthearted words made me smile. "Maybe next time. But maybe we can have dinner here. See what the place looks like at nighttime. I think I can return us from anywhere, so it won't cost any extra time to get home."

"That would be nice." She frowned and looked in her purse. "Shit. Does this place take regular money? All I have are Benjamins."

Mom came up just then. "I'll spot whatever you need. Shop owners love when people like us come in and spend." She lowered her voice. "They're more willing to share information, too, so spend away, little vampire."

You didn't need to tell Moira twice.

An hour and a half later, Moira looked like an American teenager at the mall, loaded with bags all up and down her arms. I was beginning to wonder if we'd need two trips to get everything home.

As amusing as that was, no one seemed off or jittery, and no one had mentioned a single thing about a banshee. That was unusual in itself because banshees were not common in this land, at least according to Mom.

"We'll go up and knock on the door," Mom said when we wandered out of the last shop. "I can't imagine things will turn violent since they picked a house right in the middle of town."

But Mom wore an odd expression.

"What?" I asked.

"It's an odd choice for someone trying to hide, don't you think?"

Sometimes hiding in plain sight is far more effective than making an effort to conceal yourself. But it was weird.

And too coincidental to be unrelated to Lugh's arrival.

Moira shifted her bags with a grunt.

"You look like a pack mule," I teased.

But Moira was beyond my teasing. She'd gone to retail heaven and was still walking amongst the fluffy clouds. "You cannot harsh my buzz. It is eternal."

Mom rolled her eyes. "You should try the shopping in my realm."

Moira blinked. "There's shopping everywhere?" she wheezed.

"We hold jobs just like the humans do. Art and tradesmen are far more common than anything else. Our economy is self-sustaining, so no one ever wants for anything, but sometimes people want certain things they can't afford on a universal income. That's where bartering and trading come in, or selling at the weekend markets."

We stopped in our tracks. "Wait. Everyone receives a base income that provides for…"

"Food and the use of a healer when necessary. Fae make their own dwellings. Magic is an integral part of our lives, and having someone else build your home could contaminate the energy inside, so we also provide funds to help with the cost of stone and wood, whatever they may need to build."

"Aren't you worried about people trying to scam the system?"

Mom's laugh was deep and wicked. "Everyone knows not to cheat their ruler. Every dime is meticulously accounted for, and we verify everything before doling out funds. If we suspect someone is trying to cheat, we have our ways of curtailing such behavior and finding out the truth."

Moira winced. "Not a fun way?"

"No," Mom assured us. "We do not pay for clothing, though we do assist with fabric for those who make their own. The necessities only. Food, fresh water, things our citizens must have to survive."

"Damn," Moira said, eyeing my mother with a glimmer of respect in her eyes. "I'm surprised you don't have humans beating down your doors."

Mom grunted. "Humans quickly learned of the culinary habits of the fae. Many of our citizens like exotic meat." She winked and jogged the few steps up to the door, leaving Moira and me speechless on the sidewalk.

The vampire leaned over. "Did your mom just say she eats people?"

I slowly shook my head. "Not directly."

"Hmm. She's super creepy sometimes."

"Yep," I agreed. "I won't be getting my passport stamped for an extended visit anytime soon."

The door opened. A familiar silvery head poked out and waved when she saw us. "Evie! Moira!"

Mom turned around, her eyes wide. *Be careful*, she mouthed.

Something was up.

We waved back and started down the sidewalk. "Be on your guard," I said under my breath.

Tess looked well. Better than well, actually. Her hair was down and brushed to a silvery sheen. She wore makeup, blush, gloss and mascara, giving her face far more color than normal. Her eyes were bright and borderline feverish, and she watched us with an odd stare as we came up the steps.

Tess held open the door, and we brushed past her on our way inside. The house was small but clean, and the only magic I sensed was Tess's.

Mom followed behind us.

"Would you like some tea?" Tess asked when she'd shut the door. "I have Earl Grey and Jasmine."

"Please," Moira said. Mom and I nodded.

Tess shooed us toward the living room. "Please sit! We can chat while I make your tea. It feels like it's been ages since I've seen you!"

Tess never spoke much. When she did speak, whatever she said was sure to be either morose or important. Her voice always had a tremulous warbling tone, none of it evident today.

Tess seemed…normal.

And that meant something had gone *very* wrong.

"We've been worried about you," I started.

Tess filled a tea pot with water and lit the pilot light. She laughed merrily. "Worried? Why ever for?"

Moira and I gave each other a wtf look. "Because you left without telling anyone and didn't even leave a note. We've been worried sick."

Tess took four mugs down. "Left? What do you mean left? I haven't left anywhere."

"You missed work two days in a row," Moira said. "Don't you remember?"

Tess plunked tea bags into the mugs. "Work?" Her nose scrunched. "I haven't worked at your shop in at least four years!"

Moira reached over and squeezed my knee. Mom gave me a warning look and shook her head once.

"Tess, dear," she said, "would you like any help?"

"I got it." She put everything on the tray and poured hot water over the mugs. Steam rose through the air, and Tess sighed. "I love the way tea smells."

She carried everything over and sat down, adjusting her skirt over her knees.

"I'm so glad you came to visit me." She passed the sugar bowl around along with a small silver spoon. "Now, tell me what you've been up to. I've missed you so much."

Two hours later, we walked out without Tess, all of us confused as hell.

She waved goodbye from the door, promising she'd stop by for Christmas. When she finally shut the door, none of us moved.

"What in the actual hell is going on?" I seethed.

Mom gripped my elbow and pulled me forward. "We'll talk when we're out of this town. Not beforehand."

Her steps were swift and sure, and I scrambled to keep up. Moira hurried behind.

"Once we get around that bend and out of everyone's sight, we'll leave. There's a great place back home if you want to get dinner before you leave."

I don't think I'd ever sat down with my mother and intentionally shared a meal. We'd eaten together many times over the years, but it was a snack over tea or a bite on the way out the door. A meal might be a small thing, but it was a huge step in the right direction.

"I'd like that."

Mom's face lit up. She tugged me closer, enveloping me in her sweet, mysterious scent. "Thank you, Evie."

I leaned against her.

"Dinner will give us plenty of time to discuss that faraway look you've had in your eyes when you think we're not looking."

Moira turned her head but not before I caught the smile on her face.

"It's about that boy, isn't it?" Mom demanded.

I groaned. Only an ancient and deadly immortal would call a Shifter Lord a *boy*.

Twenty~Three

"How much do you know about Lugh?" Mom asked once we'd arrived at our table at the very back of the dimly lit but stylish restaurant.

We let her choose what we ate, mostly because we couldn't understand the menu. "Not much at all," I said as I speared a green bean on my fork. "He's ancient, obviously, but I've never had any dealings with him or known anyone who has. Except for Dad, I guess."

"And me," Mom said, daintily cutting a large piece of lettuce.

Moira had a dark colored soup she seemed enamored with. She watched us, but was too busy shoveling soup into her mouth to speak.

"Lugh is tricky," she continued. "And only interested in shiny new things."

"Dad said pretty much the same thing."

Mom shook his head. "But I wonder if he told you not to discount Lugh. He, like all the ancients, is dangerous when provoked. Your father is an easy match for him. I am, too. But someone like Tess wouldn't be able to tell fact from fiction once he wove his magic around her. She truly believes she hasn't worked in that shop for years. There's nothing you can do to convince her until his spell breaks."

I'd spent a good hour and a half gently prodding Tess about what she remembered and what she didn't. The person responsible had created an entirely different life for her. Tess genuinely believed she'd moved to the fae lands years ago, and nothing I say could shake that belief.

"His? You believe Lugh is responsible?"

Mom nodded. "I don't know why he took her. I can't make any sense of this situation, but I've felt that particular spell before in his vicinity. It's one of his favorites."

"Would he need a banshee for something?" Moira asked.

Mom's brow crinkled. "I can't think of a single reason. Banshees aren't equipped with any offensive magic other than their screams. While effective, it doesn't win wars."

A server came by and set another basket of warm, fluffy bread on the table along with a butter tinged with the most unique honey I'd ever tasted before.

"Maybe it's you," Moira said to me as she reached for a hunk of bread.

I blinked. "Why in the world would he want me?"

Mom and Moira both gave me withering looks.

Oh. Damn my father and this queen nonsense.

Mom's eyes twinkled. "I can see the disgust on your face. Is it so bad to be in line for a throne?"

"You tell me." My voice was sullen and snappy, and Moira started to laugh.

"Keep it up," I told the vampire. "I'll make you the captain of my…something. I'll figure it out and make you fetch me tea at all hours of the night."

"I would be your ever so humble immortal servant," Moira mumbled through a mouthful. "As long as you keep me supplied in pretty dresses and tiaras."

"Captains don't wear tiaras."

Moira stuck her tongue out at me. "This captain does. And I want it to be shiny and pink."

"Children," Mom said. "Let's stay on track."

"Light pink," Moira whispered dramatically. "Like wedding day blush roses."

Mom's glare made Moira snap her mouth shut. "I'm not sure his arrival was accidental."

"But Moira twisted her wrist and he fell right through the roof. How could anyone have timed that so perfectly?"

Mom pushed her plate away. "My dear, you have not been around the fae much. We love our little games, and we know how to play them well. Our people have been interested in you ever since Cernunnos revealed you as his child. What better way for one of us to indulge our curiosity than to 'accidentally' land in his target's shop?"

My fingers clenched around my fork. "That ass!"

Moira gave Mom a thoughtful look. "I felt something pulling on my power. How could he have done that?"

"Ask the banshee. She believes she's lived here for years. Everything in her head feels real. Because it is. To his targets. He's a master of illusion. Lugh could have made you feel anything."

"I couldn't have sent him back if I wanted, could I?" The fae were exhausting. Every single action felt carefully crafted to guide you down a path you had no idea you were being led to.

Mom tilted her head. "Maybe. Thanks to your stunt with the tree, you've absorbed the magic that allows us to cross over to the other realms. You are the bridge. Theoretically, you should be able to toss all of us back."

"Can she keep them from coming back? Being the bridge is a cool trick, but what's to keep the fae from coming right back over?"

"No lower fae can travel right now. Only those like me. The tree served an important purpose and soon enough, the lack of one will become a bigger issue than it is now."

Great. One more thing to put on my to-do list.

Mom patted my hand. "Something to worry about for another day."

"Oh, she'll worry alright," Moira said under her breath.

"Evie might be able to keep us from returning, but none of us are familiar enough with the bridge magic to assist you."

Moira's face brightened. "Evie loves puzzles!"

I tossed a piece of my roll at her. "Do I have to be touching him to send him back? Or draw people here?"

Mom frowned. "On that one, I'm not sure. We can practice this evening. When you're ready to leave, touch Moira, and hold an image of me in the place you want to go inside your mind. If it works, you'll have your answer."

"You won't get stuck in the time space continuum?"

Mom stared at me for a beat. "I have no idea what that is, so I'm going with no." She waved her hand around the table. "Now, let's talk about your Lord."

I groaned. "Can we skip this part? I was doing a great job not thinking about him."

"Lies," Moira said. "You haven't said a word about him all day and that means you've been thinking about him since the moment we met."

"Yes, but I'm doing my best to pretend I'm not thinking about him. It's kinda working."

"Spill," Mom demanded. "What happened?"

I opened my mouth, paused, then snapped it shut. "Everything feels dumb," I admitted. "This isn't jealousy. It feels more serious than that."

"This is about another woman?" Mom's eyes sparked a liquid silver color. "Would you like me to kill her?"

Moira gasped in delight. "Your mom is so *cool*."

Who knew my BFF would become a mom fan girl after all these years? "No," I said slowly, "I do not want you to kill her. Caelan isn't cheating on me. He is, however, being difficult."

Moira leaned forward. "He's letting the harlot stay at the Keep."

Mom sucked in a breath. "Evie! You're his fiancée! I don't have to kill her, but you do."

"Amen," Moira said.

I needed to get these two away from each other before they decided to take over the world. "You're a vampire. You shouldn't be praying. You'll combust into flames."

Moira grinned at me with a little too many teeth. "I've been in plenty of churches. Fanatics are delicious."

Mom let out a merry laugh.

I gaped at her. "Alright. You two are not allowed to hang out with each other. This is getting weird."

"Don't be jealous," Moira said. "I can only have one BFF."

The servers interrupted with a large tray of desserts.

"Thank the gods," I breathed.

Mom chuckled. "Oh relax, Evie. This is the first chance I've had to be able to show you who I really am. A small part, but it's a start, isn't it?"

Tears sprang to my eyes. "Yes," I agreed. "It is."

Moira gripped my hand tightly. "Do not scatter our parts to the winds," she warned.

"Thanks for your vote of confidence."

We stood outside of Mom's house, the small village quiet and calm. Thousands of stars glittered above us, so brightly we had no trouble seeing. Mom leaned against her front door, and Moira and I stood several feet away.

A thought occurred to me. "Mom! I thought you said you had to use the tree to travel." She *had* said that and even went so far as to demand use of the tree on Caelan's property.

A wicked light sparkled in Mom's eyes. "What can I say? I lie a little bit sometimes."

I clicked my tongue. "Did you lie about the lesser fae being able to travel?"

"Nope. People like your father and me can travel whenever

and wherever we wish. You're the bridge, Evie, and it's not like you ever invited me over for tea. I had to make excuses to see you. As lies go, it was one of my more innocent ones."

"Dammit, Mom. What else did you lie about?"

Mom lifted both of her hands in a sheepish shrug. "I can't remember all the lies I've told over the years. We'll cross that bridge when we get to it."

"That's a lot of damn bridges!"

She grinned. "I'm tired and want to make some tea, so let's get on with this. Remember, picture me in the place where you want to go."

"And how will we know what happened if you're not there?"

Mom reached into her pocket and waved her cell phone.

I pressed the space between my brows. "Right."

"You need a nap," Moira said.

I squeezed my eyes shut. "Hush. I'm trying to concentrate."

A wind whipped around us as I pictured us all arriving in my driveway. Seconds later, the crunch of gravel sounded under my feet. I opened my eyes.

Mom was on her knees a few feet away, looking positively green around the gills.

"Mom!"

She held up a hand. "Give me a moment," she croaked.

I crouched down next to her. She sucked in a breath and slowly rose to her feet. "I think you need a little more practice. Perhaps we should have started with inanimate objects."

"Are you okay?" Guilt flooded me. "I am so sorry."

Mom spread her fingers out and wiggled them. Then she bent to look at her legs and kicked off her shoes to examine her feet.

Moira snorted.

"All my fingers and toes made the trip, so I'll call this a success." She swayed on her feet.

I reached for her elbow. "Why don't you come inside for a little while?"

But Mom shook her head. "No. I'll be fine in a moment. That was quite a ride, but wonderful news for you."

After seeing Mom on the ground, I'd forgotten why I was trying to move her. "We can get rid of Lugh!"

"Yes, hopefully. Practice more with smaller objects. To be sure, I'd try to get within touching distance. Skin to skin contact is better unless you nail the magic before you see him again." She smiled and touched my chin. "He will be on guard, Evie. Take care in his presence."

"We still don't know how to break the spell on Tess," Moira said. "How much longer will she have to stay there?"

"I'll work on that," Mom promised. "For now, she's fine. Lugh remains in your realm and Tess is an afterthought. She's as safe as she can be."

I didn't like it, but she was right. "Keep an eye on her for me?"

"Things will get complicated if I travel to other realms too often. And even though I can travel, using a bridge is much easier. I don't have to expend any magic when I do. So, I might have lied, but the tree was beneficial to us."

At my crestfallen look, Mom's eyes softened. "But I have trusted friends I can ask to peek in on her." She touched my shoulder. "Tess will be fine. Lugh is the problem you should focus on."

"And the harlot living in the Keep," Moira added.

"Yes," Mom said solemnly. "And the harlot." She dipped her head. "I will see you soon, daughter."

Mom brushed a hand over my cheek and disappeared in a shower of sparkles.

"Damn," Moira sighed. "If you hadn't been the kid of a king and queen, we would have realized how cool your mom was years ago."

I shot her a dark look. Moira held her hands up. "Too soon?"

Shaking my head, I turned to trudge inside the house. "I'll see you tomorrow!"

"Be careful going home," I said right before a powerful yawn erupted.

I was exhausted. Being the bridge didn't require burning any magic that I knew of, but I'd never used it so many times in a day. I felt like I could faceplant right onto my couch. My Floromancy and Chimera magic lay curled inside me, not warring with each other, finally content to slumber.

My hands shook as I put the key into the lock and opened the door. Less than ten minutes later, I was in bed, my eyes drifting shut.

My last thoughts were of Caelan and pondering why we were both stubborn idiots.

Twenty~Four

CAELAN

"You are both stubborn idiots," Rowan said.

We were in the dining room, sharing a meal and talking about how quiet the Lords had been over the last couple of weeks. Too quiet. Rowan had blamed me, which could be the truth. I'd gotten into a rip-roaring fight with them over Evie not too long ago, which had led to a lull in antagonizing my fiancée.

Did I even have the right to call her that anymore?

Regardless, there was no need to kick me when I was down. "Rowan, I don't want to hear it tonight."

A server came over and refilled our coffee mugs before disappearing from the room.

"I've warned you a few times now," the other Lord continued. "And yet, you seem to keep fucking up."

I stared the Lord down, but Rowan had never been scared of me. "What about Evie?"

He picked up his mug and sipped his coffee. "What about her?"

"When does she get any blame?"

"Thirty seconds ago, I called her an idiot."

"Yes, well, that's not enough," I grumbled.

"You knew what you were signing up for when you pursued her."

"Perhaps, but she did not know what it meant to be with a Lord."

Rowan shifted. "Yet you asked her to marry you anyway."

"That's what normal people do when they love someone, yes."

Rowan set his mug down and sighed. "You and Evie are not normal people. She is the heir to the fae crown, and the poor girl still has no clue what that means for her. It's possible she won't be able to marry you if she accepts that crown."

Rage turned my vision red. "Is that what you want?"

Rowan snorted. "I want my two best friends to work this shit out so I don't feel like I have to lecture you both." He leaned forward. "But I will say, this is the last time I will speak to you about this. There are things going on in my territory I need to attend to. Once I return home, I won't be back for a while."

Good, an uncharitable part of me thought.

Rowan's grin was edged. "Jealous bastard. You're one to talk with the Jezebel you have staying down the hall."

"For the gods' sake," I muttered. "Turning her away is the fastest way to get into a conflict with Europe."

"And the easiest way to smooth things over with your fiancée." Rowan took one more sip of his coffee and rose. He came around the table and clapped me on the shoulder. "Sometimes the wind speaks to me, Caelan. There's something off about this. Off about her. The timing is too odd for this to be coincidental. Send her home and do it quickly."

Rowan rarely spoke about his power. All the Lords had them. We were shifters, but we were also something more. None of us revealed our magic to the other, but we all knew Rowan's power had manifested differently. His gift resembled Evie's enough to make me nervous, though his was a gentler sort of power, and he used it far more than the rest of us.

Rowan's gift seemed to have been bestowed upon him at birth. The rest of us grew into our powers. I used mine only in dire circumstances, sometimes with devastating consequences. If he was warning me something wasn't right, I'd be a fool not to listen.

"I'll look into her visit."

Rowan nodded. "If I hear anything more, I'll call."

He left me sitting in the dining room wondering what the hell was wrong with me. Why hadn't I called Rachel's father yet? I never let important things slip by me.

And where the hell was Simone? When was the last time I'd seen her?

Rising, I headed into the study to make a long overdue phone call. If Rowan was concerned, I should be too.

But on the way back, I stopped by the garden first. It was a beautiful evening, and I needed the fresh air...

Twenty~Five

I hadn't seen Caelan in two days, but boy were the rumors flying around town. Business had dropped in the shop, which was unusual due to the time of year, but I didn't think much of it until I overheard some people talking in Marnie's diner.

"He's got that new girl living in the Keep. From what I hear, he dumped the florist."

I was sitting toward the back of the diner eating a bowl of tomato bisque with addictive garlic croutons I couldn't stop shoveling into my mouth when I heard the whispers. My hearing was far better than average, but the two women weren't keeping their voices down.

Small towns and their gossip mills. I shifted a little more so if one of them looked up they wouldn't immediately know it was me. I didn't recognize them, but thanks to Caelan and all the events the shop did, most people in town knew who I was.

"Things between them have been a bit rocky for a while, haven't they?"

The other woman sighed. "He could have any woman he wants. I wonder why he settled for a florist."

The soup soured in my stomach. I should stop listening. I

should put down my spoon, get my purse, and walk out—pretend I'd heard nothing at all. Ignorance was bliss after all.

"I heard she has more magic than Caelan. Someone told me she has fae blood."

My spoon froze halfway to my lips.

The soft gasp made me lean back and strain to hear the next whispers.

"Think she put him under a spell?"

A snort. "Not if he's already involved with another woman." The woman paused. "Foolish in hindsight, I suppose, when she could have bagged the Lord for good."

I refused to believe Caelan had already replaced me. Just because we hadn't spoken didn't mean we were finished. Granted, I was the one who kicked him out of my house. Maybe I should be the one to reach out.

I wish I had the type of small magic that could tip her bowl over or make her nose grow. Maybe one day I would, but I had an issue with fine control on anything other than plant life. Dad said I'd get better with time, but even that seemed in short supply these days.

"Maybe the Lord is a cheater and that's why she left," the other woman whispered.

The other woman let out a wicked laugh. "Feasible. Have you seen that ass?"

Marnie happened to pass by at that second, her brow furrowing when she noticed my expression. Her ears must have caught the tail end of the women's conversation.

Her expression turned to stone. She pivoted and went to their table, reaching for the cake in the middle of the table they were sharing.

At their squawk of outrage, Marnie leaned in. "I'll have none of that vicious talk while you're in my establishment. Not about Caelan and certainly not about Evie! This is your one and only warning. If I catch you again, you'll be banned from the diner permanently, you understand?"

No one wanted to be banned from Marnie and Twila's diner. The two hedgewitches had the best restaurant in the area. Their pastries were divine, their soups a work of art.

"We understand," the women murmured. "Can we have our cake back?"

Marnie snorted. "You certainly may not! Gather your bags and skedaddle. You don't deserve cake after letting your mouth lead you to dangerous waters, but I'll process a refund for it back to your card."

"Yes, Marnie," one of them said. The women scooted out of their chairs and shrugged their jackets on before hurrying out of the restaurant.

Marnie watched them until the door closed then hurried over to my table, her shoulders slumping. "I'm sorry about that, Evie. People are awful sometimes."

I swallowed the lump building in my throat. "It's alright. Not your fault."

Her blue eyes held sympathy. "Are you okay?"

According to the Joy Springs gossip network, I was either a sorceress or a terrible fiancée, and my handsome boyfriend had left me for greener pastures. I mustered up a smile. "I'm fine."

Marnie snorted. "Sure you are, dear." She sighed. "Hold that thought." She bustled away, leaving me staring down at my bisque feeling sorry for myself.

A moment later someone set a giant slice of lemon cream cake in front of me and scurried away. I looked up to see Marnie at the counter waving. "On the house!" she called.

I waved back and pushed my soup away. If it was a battle between cake and soup, dessert won the day every time.

Especially today.

AGAINST MY BETTER JUDGMENT, I went to the Keep and rang the doorbell.

The door jerked open a few seconds later, and a feminine hand jerked me inside. I squawked and stumbled.

"Hurry," Simone hissed.

My feet twisted and tangled together. "Can you wait until I stand up at least?"

"No." She dragged me into a side room and shut the door, holding me by the arm until I got my bearings.

I brushed the dirt off the knees of my pants. "Gods, Simone. What the hell is the matter with you?"

"There's something wrong." Her eyes were wild, her normally pristine hair standing up in places like she'd stuck her finger in a light socket.

She clenched her fists at her side, and her breathing was heavier than normal. I watched her pace the room, each step clipped and short, back and forth, back and forth.

"Simone?"

She spun to me. "When's the last time you heard from him?"

"Umm. Two days."

"See?" she hissed. "That's insane! He's obsessed with you!"

"I—um. Okay? It seemed unusual, which is why I'm here, but we had a fight."

Her nostrils flared. "Again?"

"Yes," I snapped. "*Again*. We're working some things out."

Her hand came down in a slashing motion. "Doesn't matter. Even when he's pissed at you, he's obsessed with you. He's been fine, Evie. Something is very, very wrong."

I blinked at her. "He's fine?"

"Yes. He gets up. He eats. He goes to his meetings. Caelan laughs and smiles and jokes. Everything looks normal, but he's not normal. He's forgetting things. Important things."

I stared at Simone for a long moment. "Do you need to sit down?"

"Are you listening to what I'm telling you?" She scraped a hand through her hair and glared at me.

"I am. But I think your head might explode if you don't take a beat."

We stared at each other before Simone let out an explosive sigh and sank into a leather chair. Her eyes fluttered shut and a deep sigh racked her body.

"Alright." I took a seat closer to the door. "What you're saying is everything is normal with Caelan but it's…not normal?"

One eye cracked open. "I'm not crazy."

"You are the least crazy person I know," I assured her. "Tell me what's not normal about his behavior."

"That bitch is here and he has yet to follow up on the reason why. He was supposed to call her father days ago and he still hasn't done it."

I nodded. "Okay. Can you do it?"

Simone stared at me like I had a third head. "No. I cannot contact a Shifter Lord in Europe and question him about his heir."

Her voice practically dripped acid.

I pressed my lips together to keep from laughing at her affronted tone. "Fine. Protocol, I guess?"

"The Lords live and die by their protocols."

"You could have fooled me," I muttered. They'd violated their supposed protocols every time one of them came after me and no one seemed to care.

Simone let her eyes drift shut again. "This is not about you, Evie. Let's stay on track."

Had I walked into an alternate universe? "Fine. Caelan didn't call Rachel's father. That is unusual, but is it so weird that you feel like you need to spiral about it?"

"No one needs to spiral. It just happens. But this? It's weird. Rachel randomly showed up and he isn't the least bit suspicious about her motives?" She shook her head. "Something is rotten in Joy Springs."

"Alright. Fair enough. What else?"

She cracked open an eye. "He's not out stalking you. No texts, no calls, and he's not at the Keep waiting for you to throw your-self on his mercy."

I huffed. "As if I would ever do that."

One of her eyebrows rose.

"Fine. I might be here, but the rest is an exaggeration."

"Whatever," Simone said with a slight smile. She bent over and plopped her face in her hands. "I'm telling you, something isn't right."

"Want me to talk to him?"

"I've already tried. He insists everything is fine." She frowned. "What kills me is he sounds so reasonable, and I walk away feeling like I'm the crazy one."

"Is he in his study?" I wanted to talk to him, anyway, so I might as well kill two birds with one stone.

Simone swallowed and said nothing for a long moment. "No."

"Okay," I said slowly. "Where's he at? I usually call first, but I wanted to surprise him."

Simone wouldn't meet my eyes. "He's not in the Keep."

My stomach twisted, but I didn't overreact. "Oh? Do you know where he is?"

Simone sighed.

I knew where he was, and the thought sent a crack through my already wounded heart. "He's with Rachel, isn't he?"

She didn't have to nod. Her face told me everything I needed to know. "I told him it was a bad idea."

"But he did it anyway?"

She nodded. "He said it was good for European relations."

I swore I wouldn't jump to conclusions, but Caelan was making it extremely difficult for me not to want to stab him with a rose bush limb. Maybe he felt the same way about me.

Aaaargh.

I pulled my phone from my pocket and sent him a message. "What restaurant?"

Simone chewed on her thumbnail and watched me carefully. "If I tell you, you cannot cause a scene."

"I think I'm more mature than losing my shit in public if my fiancé suddenly decided he doesn't want to be with me anymore."

Her eyes narrowed. I laughed at her expression. "Scout's honor."

"You were never a scout, were you?"

"No, but I promise. I'm well aware of Caelan's position in this town, and I wouldn't do anything to jeopardize his reputation in the eyes of the townspeople."

Simone was still reluctant, but she rattled off the name of the restaurant.

Slightly sick when she told me the name, I struggled to speak. The place was new to town, and I mentioned I wanted to go a few weeks ago. Caelan said he didn't have the time yet, but he'd take me soon. "Alright."

I glanced down at my phone. Nothing. "I'll head over now and see if he's still with her."

Simone's face turned sober. "Evie."

Annoyance heated my blood. "I already told you I won't do anything crazy. You don't need to tell me again."

"It's not that." She reached over and took one of my hands. "Don't jump to conclusions. Okay?"

It was a little too late, but I was doing my best not to lose it and drown myself in a vat of ice cream. "I'll see what's going on with my own eyes and take it from there, okay?"

"He loves you," she insisted. "More than anyone I've ever seen."

"The feeling is the same." I extricated my hand and left the Keep.

I had an errant fiancé to find.

Twenty-Six

Mom was standing in my driveway when I pulled in. I wanted to change my clothes and grab a few things before I went to Caelan.

"Everything okay?" I asked when I got out of the car.

"Fine." She smiled. "I wanted to check on you and see how things were going with Lugh."

Dead end on the Lugh front. "I haven't heard a peep from him. No one has anything bad to say, and I can't find any evidence of wrongdoing. It's maddening."

I opened the wards and invited Mom in. She blinked in hesitation, then stepped inside. "We can talk while I change."

"Going somewhere?"

"I'm off to see if Caelan is cheating on me."

Mom's sure steps hitched. I opened the door and went inside, but she was frozen on the porch, staring at me with eyes.

"Excuse me?"

"It's a long story."

"One I want to hear." Mom stepped inside and shut the door. "Have time for a cup of coffee?"

"I'll take one to go, if you don't mind."

Mom waved me away. "Go get changed and I'll make a pot."

Five minutes later, Mom handed me a filled thermal cup. I'd put on a pair of stylish but comfortable boots, wool slacks, and a blue cashmere sweater.

"Would you like some company?"

Me and Mom on a stakeout to stalk my boyfriend? "Yes, if you have time."

Mom grinned. "Of course I have time.

"I promised Simone I wouldn't cause a scene."

She nodded gravely. "I promised nothing of the sort." Mom held up a finger and went back to the kitchen to pour herself a to-go mug. "We'll play catch up in the car."

CAELAN'S CAR was parked in the restaurant lot, sending my already plummeting spirits even lower.

"Are we going in?" Mom asked.

"I'm going in. I won't interrupt, but I do want to see how… cozy things are."

Mom's eyes turned soft. "Be absolutely sure before you do or say something you can't take back."

I nodded and slid out of the car.

The restaurant was small, tasteful, and filled with customers. I waved the hostess away. "I see my party," I said, pointing in a random direction as I sailed past.

There was only one dining room making it easy to see Caelan, but he didn't notice me. Rachel sat with her back toward the door. She wore a halter dress, showcasing the smooth, tan skin of her back. Her hair was left down and loose, falling in a wave of soft curls.

And Caelan looked absolutely enamored. I swallowed hard and moved closer to see their hands clasped on top of the table.

My eyes burned. Remembering my promise to Simone, I did my best to clear my mind and heart of the humiliation and fury I felt and stopped at the edge of their table. Caelan looked up and froze. His brow furrowed and he looked down at his hand, only to yank it away from Rachel.

"Evie!" he said in surprise.

"Hi." I crossed my arms over my chest. "Is there anything you want to tell me?"

Rachel leaned forward and smiled, satisfaction dripping in her expression. "Hello, Evie. I'm surprised to see you here. It takes ages to get a reservation."

The arrow hit its mark. Caelan's chest rumbled. "Rachel."

She turned those wicked eyes to him. "Yes, darling."

I felt my lips pull back from my teeth. The glasses on the table rattled together, and I knew I was about to lose it. "I just wanted to come by and make sure you knew what you were doing." I gave him a tight smile. "It looks like you do."

"Evie—" Caelan put his napkin on the table and made to stand.

"No, that's really unnecessary." I tilted my head in acknowledgment. "I would have appreciated a text or a phone call, but maybe this is better."

Seeing him touch someone with so much propriety had ripped my heart in two, but it had ripped the film off my eyes. Seeing this with my own two eyes told me he'd made a choice. And maybe if I hadn't seen this, he would have kept me on the line and Rachel as well, though I know, even though I thought she was a massive twat, that she wouldn't stand for being second choice either.

"Would you like to stay?" Rachel asked. "Caelan and I are discussing future plans for the Keep."

Another clever knife stab. "No thanks. I have someone waiting for me in the car. Can't keep them waiting for much longer."

"Who?" Caelan's storm-colored eyes met mine.

"Don't worry about it. I'll have Simone pack up the things I left over there and drop them off." I inclined my head to both of them. "I wish you the best of luck."

Caelan didn't fight for himself or me. He made no excuses and didn't deny what I was seeing or how it would affect us. And that made it so much worse. I tried not to cry as I turned to go.

"Evie. Wait." Caelan rose and walked over, taking me by the elbow. He led me over to the restroom area and stood so close I pressed myself against the wall.

"Are you going to tell me this isn't what it looks like?"

"She's a shifter." Stab. "We're better suited to each other." Stab. "I never meant to hurt you." Stab.

I swallowed hard, refusing to let him see me cry. "All those times you fought for us. All those times I told you why we shouldn't be together, and you make me discover you out on the town with another woman without giving me the courtesy of at least telling me beforehand? This is a small town. Everyone is going to know what this is."

"I thought we could make it work." His words were soft, but there was no real fire behind them. His expression wasn't hurt or wounded. Caelan sounded like he was speaking to a friend and not someone he loved.

Every time he spoke, his words made another jagged wound in my soul.

"But you and I...we aren't compatible enough to produce heirs."

I froze. "Excuse me?"

"Rachel is a shifter. Born and pure blooded. Your blood is tainted." His words were so...flat and unemotional. This was not the man I loved.

My hand clenched into a fist. "Do you hear yourself? The horrible things you're saying to me? You never accused me of being tainted before. What changed?"

"Everything," Caelan said simply. "We've always had diffi-culty in our relationships because we come from two different worlds." He lowered his voice. "You revealed yourself as a Chimera and became heir to the Fae King. I am a Lord. What path forward do we have?"

Every word was a stone pelting against my skin. "Why did you ask me to marry you?"

Caelan's brow furrowed. He blinked a few times, opened his mouth, and snapped it shut. The next word he said made everything inside me shut down. "Honor."

"Honor," I said hoarsely. "You felt duty bound to make me your wife?"

He lifted a shoulder in a shrug. "That's what one does in a relationship, the natural order of things."

I didn't know this man standing before me. He looked like Caelan. He smelled like Caelan. But the Caelan I knew would never have spoken to me this way. The man I loved loved me. Or I thought he had.

"I see. And Rachel?"

"We've had our differences before, but a match with her is advantageous."

The ground rumbled under my feet.

He clicked his tongue. "Your emotional volatility is another reason why a match between us would never work."

A woman stepped into the hall, eyes blazing with power. She pointed at Caelan. "I've heard enough. Step away from my daughter."

"Mom." I pinched the space between my brows. "I've got it."

"No one speaks down to the fae heir." Her eyes snapped to me. "You are a princess of a powerful kingdom, and the heir to the entire fae realm. Caelan should be bowing and scraping at your feet, not insulting you."

"I bow to no one."

Mom's lips pulled back from her teeth. "*KNEEL.*"

The command in her voice made my bones hurt. Caelan slammed to the floor, his knees cracking like gunshots. "You might be a Lord, boy, but you are no king. There are few more powerful than my daughter, and you would be gods blessed to have her hand."

Caelan's jaw clenched with rage, his eyes glowing burnished

gold as he struggled against the command. "This," he growled. "This is the reason. You think you're better than us—"

"I don't," I whispered.

He scoffed. "Your father doesn't think I'm good enough for you, so why should I stay here, knowing he thinks I could never rise to his standards of power?"

This never mattered before. Or had he stayed silent about everything? "I don't care what he thinks."

"It doesn't matter. I never said I'd take the crown. I—all I wanted was you." The words were a whisper, overridden by my breaking heart.

I looked at my mother, still incandescent with rage. "Let him up, please."

Mom's eyes narrowed. Power rose in the air, and I wondered for a brief, horrifying moment whether she would kill him. I touched her arm. "Let's go."

Rachel made the mistake of coming around the corner just then. "Caelan?"

Mom turned, magic glittering from her skin. "You," she hissed. "You're responsible for this."

Rachel, who had far more beauty than brains, made the mistake of smiling. "Caelan needed to see what else was out there. It's not my fault he made the better choice."

Mom's laugh was a jagged, violent thing. She swept her hand out at an angle. Rachel was there one moment and gone the next, the sound of shattering glass and screams careening through the restaurant.

I bent down and touched Caelan's cheek. "I'm sorry it has come to this. I loved you very, very much, and nothing would have stood in the way of marrying you. I know we've had our differences, and I know that a lot of our issues were due to some things beyond our control and some due to our own experiences. But I never doubted you. Not until this moment."

Caelan's brow furrowed once more as if he was confused by

what I was saying, but then his expression cleared. "I do not regret my decision."

"Then I'll learn not to regret mine," I said and turned to walk away.

I touched Mom's arm once more. She shook with rage but finally released the hold she had on Caelan.

"If I scent you around Evie's property again, your life is forfeit."

Her words rang in the air with the magic of prophecy, a shimmering veil settling over us all. A death vow signed and sealed by a powerful, ancient goddess.

Caelan smiled. "You've no need to worry. I have no need of your daughter any longer."

My fingers clenched around my mother's arm, and I released a shuddering breath.

"It's not too late," Mom hissed.

"You can't murder someone in public," I said, amused despite everything.

Mom snorted. "Of course I can. This place holds no laws over a fae."

"Yes, but it's morally wrong." I pulled my mother away while Caelan struggled to rise.

Mom snorted. "Morals are a human construct."

"Yes, and I live in the human world."

"Exactly," Mom said, allowing me to tug her out of the restaurant.

We both pretended not to see the gaping hole in the restaurant wall where Mom had tossed Rachel through.

So much for not causing a scene

CHAPTER
Twenty~Seven

CAELAN

The light hurt my eyes. Pinpricks of pain pulsed at my temples. Simone was saying something to me, but I couldn't make out the words.

Seymour sat in my lap, rubbing his traps against my chest. He was making those odd sounds again, but this time he sounded… worried? I sat up straighter, wincing at the goddamn light. Had someone changed the bulbs?

"What?" I asked her again.

Simone and Garrett exchanged a look. She reached out and touched my forehead with the back of her hand.

"No fever," she murmured.

I swatted her hand away. "Of course I don't have a fever. I'm a shifter."

Garrett perched on the edge of my desk and stared at me. "Do you remember tonight?"

My lips tightened. Why was everyone questioning me lately? "Of course, I remember tonight," I snapped. "I came into the office and did some paperwork and then I…"

What had I done? I closed my eyes and pressed my fingertips to my temple. Why was my head pounding?

"You don't remember going out to eat? To Santino's?"

I jerked my attention to Simone. "Santino's? Evie wanted to go there." Why couldn't I remember?

Simone nodded, a strange look passing over her face. Anger, if I had to guess. But she'd never looked at me with that kind of quiet rage before. "You're right. She did want to go. You were supposed to take her when things calmed down."

I frowned. "I didn't take her?"

"I'm afraid not," Garrett answered.

I slashed my hand in the air. "Cut out the cryptic shit. Why did I go to Santino's if I wasn't with Evie?"

Another look between Garrett and Simone. "You went with Rachel."

I recoiled. "Rachel? Why would I go with her?"

"That's what we're wondering, too," Simone said. "You've been a little different lately."

I scoffed. "Different how?"

"Well, for one, you took Rachel out to the restaurant Evie has been begging to go to for weeks now."

My heart lurched. "It must have been a business dinner." But that didn't sound right. I had no meetings on the books today.

Simone slowly shook her head. "No. You were alone with Rachel."

"Cut this shit," I growled. "I don't know what's going on, but there's no reason I'd go out alone with her. I need to call her father anyway." But didn't I already do that?

"That's not all," Garrett said gently, a tone he had never taken with me before.

I snorted. "Did she make a pass at me?" Rachel had made no secret about wanting me back in her life. I needed to get her out of the Keep before she became a bigger issue than she was now.

Simone cleared her throat. "Evie found you there."

I stilled. "Shit. She's bound to be pissed." I fished around in my pocket and dug out my cellphone. "I'll call her and explain."

"Explain what?" Garrett asked. "You broke up with her." He

didn't say it loud, but his face added on to that sentence with, *you fucking idiot.*

The phone slipped from my fingers. "I did *what?*"

Simone nodded. "You told Evie her blood was tainted."

I froze. "If this is your idea of a joke," I snarled, "I'd rethink this immediately."

My head pounded, my blood a heartbeat in my temple. Simone and Garrett's faces swam in my vision.

"Her mother was there," Simone went on as if there was still a lot more to tell. Dread settled into my bones. This might not be fixable. Why in the hell would I break up with Evie when I fought so hard to claim her? I pressed my thumb against the space between my brows, attempting to calm the raging headache I had.

Simone added after a brief pause, "She tossed Rachel through the restaurant wall. The shifter is in the infirmary with serious injuries." A smile with too many teeth crossed her face. "Again."

My eyebrows lifted. "She's lucky she isn't dead."

"Evie more than likely saved that miserable bitch's life." Her words were a snarl. My Omega stared at me like she'd never seen me before and now that she did, she didn't much like what she saw.

The fog was still there inside my head, the pounding behind my eyes getting worse. "Are you sure I did all of this, and someone isn't messing with you?"

"I wish," Simone said softly. "Evie called me earlier."

I closed my eyes and swallowed hard. "Okay. I'll go over there and fix things right now."

Garrett and Simone exchanged another look.

"Evie has asked me to let you know her wards have been rekeyed. She said if she sees you on her private property she will respond with lethal force."

Goddammit. "Then I'll go to her shop."

Simone cleared her throat. "Her mother and father also dropped by before you arrived home."

Garrett's look somehow managed to be sympathetic and furious. "The King of the Fae and the Banshee Queen have claimed her shop as fae property."

My brow furrowed. "I'm not sure I follow."

"If you violate the property boundaries, you will be marked for death. Any fae with enough power will see that mark and hunt you to the ends of the earth for the insult you've given to their heir."

"What the fuck." I swore viciously. "I can't even pass by her shop without violating that order?"

Garrett's smile was unamused. "The mark will trigger if you touch her shop's door. They wished to let me know you've been given some grace as Evie's former fiancé, and you will be allowed to pass by her shop on your way to other places."

"This is insane," I muttered. "How the hell am I supposed to fix this?"

"You aren't supposed to," Simone said gently. "You humiliated your fiancée in public. Evie's phone call was brief and to the point. Any ties to her are to be severed immediately."

Garrett sighed. "That's bad enough, but you also humiliated the heir to the fae throne and said her blood was tainted and that she wasn't good enough to become your wife. There were other fae in that restaurant—creatures who appeared human who, unfortunately for you, have excellent hearing. The only reason they didn't finish Rachel off was because they overheard Evie asking her mother to leave her be."

Simone sank into one of the chairs. "Your actions were unforgivable, but even in the face of that horrific incident, Evie chose to walk away, ensuring you would not be entangled in a war for any harm that came to Rachel. And Rachel is intelligent enough to know Evie did her a solid favor." Her smile was not friendly. "I took the liberty of informing the shifter exactly who Evie was related to when she returned to the Keep with those injuries raging about revenge."

I rose, the world spinning around me. Garrett lurched forward and steadied me. "What is going on with you, Caelan? Why would you jeopardize something so important to you? For Rachel, of all people?"

I couldn't answer him. I wanted to deny everything, but I couldn't remember a thing. From the moment we left, everything turned into a bizarre fog. If I concentrated hard enough, I could see Evie standing over the table, her face a mask of frozen grief. But I don't remember what I said to her or the aftermath. I would never have said those things to her. Yes, I was worried about our future children, but it never would have stopped me from marrying her.

So what the hell was wrong with me?

"Caelan!" Simone barked. "Are you alright?"

I blinked several times and tried to refocus on my Omega's face. "I'm fine."

She snorted. "I'd like your permission to contact the European Lord's offices and speak to Rachel's father."

I stilled, the urge to reach out and strike her for her insolence burning in my veins. My fists clenched. What was wrong with me? I'd never been that kind of leader. "No," I growled. That wasn't her place and could be construed as an insult. "I'll do it tomorrow."

Her face turned to stone. Garrett rose to his full height and spoke. "Part of my job is enforcing Pack law and assisting you in times of need. You might deny there's anything wrong, but I know you, and this is *not* like you. If you do not contact Rachel's parents by tomorrow at nine a.m., Simone will do so."

He gripped my arm. "In the meantime, I want you to visit the infirmary."

"Get out," I snarled. He was trying to usurp me. Simone was his co-conspirator.

I gripped my head. No. Neither of them would ever do that, not unless I was too far gone. A hiss of pain slipped from between my teeth.

A thin ring of gold surrounded Garrett's irises. "Caelan—"

"GET OUT!" I roared. Power boomed through the study.

Seymour, still in my hands, froze. I'd forgotten I was holding him. I sat him on the edge of the desk and gripped the wood so hard it cracked underneath my fingers.

Garrett stepped forward, but Simone reached out and took him by the arm. "No," she said softly.

I thought he'd break her grip and come after me, but Garrett gave me one more grim look. "I never thought I'd see you fuck up so profoundly. The differences between you…they could have been overcome. You didn't have to crush the poor girl so thoroughly." He shook his head, disgust brimming in his eyes, and spun on his heel, Simone right behind him.

When the door shut, and I sank to the floor, my vision blurring, four words kept swimming through my mind over and over.

What have I done?

Twenty~Eight

My mother and father stood toe to toe, both bristling with magic. "You take everything," Mom said softly. "Give this to me."

My father's eyes narrowed. "You won't win if we battle."

Mom's smile was slow and seductive. "Are you so sure about that, old man?"

Oh shit. I looked to the left, then the right for a place I could take cover if they decided to go at it. It had been five days since the disaster at the restaurant.

True to her word, Simone had kept Caelan from my property. Or he'd chosen to stay away because he meant every word he said to me that night.

I still couldn't think about it without wanting to tear down the Keep brick by brick while sobbing. Mom had stayed over the first two nights and proved a surprisingly good houseguest. On the third night, she told me to think, really think about what I wanted for myself. Did I want to be Cernunnos' heir? Or did I want to run a flower shop forever and be content with my Floromancy and the occasional use of my Chimera form?

Barrett had contacted me a couple of times asking when I wanted to begin training, but focusing on magic while your heart was shattering into a million pieces was surprisingly difficult, so I fobbed him off for a week or two.

The swans had been quiet, no doubt plotting their next move, and there was still no sign of the other missing Chimera.

So far, I'd proven a surprisingly terrible Chimera representative to our people.

But I couldn't find the emotion to care because my heart was still tied up in Caelan.

To rub salt in my wounds, he hadn't even bothered to text or call. Not that I would have answered, but all signs pointed to him being serious about the breakup and his new choice.

According to Simone, Rachel was out of the infirmary no worse for the wear. But she'd told me the fae had marked her. Every time she stepped outside the boundaries of the Keep, a strange mark appeared on her brow that looked like an S with two diagonal slashes. It had faded after a moment, but when she stepped into town, several residents approached her, magic at the ready.

Someone finally took mercy on Rachel and told her what the mark meant.

Simone begrudgingly asked my parents if they could remove it only to help them prevent war when Rachel returned to Europe. She, at least, was still under the impression this was all some grave misunderstanding that would work itself out.

Mom and Dad had been at my house during the phone call and had laughed their heads off, telling Simone their quarrel was not with the Lords, or at least not the European Lords, only Rachel. They would not remove the mark, thank you very much, and if Simone or Caelan insisted, they'd have no trouble extending the range of Caelan's mark, which would effectively terminate his rule over the Joy Springs area, all of Texas, and wherever else the poor bastard ruled.

Needless to say, Simone was smart enough to realize she was beaten and dropped it, then quietly asked if she'd been marked.

Mom and Dad had shown too many teeth when they smiled and Dad said, "Not yet."

Honestly, it was kind of awesome having feral parents.

"Old man?" Dad murmured. "Any time you want to tangle Cliona, you give me a call." He straightened and crossed his powerful arms over his chest.

Dad was in full on athletic gear mode, wearing a pair of charcoal-colored joggers and a dark t-shirt even though it was cold as hell outside.

Mom was dressed down, too, which was a surprise. She wore a pair of old skinny jeans, slip on sneakers, and a striped cotton sweater. Her hair was in a thick braid and slung over one shoulder. The Banshee Queen looked like she was a college student home for winter break.

I'd walked out here with a cup of cocoa and spotted them. Sensing they were in a pissing contest, I curled into a rocker with a blanket to watch the fireworks.

Not knowing what the hell they were arguing about made things even more interesting.

"Dual," Mom said.

Dad scoffed. "Too much. Just because yours is separate doesn't mean she will have time for additional duties."

Wait. She?

"There won't be any additional duties because I have no plans to retire, but I do need a representative in her realm because I prefer being at home. In saying that, there may be a few meetings here and there, but nothing major."

My eyes narrowed.

"She'll be far too busy with her other duties to take on much more."

"Who are you talking about?" I blurted.

Mom's expression turned crafty. "Aren't you the least bit curious about what's going on in my realm since you're blocked from entering? You could use her as a spy."

I gaped. "You blocked Dad?"

"A story for another time," Mom said. "Tess says hello and wants you to visit her soon. Any word on Lugh?"

I'd neglected that as well. And the shop. And Ash. Moira had been by a couple of times but was giving me the space I'd needed. I was going back to work tomorrow and giving Ash a paid week off whether he wanted it or not. He'd stepped way up for all of us and kept things running while I was on the couch shoveling ice cream down my throat.

"No, but I was planning on sending him home tonight. If I can find him."

"You will," Mom said. "This stunt was never about Tess in the first place. It's always been about you. Keep in mind, he may know you're the bridge and wants to exploit you. If he does know, he will be on guard for you trying to touch him." Her eyes glittered as she smiled. "But he doesn't know the trick you've been practicing."

And practiced, I had. Every single day, multiple times a day even when I wanted to dissolve in a puddle of tears. Mom had finally pronounced me ready just yesterday.

But something else nagged at me. "What if this is not about being the bridge? What if he knows about…the other thing?"

Dad looked away from Mom. "Then you must decide if you wish to fight him as a Floromancer, the heir to our people, or the beast that prowls under your skin."

"Any suggestions?" Because none of those sounded awesome. I lay firmly on team sci-fi transporter and hoped I could just beam him back to whatever hell he'd come from and never allow him passage back.

Moira hadn't brought any other people through, though she'd pulled an odd plant that looked a little like Seymour but bit a hell of a lot harder and was now happily hanging out in my greenhouse eating my herbs when it thought I wasn't looking.

Another worrying thing to think about later.

"You're still terrified of others knowing you're a Chimera," my father said.

I stared at him for a beat. "Because I'll be hunted to the ends of the earth by the Lords and others who hate my kind."

"Yes," my father said slowly, "but you are no longer merely a Floromancer, and your powers, though unique, are not illegal in our world."

Mom jerked her attention to him. "Don't you dare," she seethed.

My father's shit-eating grin made me nervous. "If you were to accept the crown officially, you would have the entire might of my kingdom behind you."

My eyes narrowed. "Didn't your kingdom already accept me when you claimed my property as fae owned and marked Caelan for death?"

"All by the book," he said. "You're still my daughter and entitled to my protection regardless of whether you wear the crown."

"Buuuutttt…" I drawled. I knew there was a 'but.' There was always a 'but' with this freaking guy.

Dad chuckled. "But, if you were to take the crown, and if your Chimera heritage was revealed to people, we could put the might of my kingdom behind you. Such would act as a major deterrent to those who might seek to harm you."

I chewed on my lip as I studied him. "How long have you been saving this up?"

Mom laughed. "She's onto you."

I glanced at her. "Don't think I don't realize you two meddlers are speaking about me, either. I don't think it's possible for me to be queen of two places."

"It's very possible," Mom said hurriedly. "But it hasn't been done yet. And," she said with a long-suffering look at my father, "if you choose to become a dual heir, you'd also have the formal might of my realm behind you too. I can only interfere so much in the dealings of this realm before my hands are legally tied. Lugh is a special case, though. He is not one of the lower realm people and will be difficult to defeat. We will help wherever we can, but this cannot be our fight."

"Until I do exactly what you want."

"Even if you claim the crown, we won't interfere if it turns into a fight between you two, otherwise you will lose the respect of our people. You must vanquish your enemies with your might and wits."

Dad didn't seem worried at all. Cool cool. Okay then. One immortal Floromancer of dubious origins and cursed blood going up against a literal ancient god.

Awesome.

"I kinda liked it better when I thought you were both jerks," I muttered under my breath.

Dad laughed. "We are still jerks, as you say, but we are also rulers in our own right, and sacrifices must be made." He put his hand on my shoulder, and I could feel the ancient power vibrating with his body. I wondered what I felt like to him when he touched me—if my magic burned or annoyed him. If it did, he was good at hiding his emotions.

He continued. "When you are a queen, you must put your people first, but you must also be strong enough to hold your territory. Lugh is an ancient, yes, but he is also..." His voice trailed off. "What do you call it? A one-trick horse?"

"Pony," I said, trying not to grin. "A one-trick pony."

Dad snapped his fingers. "That's it. He prefers trickery over straight combat and has become lazy over the years. Lugh will try to beat you with deceit and subterfuge. You must be on the lookout for him trying to stab you in the back."

I wasn't surprised. Most fae relied on some form of trickery when they were trying to win. "Neither of you are concerned that he's made no noise or caused any real trouble?"

Mom and Dad exchanged a look. "He's causing trouble," she assured me. "We just haven't seen the extent yet."

"Goody."

"On that note," Dad said. "Have you thought about your heritage?"

I shot him an exasperated look. "Only every day since you

keep cramming it down my throat. But I still don't fully understand why Thalia can't take the role." Before he could go on a tangent, I held up my hand. "Yes, I understand there are limitations due to her powers, but what if we were to share the role?"

Dad shook his head. "I understand you…care for Thalia, but there are other factors at play. Factors Thalia is already aware of. But more importantly, she does not want the crown and never has. If it were up to her, she'd disappear into a small, artsy town and completely forsake her heritage. She never wanted to be caught up in my world. Though she puts on a brave face and has a volatile temper, Thalia very much wants the normalcy the human world can provide."

Empathy struck me. "If I don't take the crown, why can't you give it to her? Why haven't you given her the choice?"

His eyes softened. "Because, like you, she is attached to me, and she will always be a target. There are ways to offer her the crown, but she will lose pieces of herself, and Thalia very much loves her individuality. The best I could do is allow her into my court, and she has vehemently refused."

"She doesn't want to be coddled." I understood completely. Being handled with a velvet glove doesn't mean the glove doesn't itch.

He inclined his head in acknowledgment. "Very much so."

Dad wanted me to do this. Mom did too. I crossed my arms over my chest and watched them both. "I'd like to bargain."

Mom gasped in surprise. Dad's eyes narrowed for a brief moment before a slow, satisfied grin slid over his face. "Very well, daughter, let us bargain for the crown."

Twenty~Nine

oney was falling from the sky.

I was back to work, elbows deep in a pile of ranunculus when the first shouts began. Moira stood at the window, a grim slant to her mouth.

"Lugh is starting his shit," she announced.

"We all knew something would happen," Ash called from his worktable. "It was only a matter of time."

I brushed petals from my hands and rose. The town square was crowded with people staring up at the sky with awe. The calm wouldn't last. Not with the number of humans interspersed with the paranormals. People like me would wonder what the catch was, or what kind of magic had gone awry.

Humans wouldn't care about the consequences. They would dive in, take what they could, then try to take others' share from them as well. Security cameras or a police force wouldn't matter. Many humans thought they were bulletproof.

The camera wouldn't catch them.

The police would be too busy to worry about them.

The money was falling from the sky. Why shouldn't they take it? They *deserved* it. It was meant for them. They'd worked hard. They needed it more than other people did.

Funny the kinds of actions one person could justify when something they wanted more than anything dropped in front of them. No matter if it was too good to be true.

"There they go," Moira murmured.

The first shout rang out. Maybe forty percent of the people in the square started grabbing every dollar they could. Others looked around, a perplexed expression on their faces.

I sighed and grabbed my jacket. Moira followed close behind.

Ash, conflict averse, stayed inside and locked the door once we were outside. If things got too out of hand, Ash would protect the shop if the wards went down.

"He's here somewhere," I murmured.

"I'm getting real tired of fae bullshit," Moira whispered back.

Sirena lifted a hand in greeting as she watched impassively from her gelato truck. I didn't wave back. I could use her help, but the siren was kind of an asshole sometimes. She was all about herself and seemed not to care about the world burning around her.

But there was one more person I needed to worry about showing up. This was still his town, no matter that he had set my life on fire a few days ago. I had maybe minutes until Caelan was here trying to keep order.

"I don't see him," Moira said.

"His magic is difficult to read. I don't know that I've ever sensed it."

"Illusion," Moira said. "He's a powerful glamour worker." She sucked her teeth and scanned the rooftops. "I wouldn't be surprised if this cash turned into acorns within the hour."

"Better than him stealing it from a bank and dropping it here." I wouldn't put something like that past him.

"True. Everyone would leave here with a criminal record."

"That'd be great for future tourism."

Moira winced. "Maybe we should start dealing drugs instead of flowers."

I nodded. "Job security, for sure."

We grinned at each other.

She went still a second later. "I see him. Top of the town hall roof, bare legs dangling off the roof like a drunk frat boy."

I didn't look right away. Instead, I pulled my phone out and texted Dad. He was at my side less than thirty seconds later.

"Is he here?" Dad said.

"Yup. Town Hall roof."

Dad didn't bother to look. He was more concerned about the cash falling from the air. "Glamoured," he said after a moment. "You're going to have a lot of disappointed tourists in a few hours."

"They're all thieves anyway," I said quietly. "I just feel bad for the shops if they take any of that cash."

"I'll send your Mom to warn them."

Moira eyed me and nodded, approval shining warm in her eyes. My stomach twisted in regret. I'd spent so long relying only on myself I'd forgotten what it was like to work as a team. I reached for her hand and gave it a quick squeeze.

Dad's eyes swirled with magic, and my mother appeared a moment later. They conferred before Mom peeled off to presumably want the shopkeepers. If they were smart, which most of them were, they'd shut down until everything blew over.

"Are you sure you're ready for this?" Dad asked quietly.

I would never be ready, but I nodded anyway. Much of humanity resisted change, and I'd grown up among them and had adopted this trait from them. I liked things harmonious and comfortable, and my life had been anything but lately.

Such didn't stop the world from turning, though.

He brushed his fingers against my cheek. "I am proud to be your father."

Tears burned the backs of my eyes, the words unlocking something in the hidden depths of my heart. I'd waited my entire life to hear those words, and even though there were times my existence had been something of a suck fest, I'd never felt more fortunate.

There were many people out there still waiting to hear words like that from their parents.

Dad disappeared into the crowd, leaving me and Moira to confront Lugh.

We kept a wide berth away from the chaos, and chaos it was. People had cash stuffed in their pockets, down the front and backs of their pants. In their socks and shoes, their bras and fists clenched full of bills.

They all had a slightly dazed, feverish look in their eyes, the kind of look a smart human would recognize as a warning sign to get the hell away. And some did. Maybe ten percent of the humans saw what was happening and the very real potential of things escalating and had quietly pulled their families to safety.

A scream of rage rang out, and two people came to blows. The crowd was working itself into a frenzy. I stopped directly below the Town Hall and looked up.

Lugh gave me a little wave.

I responded by giving him the middle finger.

The bastard had the nerve to laugh.

"Why don't you come down here so we can have a chat?" I called.

Lugh grinned. "So your mommy and daddy can interfere?"

Few people knew Cliona was my mother. Interesting. "They're busy because some dick is causing chaos in the town square and told me to handle my own problems."

Lugh's eyes narrowed. He disappeared in a flash of light and reappeared a few feet away.

He wore a pair of Bermuda shorts and a surfer t-shirt, one of those popular label ones that made the wearer look like he said things like, "Dude, I'm meant for the waves, not a 9-to-5."

To add insult to injury, he wore flipflops. In the middle of winter.

"You look like a douchebag," I said by way of greeting.

His eyes flashed with anger. "I'm on vacation. Isn't this how you dress when you're off work?"

"Only if you're a douchebag." I smiled.

Moira snickered.

"What's the point of this useless display of power?" I asked, waving my hand at the glamoured money still falling from the sky.

"It's to show you the futility of man. Temptation is too irresistible for them to be anything more than mewling children who waste resources and pollute the earth when they die."

Alrighty then. I tilted my head. "And yet you're here taking advantage of all those temptations and seem to have no plans to return to your own realm. How can you be better than them when your actions are the same?"

Lugh didn't like that. His jaw clenched with fury. "You know nothing about me, mongrel."

I laughed out loud. "You know my parents. I might come from two magical bloodlines, but I am still fae."

Satisfaction flickered in his eyes, and I suddenly became very worried.

"But that's not all you are, is it?"

Moira stiffened. "Watch how you speak to her."

"Why?" Lugh asked. "Are you afraid of her, too? She bears a terrible curse, one everyone seems afraid of. Your Evie is being hunted from many directions, and she won't be able to avoid all the arrows that fall. She's better off joining with me."

"Why?" I asked. "So you can protect me?"

Lugh laughed. "You don't need protection."

Moira groaned and nudged me with an elbow. "Oh no. I think this is going to be one of those join with me and we'll rule the world soliloquies followed by maniacal laughter and bicep flexing."

I grimaced. "Is that true? Can we leave the bicep flexing off, at least?"

Darkness flowed around the god, up from his feet until his body was surrounded. His eyes glowed a disturbing silvery green as he lifted his hands. I gathered my magic around me, readying the earth underneath us to prepare.

But Lugh didn't strike. Instead, he laughed. "You will learn, Evie, that I am a patient man, and I know your secrets."

As much as it terrified me to worry about my Chimera curse being leaked, my father was right. I wasn't only one thing. I could only be myself, even if I wanted so badly to be someone else. Looking toward the past would never be the way forward.

Mom and Dad appeared several feet behind Lugh. They gave me a slight nod and faded away.

Magic boomed through my voice, the power of my mother and father stirring the wind and trees. Silver, green, and gold power spun around my body, coalescing into a sparkling crown floating above my head—an annoying, but pointed trick of my father, and one he assured me would disappear once everything was over. One more bit of razzle dazzle until we could all take our toys and return home with minimal bloodshed, I hoped. The bargain I made with my parents in mind, I inhaled and spoke one final time.

Gasps rang out through the crowd.

"As heir to Cliona of the Misty Isle Barrows and Cernunnos, the King of the Fae, I pronounce you in direct violation of fae law."

Lugh's eyes widened. A stunned choked inhale of air from the vampire beside me, but I continued on.

"You are hereby ordered to return Tess Mallory to her home in Joy Springs within the next eight hours, unharmed and with all her memories restored."

The dark power gathered around Lugh shrank from the authority in my voice. "We don't—"

I plowed on. "You are further ordered to leave this realm within the next eight hours, ensuring everyone you've had contact with leaves your proximity unharmed and with all their memories prior to and during your visit. If, during my investigation, it is found you've broken additional fae laws, I am well within my rights to pursue further punishment."

Moira stared at me with wide, shocked eyes, her gaze going from the crown to my face. I gave her a small, sad smile, and plowed on.

"And if I don't?" Lugh interrupted, the fear in his eyes replaced with unadulterated fury.

"Then you will have signed your execution warrant. You are hereby banned from ever returning to this realm without the explicit permission of the crown." I paused and let the crazy shine in my eyes. "And I can assure you, permission will not be granted. But I'd love to see your request come through so I can put my personal stamp of refusal on it."

The god's eyes narrowed. "You *bitch*."

I laid a hand over my heart. "Ouch. Hurt people hurt people."

Moira barked a laugh.

He took a menacing step forward, teeth bared. "I should kill you where you stand."

"You can try. I'd love to show you exactly what someone like me can do." I waved a hand and the money still falling from the sky turned into confetti, the environmentally safe kind because I was not a menace. Groans and yells of disappointment sounded all around us.

I shot Moira a look and without words, she nodded and turned to the crowd, holding her arms out wide before she spoke. "Thank you all for coming to our pop-up magic demonstration! Unfortunately, the money you've already taken has no legal tender."

Cue more groans.

"But this guy right here—" She pointed to Lugh. "He has free tickets for the show tomorrow evening and a free gift to take home with you."

Over a hundred people started walking our way.

Grinning at Moira's antics, I addressed Lugh one final time. "I'll leave you to your adoring public," I said. "Remember my words. Eight hours. If Tess isn't home and you aren't out of my town, I will find you."

I bared my teeth. "And I will kill you."

Lugh disappeared in a shower of light.

Moira took me by the arm and hurried away while the people were still interested in finding Lugh for their fake tickets and free gift. The last thing we needed was a riot.

But as we walked away, a tall, lean man with glowing golden eyes stepped into our path, a woman with glittering green eyes at his side.

Thirty

"Hello, Evie," Rachel purred, her painted claws curled around Caelan's forearm.

I ignored her and tilted my head to Caelan. "Lord."

Caelan's eyes narrowed. "Evie." His sharp gaze took in the confetti littering the ground and the people standing around looking confused. "What happened here?"

"We both know Simone already told you."

"I'm asking you." The way he looked at me was like a stab right to the gut. There was no warmth or familiarity in his eyes. I could have been a stranger for the way he watched me.

His eyes strayed to the crown still swirling around my head. A furrow appeared between his brows. His mouth opened, then snapped shut.

"You have a god living in your town. He caused an…interruption. One I took care of."

His upper lip curled. "I don't need you to take care of anything."

I didn't think I could talk to him again, not if he responded to everything like I was dirt on the bottom of his shoe. "Then you should have gotten here sooner," I said quietly.

"Bitch," Rachel hissed, stepping forward.

Caelan frowned and reached up to rub his temples. He jerked Rachel back. "Stop," he commanded. "I—There's something—" He lifted those stormy eyes up to mine and I saw something I'd never seen in them before.

Fear.

Moira and I exchanged a look. "Caelan?" I stepped forward and reached out to him.

Rachel knocked my hand away. "Don't touch him," she snapped. "He didn't want you. He doesn't want you."

As difficult as it was to ignore Rachel, I watched Caelan. "If there's something wrong, you can come to me, Caelan. I don't know where it all went wrong but—"

"Don't listen to her," Rachel urged Caelan. "You know she only wants you for your power."

I snorted and pointed to the still spinning crown atop my head. "Very sorry, but did you miss the glowing thing I'm wearing? I have all the power I never wanted and then some."

"She'll take and take and you'll never get her claws out of you," Rachel said, every word she spoke a venomous barb.

Moira stepped forward. "What the fuck is wrong with you?"

I had no idea who she was talking to, but the question was pertinent for both of them.

Rachel opened her mouth.

"Not you," Moira snapped. "You." She pointed to Caelan. "Evie has done nothing but love you. Yes, you've had stupid fights, but nothing worth...this." Her voice broke. "You are ruining everything. And once you do, once Evie finally steps away and decides you are no longer worth it, you will *never* get her back."

She shook her head. "Think about this before you permanently topple the bridge you've spent so long building."

Caelan's nostrils flared. He took a hesitant step forward, but Rachel reached out for him, stopping him in his tracks. "He doesn't want her back," Rachel snapped.

Caelan opened his mouth again, but right before he spoke, his eyes hardened. "I don't want to see you again," he said quietly. "You can still have your shop, but as far as I'm concerned, you no longer fall under my jurisdiction. If you need assistance or protection, you will need to ask your parents."

Moira sucked in a sharp breath. "You ass."

Anger burned in the back of my throat, but I resisted the urge to spew poisonous words. He was doing a wonderful job fucking this up all on his own. I didn't need to add fuel to the fire.

"Fine by me," I said instead.

A blonde woman walked up behind Caelan and Rachel, her eyes wary. When she saw my face, her lips thinned. "Evie," she acknowledged.

"Simone." I nodded. "We were just leaving."

She held up a hand. "A moment, please."

When I frowned, a pleading emotion appeared in her eyes. And though she said nothing, I hesitated, then gave her a short nod. Relief filled her face. I held no grudge against Simone and usually called her a friend. She couldn't help getting caught up in whatever this was.

Whatever I had done to Caelan, I couldn't guess. Or if I hadn't done anything and only been usurped by a woman who had something more than me, it still wasn't Simone's fault.

Simone's eyes fell on Rachel, and hatred flared inside the light depths, surprising me with its intensity. "If you'd give us a moment," she said.

Rachel opened her mouth to undoubtedly argue, but Simone bared her teeth. "Leave us," she snarled.

Rachel blinked and took a step back, her fingers sliding from their proprietary grasp on Caelan's arm. With a furious glare at me and Moira, Rachel hurried away, far enough to prevent her from overhearing Simone's next words.

Caelan's eyes tracked every step Rachel took until Simone yanked his attention away by digging her nails into his arm and whispering something into his ear.

His jaw tightened, but he tore his gaze away.

Simone sighed and closed her eyes for a brief moment. When she opened them, her eyes snagged on my crown. "It's true then."

Something like sorrow flashed over her face, there and gone in a heartbeat. "Congratulations are in order, it seems." A thin smile. Then, "Or condolences, maybe."

Moira laughed. "She took me by surprise, too. We haven't discussed what she gave up."

As bargains went, it wasn't the worst. Something to think about later, once I was out of here and safe. And in pajamas with a very large glass of wine in my hand.

"She wanted it all along," Caelan growled. "Never me. Never us."

Simone's nostrils flared. She shot him an angry glare. "Just…" she paused and exhaled. "Just shut up, Caelan. For the love of the gods, I do not know what's gotten into you, but you've been insufferable these last couple of weeks."

Caelan blinked in surprise and reared back like Simone had slapped him.

And she had. Verbally.

Moira's lips twitched.

"This changes things," Simone said, ignoring the way Caelan looked at her. "Since you and our Shifter Lord are no longer… involved—" She slid an accusing glare his way. "There must be boundaries. And if you decide to repair this rift—"

"Unnecessary," Caelan interrupted. "And unwanted. Rachel and I will be married within the month."

Simone's head snapped to focus on Caelan. She blinked once, twice, before slowly shaking her head. "Oh, Caelan," she murmured softly.

All the air was sucked out of my lungs. I swayed, Moira reaching for me, steadying me with the grip of her hand. My gaze went to his face, memorizing the lines and planes of his cheekbones and jaws, remembering every time I traced my fingers over them when we lay together. Hot tears burned the backs of my eyes,

"You sonofabitch," Moira hissed, eyes flashing crimson. The only reason she didn't lunge for him was because she was holding me upright. "What was all of this? All the chasing and begging and pursuing just to cast her away when she didn't bat pretty green eyes at you?"

"A Lord can never resist a challenge," he said, a defiant look in his eyes.

I shrugged Moira off and straightened. Before I opened my mouth, Moira leaned over. "Be sure," she whispered, her eyes imploring.

I was more than sure. "The Caelan I knew would have never spoken to me like this, would have never hurt me or embarrassed me in public. I don't know what's happening or what has changed to make you so cruel, but I do not deserve it."

Simone bowed her head, her slender hands trembling. She, like Moira, knew where this was going.

"I never should have pursued someone who could not bear pureblooded children," he sneered.

Another stab to my heart, another cruel jab forcing me to close the door on something I thought could not be destroyed.

"Perhaps not," I agreed. Proud of myself for keeping my voice steady and my hands still, I looked at Simone. "Regardless of what's happened with your Lord, you are always welcome in my home, Omega. As is Garrett, provided he does not have the same attitude as Caelan."

"He doesn't," blurted Simone, sliding a horrified look at Caelan.

I nodded. "When I return home, I will adjust my wards. Seymour can visit me any time he wishes, though if your Lord is cruel to him, I hope you will return him to me."

"I would never be cruel to Seymour," Caelan snapped.

I gave him a sad smile. "No. Only to your former, tainted blood fiancée, it seems."

Simone let out a breath of dismay. "There are few of us who do not admire you, Evie. Please don't let this taint your view of our people."

"Don't worry. I've long been able to differentiate one person's prejudices and separate them from the whole."

I tilted my head. "I will see you around, Simone. Best of luck with your new Lady."

Simone's lower lip wobbled. She lunged for me and pulled me in for a tight hug."

"I am so sorry," she whispered. "I have no idea what is happening."

I patted her back and stepped away. "It's okay. Better to know now, I suppose."

Caelan's eyes swirled when our gazes met. "Goodbye, Lord." I tilted my head in acknowledgment. "I will ensure my parents know my situation has changed."

The smile didn't reach his eyes. "Perhaps they can find a better genetic match for you. Someone who will not care about your tainted blood."

My mind went silent for a brief second, every thought in my head disappearing into the black hole that opened underneath my feet. I stared at him for a long moment, this man I had loved more than myself, and laughed.

The sound was a harsh crack, not a lick of amusement anywhere. That silence roared back like a wildfire and power crackled in my veins. The earth rumbled underneath our feet, and vines slid from the ground, tearing up the sidewalks and road, damaging the very infrastructure under Joy Springs, but I couldn't care.

I was too angry to care, the realization of what I had done once more, loving a man who loved himself more, sending a tearing pain through my soul.

"Attack me," Caelan said quietly. "Begin the war between our people. Be the spark that tears everything apart, Evie. I know your blood roars for vengeance. Do it and prove me right."

The words struck something inside me, some deep, desperate

part still looking for a peaceful resolution. Moira's cool fingers touched my arm. The vines withdrew into the ground.

A familiar shimmer of power from behind told me my parents had arrived.

Cernunnos and Cliona stepped up beside me. With a wave of her hand, the roads and sidewalks repaired themselves. She smiled thinly at Caelan.

"I think you've done enough damage," she said quietly. "No reason for our tainted blood to cause more." She reached for me. "Come, Evie. Let us leave Caelan to the mess he's created."

I let her lead me away, Moira quietly walking by my side. She trembled with fury, her jaw held so tightly I thought her teeth might crack.

My father didn't leave with us. I glanced back to see him and Caelan speaking, but I was too far away to hear what was being said.

Whatever it was didn't look friendly.

Mom tugged me once more. "Never look behind you," she said quietly. "Nothing lives there but pain."

She had no idea how true her words were.

Thirty-One

CAELAN

Simone's disgust with me shivered in the air around us. Hers was nothing compared to my own.

The barbed words I'd said to Evie had fallen out of my mouth like spilled rubies. I couldn't control anything other than my movements, but when Rachel touched me, my limbs wanted to obey only her. Something was terribly wrong.

"Are you out of your mind?" Simone hissed, her eyes wide with shock as Evie disappeared around the corner. Rachel was still across the street, idly scrolling on her phone as she waited for Simone to call her back.

But my Omega looked disinclined to do anything other than scratch the other shifter's eyes right out of her head.

I wanted to scream for help, but it was like my brain and mouth were wholly out of my control. "I said nothing to her but the truth."

As terrible as this all was, the words I had said and kept saying were nothing I hadn't thought before in the deepest, darkest times of night, when all those thoughts crept out for examination only to be shut up tight by the time the sun rose. Was this my punishment for even thinking such terrible thoughts?

I loved Evie more than I'd ever loved anyone, but we had

major obstacles. And as a Lord of a large territory, I had to think about such things. If my children were to inherit my territories, they had to prove powerful and with Evie's Chimera blood, having children could be dangerous to both of us and to the world.

I wanted so desperately not to care, to fling my cautions to the wind and accept her with open arms, and I'd done that.

In public, at least.

But something had always held me back.

The awful things I'd said to her, though, would haunt me for the rest of my life. I wanted things to work out between us. I wished I could be the kind of person to walk away from my responsibilities and just take her hand and walk off into the sunset.

Because Evie was that kind of person. She genuinely didn't care what powers her children may or may not have or about any future complications.

But now, even if I wanted things to work out between us, she'd taken the fae crown. Evie was officially the high ruler of her people, even if Cernunnos hadn't formally stepped aside yet. At least not completely.

I knew why she'd done so. Lugh was too big of a threat to her and those she loved for her to take on by herself. At least not before she knew and understood her powers.

And, if her Chimera heritage were to be leaked, our kind would hunt her to the ends of the earth. As the fae heir, her heritage no longer mattered. She was accepted by her people despite her genetics or mixed blood—something I don't think I could have given her, regardless of how much I wanted to. She could turn into a Chimera in the middle of the street, and neither I, nor the Lords, could do a thing about it unless we wanted to start a war with the fae.

Clever, cunning Cernunnos. I had to shake my head at the genius of it. The bastard was never one to pass up an opportunity. With Evie and I on shaky ground and Lugh in town keeping Tess captive, now was the perfect time to force her hand.

And I'd nudged her along by being an absolute dick.

Horror brimmed in Simone's eyes. "I never knew you to be so cruel," she said after a long moment. Judgment brimmed in her voice. "Never have I seen you treat someone you loved so poorly." She bared her teeth. "I am ashamed of you."

Garrett appeared from around the corner, his eyes narrowing as he scented the fury surrounding my Omega. When he reached us, he shoved his hands in his pockets and stared at both of us.

"I've obviously missed something," he drawled, eyes lingering on Simone. "Are you okay?"

I snorted. "Since when do you inquire about Simone's well-being before my own?"

Those amber eyes slid my way. "Since you became someone few of us recognize, *Lord*."

The emphasis on my title made shame slam through my veins. But anger brimmed there, too. "Should I be questioning your loyalty?"

Simone's harsh laugh made me still.

But Garrett had always been calm and cool. "I wonder if we should be questioning yours."

I blinked in surprise before fury boiled my blood.

Garrett kept speaking. "You introduced Evie as our new lady. You gave her a portion of your property. She stayed over at the Keep for days at a time, and you asked her to marry you. The shifters were looking forward to new energy and a new future. Maybe we didn't all accept her, but we would have. I believe that much. She's beautiful, powerful, and well-connected." He ran a hand through his hair. "Christ, Caelan. She's the heir to the gods-damned fae throne."

Simone cleared her throat. "No longer the heir."

Garrett's attention snapped to Simone. "What happened?"

A small smile curved her lips. "She accepted the throne."

He sucked in a breath. "Shit." Garrett blinked a few times

before he laughed. "Can't say I expected that ending." He waved a hand. "I've never seen someone commit such a colossal fuck up before."

He was not speaking of Evie.

Garrett laughed again and returned his attention to me. "How does it feel to know you've let kinghood pass you by? To know you let someone so powerful who loved you so much slip right through your fingers?"

But Simone didn't allow me to speak. "He's asked Rachel to be his bride."

Garrett snorted, but when he realized Simone was serious, his jaw dropped. "No fucking way."

Simone nodded, a sad smile on her lips.

He scrubbed a hand over his jaw and eyed Simone, thoughtfully, before jerking his head to the left.

Simone nodded, and they both walked off, leaving me standing there alone, a feeling of dread churning in my stomach. Rachel straightened and began walking over. I shook my head once, sharp, and the shifter hesitated.

Less than a minute later, my Omega and Second returned, wearing equally grim expressions.

I crossed my arms over my chest and waited.

They exchanged looks. "We resign," they said as one.

My stomach fell to my feet. "Excuse me?"

"You heard us," Garrett said. "We resign. You are not the Lord we signed up to serve. We certainly did not sign up to have someone like Rachel lead us into the future."

I was screaming inside my head, beating against the walls of the mental prison I was trapped inside.

But those hateful words kept flowing. "You can't resign. This is not a job."

Garrett shrugged. "We can and we will."

"We are a Pack. I am your Lord. You can't just walk away." The floor was caving underneath my feet.

Simone removed the pin fastened inside her collar, the one

denoting her as an Omega to our Pack, and took my hand, pressing the pin inside my palm. "I am an Omega and will be accepted into whatever Pack I choose."

Garrett nodded. "And I am an Enforcer and powerful enough to become a Lord if I wished."

"You'd become rogues?"

Simone looked to the space where Evie had disappeared. "No. I know someone who will have a space for us if we wish."

Garrett's eyebrows flicked up, but he nodded too.

Panic set in. "I could make you both stay," I snarled. Not a lie, but if they thought I was a tyrant now, what would forcing them to stay in my Pack do—not only to them, but to the rest of my people?

"You could try," Garrett said mildly. "But I'd suggest refraining from making a public scene. Your reputation is already in tatters with our people."

I took a step forward, claws sliding from my fingernails. Rachel started walking across the street, but Simone and Garrett were done. They both took a step back.

"I hope this works out for you," she said quietly, grief brimming in her eyes.

Garrett said nothing, only gave me a long, searching look before he took Simone's hand and led her away.

Grief was a fire in my veins as I watched the two most important people in my life walk away, after the first one I'd screwed up with so profoundly.

I needed help.

But then Rachel was standing in front of me, her green eyes flashing in a hypnotic manner, and everything else faded away.

He answered the phone on the first ring. "What's wrong?"

I couldn't help the grin forming on my face. "Do I only call you in an emergency?"

"Yes," Ben growled. "These days at least."

"There's nothing wrong. With me, at least," I clarified. "But I think there might be something wrong with Caelan."

Silence over the line for a long moment. "Wrong how?"

I explained a few things, Ben not interrupting. "We broke up a couple of hours ago."

Ben sighed, and I could hear the sound of something rough rubbing against the phone speaker. "I don't know, Evie," he said hesitantly. "Are you sure you haven't grown apart?"

I took the phone away from my ear and stared down at it in disbelief. "A few weeks ago, he asked me to marry him!"

I could almost see his wince through the phone. "I know. I'm not saying you did anything to cause this—"

"You sure as hell better not be!" I snapped.

Dad, sitting in the kitchen, eating the caramel popcorn I special ordered, laughed.

I covered the speaker and hissed, "Do not eat all my popcorn!"

Dad wiggled his eyebrows and grabbed another handful.

Ben chuckled. "Sometimes things change. He and this Rachel woman have a past. Who's to say things didn't rekindle as soon as he saw her?"

Because that would mean everything we had was a lie. And if it wasn't a lie, it was an indicator that what I felt for him was much stronger than whatever he'd felt for me, no matter how doggedly he'd pursued me.

Both left a terrible taste in my mouth and an ache in my heart that would never go away.

"You're being an asshole," I grumbled.

"Evie." He paused. "I know you love him. From everything I saw, he loved you too. But things don't always work out, and you two weren't mated, were you?"

"You damn well know we weren't. I don't even know if a bond like that can happen between a fae and a shifter."

"Shifters can mate outside of their species."

"You are not helping right now."

Ben's laugh eased something in my heart. "For what it's worth, I'm sorry. And, if it will make you feel better, I'll travel to Joy Springs in a few days to check him out."

"Thank you," I breathed.

"Don't get too excited," he warned. "Caelan damn near went to war over you with the Lords, and he has not been friendly to us since. He and Rowan are still on good terms, but he's testy even with me."

"It's because we smooched," I teased.

"He should be more jealous of Rowan than me," Ben said seriously. "That man stares at you like you're the sun."

I laughed, but Ben didn't. "It's not like that between us."

"Maybe not," he agreed. "But it doesn't mean he doesn't wish for it."

I sank deeper into the couch cushions. "Enough of such talk.

Rowan and I are only friends. Please try to see Caelan if you can. If anything, he needs a friend. Rachel is…"

"I know exactly what Rachel is," Ben growled. "She is not fit to be their Lady."

"Then maybe you can talk some reason into him. Even if he doesn't choose me, Ben, he should choose someone…better. Someone fit to lead his people into the future."

"Someone like you?" His tone wasn't mocking or cruel, only contemplative.

I laughed. "Have we met? I'm a hot mess eighty percent of the time. No. Not me. Though I was willing to do it. I have my own problems to worry about now."

Dad grinned and wiggled his fingers at me.

I suppressed my sigh. Yes. Plenty of problems both current and future.

"I'm sorry, Evie." He sounded like he meant the words. "Don't dismiss what I said about Rowan. Not right away. He's a good man. A good shifter. A good Lord. Wildly different from Caelan, but maybe that's what you need."

I couldn't think about anything other than the ache in my heart right now. "Ben, I'm putting one foot in front of the other, and that's all I can do. I'm letting go and giving it to the universe to sort out for me because the gods know I have enough on my plate."

Ben's chuckle reverberated over the line. "Fair enough. I'll call you when I make it to town. Until then, be careful. Female shifters are known to be volatile with their current partner's old flames."

He hung up before I could squawk. An old flame meant I was in the past, and the sun hadn't even set over this yet.

Old flame, my ass.

Right now, the only flame burning was the one in my heart, and it was so hot, everything felt like ash.

My father set his bowl of popcorn down and brushed off his hands. "Come. Let us watch some of that fishing net movie film program."

I blinked. "What?"

Dad waved his hand at the television. "The program with all the movies. The net movie network."

"Netflix?"

Dad's face lit up. "Yes! Net Flix."

"One word, Dad." I started laughing. "Have you ever watched anything from there?"

He shook his head. "No. But your mother loves it. She claims it's the best invention for immortals ever invented." Dad rolled his eyes. "I once watched her spend a full eight hours lying in a prone position on the couch watching British aristocrats be over-entitled." Dad rolled his eyes. "It was maddening, but every time I tried to turn it off, she'd throw something at me."

Something inside me thawed at the thought of my mom and dad fighting over something as normal as too much streaming tv time. "I'm going to tell her about Britbox."

Dad frowned. "What is that?"

"It's like the British Netflix."

"Don't you dare!"

A knock on the door interrupted Dad's horror. To my surprise, Garrett and Simone stood on the front porch.

"This is a surprise," I said, opening the door to let them in.

Garrett, always a man of many words, grunted in greeting. Simone grinned at his back and shrugged. "We're here to ask you a favor."

I shut the door behind me. Dad, in the few seconds it took me to greet them had sprawled on one of the couches and was pressing every button on the remote.

Garrett's eyebrows flicked up at the sight. "Hello."

"Greetings, young Enforcer," Dad said, doing a hell of a Vulcan impression. "You are here to ask my daughter for employment, are you not?"

I froze. Simone shot Dad a glare. "Seriously?" She shook her head and headed for the kitchen. "Is he always like this?"

"Always," I confirmed. "But what's this about a job? Is everything okay?" I thought about it. "The shop stays pretty busy, but we can always use help with making extra bouquets if you really need extra employment." I eyed her. "Or you can just ask Caelan for a raise."

"Not that kind of employment," Garrett said.

"Have a seat," I told him because if I didn't, he'd never relax.

Simone was digging through the liquor cabinet. "You got any vanilla vodka?" she called over her shoulder.

"Err. Yes?" I pointed to the top left of the cabinet. "Behind the plum brandy."

"Who keeps plum brandy?" Garrett grumbled.

"It's for mulled wine, and it's delicious."

The Enforcer rolled his eyes and crossed his arms behind his head.

"Espresso?" Simone yelled.

"Pods are by the machine."

"Simple syrup?"

I gaped at her. She was acting super weird. "There's agave syrup in the cabinet above the coffee."

Simone sighed. "I guess that will do," she grumbled.

"Cocktail shaker is above the fridge," I added since she seemed to be on a mission.

"Thanks." Silence fell in the kitchen until the sounds of the ice machine and Simone shaking the hell out of a cocktail shattered the quiet of the living room.

"Who wants one?" she yelled.

Dad frowned. "What is it?"

"An espresso martini, I think. They're delicious."

"Yes, please," Dad called.

Garrett waved his hand.

"I'll have one. Mom and Moira are in the greenhouse. How many did you make?"

"A lot."

"Good. I'll text them."

A moment later, Simone shoved a drink under my nose, and Mom and Moira burst through the door.

"Gimme!" Moira said.

Simone jerked a thumb over her shoulder. "There are two on the kitchen island."

Mom shoved Moira so hard the vampire flipped over the back of the recliner and crashed to the ground.

She cackled and sprinted to the kitchen. "Me first!" Mom crowed.

"Looks like you two made up," I drawled as Moira tried to untangle herself from the blanket I'd draped on the back of the chair.

"Your mother is a damn menace." She finally freed herself and rose.

"Here." Mom handed her the drink and grinned. "I wanted the one that was a little fuller."

Moira took the drink and narrowed her eyes at my mom. "Did you do anything to it?"

Mom sipped her cocktail. "Mmm. This is delicious. Who's the bartender?"

I pointed at Simone who'd sprawled next to Garrett.

"We'll have to keep you around," Mom said before she nudged Moira out of the way with her hip and took the chair for herself.

"That's actually why we're here," Simone began.

"She doesn't want a job at the shop," I said.

Garrett groaned. "For the gods' sake. Do women always take this long to get to the point?"

Simone nudged him. "Shut up," she hissed.

"Yes," Dad said.

"We left Caelan," Garrett said. "Permanently. As such, we can no longer live in his territory."

I sucked in a shocked gasp. "What. Why?"

Both the shifters looked profoundly uncomfortable.

Dad snorted and sat up straighter. "Caelan has proven

himself unfit at the current time. Simone and Garrett have lost faith in their leadership and since they are both far more powerful than they let on, they must find someone more powerful to serve."

I stared at my father for a long moment. "Serve?" The word felt…uncomfortable. "I don't want anyone serving me."

"No." Dad shook his head. "Shifters are born and naturally inclined to serve in a strong hierarchy. Without one, they become lost. Volatile. Sometimes dangerous."

Simone and Garrett sat there like stones. And me? I was confused as all hell. Those two had served Caelan for generations. What in the hell had happened in the short time since I'd left them? "I don't understand how I can help you. I'm not a—a shifter or have a Keep or anything of the sort. I want to help, but I don't have any work."

Mom let out a low, wicked laugh. "Darling, they're asking to be a part of your court."

"My court?" I echoed, giving Mom a blank stare.

Moira slapped her hand over her mouth and gasped. "Oh, Evie," she mumbled.

Garrett started to laugh, the sound a low, sexy rumble. "First, you should hire someone well versed in social etiquette." He gestured to Simone. "I happen to have someone highly qualified right here."

Simone gave me a little wave.

The cobwebs started to clear.

"There she goes," Dad said, amusement in his voice. "She's starting to understand."

"A court," I murmured. "Like ladies in waiting and all that nonsense?"

"Not so fancy as that," Mom said, "but you do need a few close friends and family to keep you grounded and abreast on your social engagements."

Well shit. I should have asked more questions. "Do you have people?" I put the word in air quotes.

"We both do," Dad interjected. "You've met my people. Cliona's people are more circumspect."

Mom rolled her eyes. "And they don't like you. Which is why you never see them."

Dad wiggled his eyebrows at her, and Mom harrumphed, though her eyes sparkled with laughter.

"I don't have a fund for salaries." I frowned. "Or money to pay them."

Dad sighed and shook his empty glass. "Simone. Can you make about twenty more of these?"

Moira snickered.

Simone rose. "I'll make a pitcher."

"The gods have blessed you," Dad said. He floated the empty glasses over to the kitchen island.

Once Simone was in the kitchen, Dad leaned forward. "You are the current queen in training for all the fae."

When I blinked owlishly at him, Dad groaned.

Garrett grinned. "Evie. Your father is too ancient to talk about money in public, but what he's trying to hint around to is the fact that you're filthy fucking rich." He glanced at my father. "Correct?"

"Correct," Dad agreed.

"So I can afford to pay salaries?"

"Many, many salaries," Dad said.

"Huh. I'll be damned. Cool."

The sound of the cocktail shaker clattered around.

I glanced at Garrett. "Are you sure you want to leave Caelan? You've been with him for a long time. And you're friends with him. Good friends."

Grief flashed over his face, there and gone in an instant. "Not once in the many years I've been with him have I ever thought about walking away. Not until a few months ago. These last few weeks have only solidified my decision. Today was the last straw."

I reached out to touch him but hesitated. "Garrett, I think

something might be wrong with Caelan. He's never been casually cruel."

"None of us scent any foreign magic on him. We've looked." Garrett grimaced. "We haven't found anything inside the Keep that doesn't belong, so it can't be a curse or a charmed object. There's nothing to explain his behavioral changes."

While I'd known they wouldn't have dismissed Caelan's odd behavior as a fluke, it was cold comfort to realize they'd done their due diligence and found out that my fiancé was not under the influence of magic.

He was just a huge dick.

But I still wanted to ensure they weren't making a mistake by coming to me. "Are you sure you don't want to give it more time? I can't help but think this is partially my fault."

Simone came over with a tray full of martinis. "I don't need more time. If the Lord I serve under can treat someone so poorly and keep hammering when her heart is clearly breaking in front of everyone, he is not a man I wish to continue serving."

I blinked away the tears forming. "I—" My voice cracked. "Thank you, Simone."

Garrett's jaw tightened. "I was not there for that, but I hope you know I would have done something. Words hurt as much as a physical blow sometimes."

"I'll be fine." As difficult as things were right now, I believed the words I was saying. I would be okay. If I could recover after Scotland, I could recover from this. At least I hadn't gone ahead and married him. "But thank you."

"Mom? Dad? What do you think? Anything I should know before I say yes?"

Mom sighed. "You're a terrible negotiator."

Moira sipped her martini. "How much was Caelan paying you?"

Dad snapped his fingers. "Yes. A good starting point."

Garrett rattled off a number that made me choke on my drink, but Dad looked thoughtful.

"A good salary. You had access to a Healer at the Keep and mages for an additional level of security, yes?"

Garrett nodded. "I was in charge of much of the Keep's security, but there were other aspects I had no say in."

"Do you have additional gifts?"

Garrett's eyes narrowed. "Excuse me?"

"If you wish to work for the fae, specifically the queen, you are required to divulge anything which could potentially endanger her or add to her wellbeing."

I gave Dad a funny look. What was he talking about?

The shifter looked uncomfortable. "Not all shifters possess additional gifts. Mostly they are limited to the Lords."

"Which you will one day be," Dad said, surprising the hell out of me.

How things change. Months ago, Garrett could barely tolerate being in the same room with me, going so far as to threaten to kill me every time he saw me. Now, not only were we sitting together, he was asking for a job. "Damn, Garrett. You might be a Lord, and you still want to work for me?"

He rolled his eyes. "I'm not a Lord, and working for you will look great on my resume. Even if you have no idea what you're doing."

"Careful, wolf," Dad said in a warning tone.

"I'm not wrong," Garrett doubled down.

"Perhaps, but you are still speaking to a queen."

I raised my hand. "Queen in training. And it's Garrett. I appreciate that he doesn't feel the need to be nice to me."

"And I appreciate you feel the same."

We smiled at each other, and it wasn't exactly friendly.

I looked over at Dad. "How do you assure someone's loyalty when they become part of your court?"

Garrett snorted. "You're finally learning, kid."

"Blood oaths," Dad said. "It will feel odd at first, but you'll get used to them."

Simone interjected. "The Lords have something similar. We swear one to whatever Alpha or Lord we choose to serve."

"Are you still under the blood oath?" Moira asked.

Simone nodded. "Until Caelan severs it or we choose another one to serve."

"Can he compel you through the oath?"

Simone and Garrett exchanged an unreadable glance. "In some ways, yes," she finally said.

I grimaced. "Is the fae oath similar?"

Dad nodded. "You can make the commands as loose or as strong as you wish. Loosening them allows freedom and choice. But I would recommend ensuring you have a few ironclad commands."

"Such as?" I couldn't think of anything I'd want to force Simone and Garrett to do.

"Loyalty to your kingdom and people. Protection of family and loved ones. Things like that."

I glanced at the two shifters. "Are those similar to what Caelan did?"

Simone shifted. Garrett's expression was blank. "We are not allowed to tell you of the previously taken oaths."

"Will those oaths shatter once you are under a new one?"

Garrett nodded.

"Will it be difficult for you to fight against Caelan if ever called to do so?"

My attention jerked to my father. "What kind of question is that?"

He shrugged. "One that needs asking."

Garret's nostrils flared. "Even after all of this, he remains my friend. At least on my side. He is unhappy, but I do not think he will strike back. But if he does, if I am under another oath, I will have no choice other than to fight back."

I looked at Simone. She swallowed hard but nodded.

"Do you want more time to think about this? Even if you can't find something wrong, that's not a definitive answer. What would you do if he really was under the influence of something?"

"We've already spoken about this. Caelan has been different for many months now, and we have not always agreed with his methods, even before you came into his life. We were already speaking of leaving, but neither of us expected to seek another so soon. As Lords go, he was one of the better ones, but now we're wondering how far he will go to win."

Sympathy flooded me. "I'm sorry. For both of you. And the answer is—"

Moira jumped in. "You haven't asked me."

I blinked. "Asked you what?"

"If I wanted to be in your court or whatever the hell this is." Her dark eyes pinned me to the seat. "I'm supposed to be your best friend, and I didn't even know you'd claimed the crown until that thing started spinning around on your head!"

I opened my mouth to explain, then closed it. She was right. I'd bargained for myself and my friends and barreled straight ahead without even thinking of consulting Moira.

"I—" My voice cracked. "I'm sorry. I wasn't thinking. Would you even want a spot? What if I have to move? Or travel all the time?"

Moira reached over and took my hands in her cool ones. "I will go wherever you go. Home is wherever we're together."

Tears filled my eyes. "Of course, Moira. Whatever place you want, you can have."

I waved my hand at Mom and Dad. "Pay her a lot."

Mom laughed.

"Alright then," I said and dragged in a breath. "I'm willing if you are. But I want you to know I take no pleasure in this, and I want to be 100% sure this is what you want."

Everyone nodded. The feeling of a loosened knot being tightened formed in my chest. What was happening right now felt like I'd been slowly moving toward this my entire life, and I couldn't explain why. I had no idea who my father was until a few months ago. I shouldn't be able to carry the Chimera curse, and yet, here I was, the product of two powerful fae and my blood swimming with Chimera DNA.

And now I was queen of all the fae.

Or queen in training. Weird enough either way.

Talk about things not being on your bingo card. This was all one big doozy.

Caelan was going to be furious when he found out.

Strangely enough, that was the least of my problems.

Thirty~Three

A few hours later, we were all buzzed on espresso martinis thanks to the new vodka mom had slipped into the bottle in my pantry, and I had three brand new employees, or court members, or whatever they were, who were taking great pride in bossing me around.

I finally covered my ears and declared, "If you don't stop, I'm going to make you all wear black and white uniforms and start calling you Beetlejuice."

"Lame," Simone slurred. She lifted her glass and gave it the hairy eyeball. "What the hell is in those things?"

"You're the one who made them," Mom said mildly, hiding her smile behind her glass.

"True." Simone blinked. "Huh. I'm great at being a bartender!"

Moira patted Simone's knee. "You are. The spiked vodka helps too."

Another knock on the door made us all freeze. There were only a few people who could get to the porch. Moira and I locked eyes. A second later, we were both scrambling for the door.

Tess stood on the porch with a blanket and a wide-eyed expression.

I didn't reach for her right away. "Tess?"

Moira wrung her hands beside me. "Are you…you?" she asked.

Tess nodded. "Lugh said he will see you very, very soon." Her lower lip wobbled.

Moira and I reached for her at the same time, enveloping her in a tight hug before ushering her into the house and pressing a martini into her cold hands.

She gravitated toward my mother first, who wrapped a blanket around her and tucked her under her arm. Mom stroked Tess's hair and murmured nonsensical words.

Silence fell for a couple of minutes until Tess blinked a few times. "Why do the shifters smell different?"

Moira frowned. "You can smell them? Like I can?"

Tess sipped her martini and shrugged. "They smell a little like Evie. Before that, they smelled a little like Caelan. But I can't smell him at all anymore." Her eyes widened. "Did something happen?"

Dad chuckled. "Someone should give her the condensed version."

Garrett did just that, and as I listened to the man, I noticed something about him I never had before. He seemed less tense, more relaxed than normal.

Had working for Caelan been so tough? How had I missed so many things? I wanted to deny it, but the things he'd said to me.

I still couldn't shake the feeling that something was wrong, but I couldn't discount the things from before. Maybe this was for the best. Maybe it took something as awful as this to shake me from my complacency.

But seeing Garrett smiling at Tess, when I'd rarely seen a genuine smile cross his face, knocked something loose inside me. Even after our rocky start, he'd come to me when he could have gone anywhere. And Simone had too. Granted, the fae were powerful, and I knew there was some self-preservation in their decision, but they'd come to me first.

And that had to mean something.

When Garrett finally stopped talking, Tess was sitting straight up gawking at him. Her pale gaze found mine. "Moira joined too?"

I nodded.

"What about me?"

I reached over and ruffled her hair. "We can talk when you've rested. You've spent quite a while under a powerful glamour, and I want to make sure you know you're back in the real world and all of this really happened."

At the disappointment in her eyes, I shook my head. "I'm not saying no, Tess. Not at all. I'm saying, let's take a beat. Lugh is supposed to be gone, but I won't believe it until I see it myself. I'll go out tomorrow and find his usual haunts to make sure."

"I'll help," Dad said.

"Me too," Mom added.

"Once we know he's gone, then we'll talk. I'm worried he might try to get to you again."

Tess nodded. "Okay, but he's not after me, Evie. He wants you."

The booming of the wards stopped me from interrogating Tess about that.

"Caelan's here," I said quietly.

"He felt the oath break," Simone murmured. She sighed and started to rise, but Mom put her hand on the shifter's arm.

"No. You're Evie's now. She will take care of this."

Simone's eyes tightened at the edges. "Be careful. Caelan in a rage is…"

She shook her head. "Just be careful."

"Same for you," Mom said to Garrett when he started to rise.

But Garrett shook his head and stood anyway. "My role is different from Simone's. I will always stand beside her when danger comes to call."

Dad's eyes glimmered with approval. He inclined his head. "I'll follow you out."

Dad and Garrett came outside with me and waited on the

porch while I walked down the steps and to the edge of the wards.

A golden glow bounced off the wards, highlighting Caelan in a soft glow. Any other time, it might have been beautiful, but Caelan was in a full-blown rage. He paced back and forth, his gaze burning into me as I walked closer.

"You think you can take them from me?" he snarled. Claws slid from his fingers, the razor sharpness heightened by the soft glow of the light.

I didn't have the heart to tell him I already had. "If something is wrong, you need to figure out a way to tell me. Your behavior has been off for a while now, but especially now."

"There's nothing wrong with me!" he roared, the sound sending birds flying from the trees.

Oh my gods. Fee and Poe. My heartbeat picked up. I needed to get them away from the Keep.

Caelan's nostrils flared. "Are you afraid of me, Evie?" The smile that crossed his face held a savage edge.

I knew at that moment if he could reach me, he would kill me.

"I never used to be."

Rachel stepped out from the brush, her chestnut hair swinging around her shoulders. She said nothing, only went to Caelan's side and looped an arm around his waist.

"Release them," he growled. "Now."

"They don't want to be released."

"THEY ARE MINE!" Sharp canines slid from his incisors.

"No longer," I said quietly. "They came to me and asked to be a part of my court."

Rachel snorted. "A court? You're a wannabe princess playing with forces you don't understand."

I smiled. Her proprietary hold on Caelan's waist cut deep, but the Lord allowed it. I held my tongue about it, and instead, spoke to Rachel. "I wish you the best of luck. Becoming a Lady of a territory is no easy thing."

"I don't need your luck," Rachel hissed. "I was born to do this."

A strange flash of light rolled over her iris. Not the color of a Lord, but something sickly. The color of illness, a green I never saw in the natural world. I tilted my head and focused harder, but it had disappeared.

"Give them back," Caelan said, quieter this time, an almost plaintive whisper.

I stilled at the hopelessness in his voice. Rachel's claws slid from her fingers and dug into Caelan's side. Blood, visible even in the low light, seeped through the shirt's fabric.

"Caelan?" I took a step closer to the wards. "Whatever this is, fight it." He would have never allowed someone to hurt him like that.

What in the hell was going on?

The Lord's eyes widened, and he took a step back, but Rachel's grip tightened, and like a light switch, his expression went cold and aloof once more.

I hoped Garrett had witnessed this.

"Simone and Garrett are blood sworn to the fae now. To me. They no longer answer to you."

Rachel bared her teeth. "They won't be with you long. You'll never be strong enough to hold them."

"You know nothing about me." I allowed a sheen of crimson to roll across my eyes, and for the first time since everything happened, Rachel looked unsure.

"I will kill you," Caelan hissed. He lunged for me, claws extended, face screwed in a grimace of concentration.

I held my ground, secure in my enhanced wards. Caelan bounced harmlessly off the boundary, landing in a graceful crouch. "You won't always stay behind these wards. One day soon, you and I will have it out."

I stared at the man I'd loved and wondered when the moment was I'd resolved not to fight for us any longer. I'd help him, if only because of what we had, but I don't think I could ever forgive the poison falling from his lips, the barbs pointed right to my deepest insecurities. How could one ever recover from something like that?

"You are not my enemy. I'm not sure where it all went so wrong, but this is not you. One day you're going to wake up and wonder what happened. I want you to remember this moment. You are no longer welcome in my home or on my lands."

Footsteps from behind and my father was at my side a moment later. "Much the same as her shop, Lord, returning will net you a death sentence."

Cernunnos' attention turned to Rachel. "I'm of the opinion my daughter should kill you where you stand, but she's a new queen and raised outside of my lands. Her heart is more tender than mine."

Rachel sneered. "And who the hell are you, old man?"

Garrett wheezed with laughter from behind us.

My father, dressed in his familiar outfit of joggers and a t-shirt, smiled faintly. Magic swelled in the surrounding air until he was at least a foot taller than me, horns extending another two to three feet above his head.

Rachel blanched, her mouth falling open.

"My father," I said. "Cernunnos, King of the Fae. My mother is inside. Cliona, Queen of the Banshees, in case you were curious."

The shifter went white, her eyes wide in her pale face. She tugged on Caelan's arm and murmured something in his ear.

"I'll follow you in a moment," he said.

Rachel didn't hesitate. She turned on her heel and hurried away. When she was outside of earshot, Caelan stepped closer to the wards.

Dad frowned. "Step closer, Lord."

Caelan's upper lip curled.

My father merely watched him with an expression I couldn't identify. "I can make you. I'm asking to be polite and for the space you hold in my daughter's heart."

To his credit, Caelan stepped closer. Dad reached through the wards with one hand and touched the Lord's forehead. A mix of gold and green light speared through Caelan's skin.

His eyes closed, pain rolling over Caelan's features as Dad did…something to him. Every second it took, Dad's expression grew even more grim.

"I'm going to have to open the wards," he said. "He will not harm you."

I nodded, not having a clue what was going on, but trusting him regardless. He must have found something.

Dad dropped the wards for a split second, just long enough to yank Caelan through. Rachel, apparently watching from the trees like a female peeping Tom, screeched and came barreling back through the woods, as if she knew what Dad had done and threw herself toward the hole.

She bounced off the wards so hard, she flew back several yards. Dad disappeared in a flash of light, Caelan in his arms, but not before saying in an urgent voice, "Get to the house."

I didn't wait to see what Rachel would do. The wards would hold no matter what she did. I took off running toward the house, Garrett waiting for me on the porch.

His face was grim, a shining ring of gold around his iris.

"Something's wrong with Caelan," I breathed, though he already knew.

With an iron grip on my elbow and a final look behind us, Garrett ushered us inside.

CHAPTER
Thirty-Four

Caelan lay motionless on my couch, a gold and green light swirling around him—Dad's magic. His eyes were closed, his claws back inside his hands.

Tess sat on the couch, huddled inside a blanket, eyes wide as she took everything in.

"What's going on?" I said as I came up beside my father.

"You were right." Dad's hands moved as his magic flowed inside the Shifter Lord's body. "There isn't anything wrong with him physically, but he isn't seeing or hearing the same things you are."

I didn't understand. Mom touched my elbow. "Caelan sees you as you are, but the words you say to him are not what he's hearing. He's being affected by a powerful illusion." She shook her head. "That's not quite right. A glamour, perhaps. Not a spell, not one we could easily sense. Someone extremely powerful has been messing around inside his head."

"Lugh," I breathed.

Dad gripped something at the side of Caelan's head and pulled, exposing a thin, wriggling line of grey and green magic. Simone, who had been silent this entire time, gasped.

"What is that?" she breathed.

"Magic," Dad said grimly. "From the looks of it, it's been inside him for a while."

I sank onto the edge of the coffee table, the ramifications of what my father had just said rattling around inside my skull like jagged rocks.

"How long?" I croaked.

A heavy, warm hand fell onto my shoulder and gently squeezed.

When no one answered, I closed my eyes and let out a long breath. "How long?" I asked again, a frightened tremble in my voice.

That sickly magic struggled in Dad's hands, but it was no match for a fae king. Once the last of it slid from Caelan's temple, Cernunnos crushed it in his palms, sending a plume of black and green smoke into the air before it disappeared into nothingness.

Silence lay heavy over my living room. Caelan's breath turned deep and even.

"Excuse me," I said, lurching to my feet. The hand on my shoulder fell away.

A broken sob escaped me as I stumbled to the back and barely made it to the toilet before my stomach emptied.

I don't know how long I was there, how long I was sick, or how long the words kept bouncing around inside my head.

None of it was real.

But that couldn't be right. Some of it was real, wasn't it?

All that time, all that effort. All those fights. When had it started going wrong?

And why didn't I notice?

"Oh gods," I whispered, backing away from the toilet to slump against the wall. My gaze landed on heavy, dirty work boots and slid up powerful thighs encased in worn jeans, a flannel shirt, and up to Garrett's face.

"Go away," I muttered.

"Is that an order?" he asked mildly.

I shut my eyes tight.

He sat down beside me. I cracked open an eye to see him adjusting his bulk to try to fit inside the bathroom. One leg was pushed up and the other was out the door, but he made it work.

"I know what you're thinking right now," he said, his voice low and gravely.

My sharp laugh echoed into the small space. "You can't possibly know all the things bouncing around inside my brain."

"You're wondering how much of it was real."

My lower lip wobbled, and I fought against the tears flooding my vision.

"You're wondering if Caelan ever loved you or if you've been targeted all this time." Garrett let out a heavy sigh. "You're wondering if you wasted your time on an illusion—if Caelan ever heard the things you've said to him or if he's always heard whatever Lugh wanted him to hear. What promises did you make to him? What does he think you've said to him?"

I held up a hand. "Stop," I croaked.

"Close enough?" Garrett asked.

I nodded miserably.

My…Enforcer? Guard? Whatever the hell he was, Garrett opened an arm, a silent offering of support. I stared at it for a long moment before I scooted into his warmth and lay my head against my chest. He wasn't Caelan. Hell, a few months ago we were at each other's throats, but the blood oath we'd taken earlier told me his offer was sincere, told me he was grieving right alongside me, and that he was wondering the same things I was.

How much of it was real? How much of it was a lie?

A sob bubbled from my throat. Garrett lay a heavy hand against the back of my head. "Caelan is still down. Your father and mother are guarding him. Let it out, Evie. No matter how this shakes out, you can't let this turn into a cancer that eats you from the inside."

The dam broke. My shoulders shook and hot tears flowed down my face. My throat hurt with the screams I'd been holding back, but I let them go. All the grief, all the pain, all the horror.

And when I was finished, and Garrett helped me stand and wash my face, I squared my shoulders and stared at myself in the mirror.

I'd walked through fire and hell and managed to build a life again.

I would not let this break me.

When I nodded to Garrett, he held the door open for me and led me back out into the living room.

The Shifter Lord was awake and from the way he was staring at me, way more lucid than he had been for a while.

"Evie," Caelan breathed.

He reached for me, but I couldn't bring myself to go to him. Instead, I sat on the edge of the coffee table. Garrett stood by my left, Simone on my right.

Caelan's stormy eyes looked first to his Enforcer and then to his Omega. He nodded once. "I deserve this, I suppose."

His eyes were clear, bereft of hatred or anger. Caelan mostly just looked…sad.

Defeated.

I glanced at Dad who was watching me with an unreadable look. "How long?"

"Hard to say exactly, but if I had to guess, I believe it was around four to five months. Maybe a little longer."

My brain worked furiously. Knowing was a relief. He had cared about me, at least. The timeline was after we had met, after he began his dogged pursuit.

"Do we know why?"

"You can ask me," Caelan croaked.

I couldn't even look at him without wanting to curl into the fetal position and die. Shifting my attention, I stared at him.

"I'm me again," he said softly.

Was he? Had I ever really known him? Would I like this Caelan? The doubt had settled inside me like an infection I couldn't shake. "Do you know how long?"

He shook his head. "The magic was insidious. I had no idea

anything was off until the last few weeks. I started feeling differently maybe two months ago. My sense of time has been messed up for a while. Decisions weren't as easy to make, almost like someone was pushing back against my own thoughts. I started losing patches of time. My anger was far worse than usual..." His voice trailed off. "Evie, I can't begin to tell you how sorry I am—"

I interrupted, knowing I wasn't strong enough to hear his apologies right now. "What happened to you was not your fault." I looked at Dad. "Can you show him my memories?"

Dad's lips tightened, even as his eyes filled with sympathy. "Are you sure?"

I nodded. "Does he remember everything?"

"He only remembers it as he saw it."

Grief filled me. "Show him. Go back four months and take whatever memories he's in. Show him the truth." I paused. "My truth, at least. I—I'm sorry if you see anything weird."

Dad snorted. "I'm immortal. Weird is irrelevant for all the things I've been exposed to." He held out his hand. I linked my fingers with his and opened my mind.

Dad touched Caelan's forehead.

Power burned through my soul as he rifled through the memories I had with Caelan and shared them with the Shifter Lord.

But he did something unexpected, he shared Caelan's memories with me as well.

And by the time he finished, I realized most of the last three months of my life had been a lie.

CHAPTER
Thirty-Five
CAELAN

She loved me. The force of that truth was a supernova burning inside my heart. Images and feelings flooded my mind, a much different truth of what I thought I'd known. She'd never questioned me, my leadership. She had always supported me. How had this all gone so wrong?

"Stop," I whispered, wrapping my hand around the fae king's wrist.

But still the images kept coming.

"*Stop*," I begged, unable to bear the truth any longer.

The look in her eyes when Rachel had shown up in her shop, as if she'd known this was the beginning of the end. I knew she doubted herself, questioned why she thought it might be the end. I saw the confusion and the will it took to shake that off, only to find out she was right all along.

But I hadn't taken that final step, even though Rachel had wanted to. Something inside me had fought back long enough to refrain, but I knew it was over. The things I'd said to her downtown seared through my soul.

I'd said horrific, unforgivable things to her, had made her doubt her power, her very self.

"Gods," I hissed through clenched teeth. "Stop."

"No," Cernunnos said. "See and know what you have lost."

And still the images kept coming.

Evie curled on her side, her dark hair spilling down her back as we spoke in the deep of night, even while knowing I doubted her ability to become the Lady my Pack needed and not sure why.

Evie smiling at me when I interacted with Seymour.

The hurt in her eyes when I reacted with anger over something that shouldn't have been a big deal.

The confusion on her face when I kept pushing her for a commitment she wasn't ready to give. The fury when confronted by the Lords to marry me or someone to leash her power.

Her fury at Ethan when he accused her of selling herself for power.

Everything had gone so terribly wrong.

And there were snatches of something else, something Cernunnos probably shouldn't have shown me, and I know the bastard did just to hurt me. Their conversations about suitable leaders, her father implying I wasn't and would never be good enough.

Turned out the sonofabitch was right, just not in the way he thought he was.

Evie's accusations of Cernunnos bringing Rachel to the Keep. False, but it didn't matter anymore, did it?

Evie curled on the couch with Rowan.

Jealousy raged within me, and it took every ounce of willpower I had to stifle the emotion. He'd done nothing untoward, did not steer her away from me. The bastard had been far more honorable than I had.

Cernunnos didn't stop until I had sagged in my chair utterly defeated. Only then did he halt the barrage, ending with Simone and Garrett's pledges to Evie, and the blood oath breaking our bonds.

How could I have fucked up everything so terribly?

Evie sagged forward, her lips pulled back from her teeth. Tears rolled down her face and dripped off the end of her nose, splashing onto the floor underneath her feet.

"It wasn't all a lie," I managed. "I love you. I've loved you since the moment you sent me that fuck you automaton."

But Evie was beyond hearing. She covered her face with her hands and rose on shaky legs.

My former Enforcer gripped her elbow to steady her. Simone gave me a look full of recrimination before he escorted her outside.

Cernunnos sat on the loveseat and watched me.

"How can I fix this?" I croaked.

A faint smile appeared on Cliona's face. "This may not be your fault, Lord, but it is your responsibility. Not everything was a lie, you're right on that point. But there were things happening before the influence that still would have brought you to this point or something close. Maybe you would still have your people beside you, but I am not so sure you'd still have Evie." She stood and touched my shoulder. "I am sorry for this, for what is happening now, but I do not know if you can fix it. Only time will tell. Love fixes many things. Give her the space she needs."

"The Shifter Lord has proven time and time again he is incapable of personal boundaries," Cernunnos drawled.

Cliona shot him a reproving look. "Perhaps this is one of the many lessons he will learn after losing so many precious things."

On that note, she followed Evie outside, Tess and Moira rising to follow behind.

Cernunnos didn't speak until the door was completely shut. When he did, the coldness in his tone froze me to the spot.

"You cannot love her like she needs to be loved."

I grappled for the right words. "Does that matter if she loves me regardless?"

The fae king snorted. "Asking such a question is an insight to your character and shows you would not let her go even when keeping her caged is slowly killing her."

"We will get through this." I had to believe such. If we

couldn't, what had it all been for? The pain, the fights, then the eventual joy of being together…it couldn't have been for nothing.

"You have much bigger problems than trying to win Evie back. Lugh might have returned Tess, but I know him well enough to know he does not give up so easily. What will you do to free your territory from his influence?"

I didn't give a shit about Lugh, but the god posed a danger I couldn't ignore. "If I couldn't fight this, how can I fight him?"

Cernunnos' hands glowed with power, a small ball of golden and green light forming inside his palms. When the light went out, a small charm rested there.

"A stag?" How appropriate.

He dropped it onto my lap. "Wear this. His illusions will no longer affect you."

"And my people?"

A flash of teeth. "Your people are your concern." He jerked his head toward the charm. "Consider this a one-off thank you for teaching my daughter what not to want in a mate."

The barb struck home. "She cannot know who you truly are and love you still."

Cernunnos chuckled and stood, his terrifying visage morphing to that of a thirty-something athletic man. Power still clung to him, and if I saw him on the street I would cross to the other side. Quickly.

"Evie takes after me more than she likes to believe. She has done terrible things for those she loves, and I do not see that stopping now that she is queen. Evie is now a target for everyone holding a grudge against me and my kind, as well as for those who seek the power she now holds."

"She is untrained. Why would you allow her to be crowned?"

"Evie is far more powerful than you, even *untrained* as she is, and you are Lord, are you not?"

I glared at Cernunnos. He merely smiled and strode to the door. "Wear the charm, if not for yourself, then for Evie. Regardless of everything, she still loves you. Love does not disappear overnight."

"That is why we will survive this."

His eyes swirled with ancient power. "Perhaps," he said, tilting his head in acknowledgment. "A fool's hope is better than none at all."

Mom finished her inspection of Tess and declared her well and truly free from Lugh's influence. Dad stepped outside not long after and passed out silver stag charms to everyone, instructing them not to take them off until Lugh's threat had passed.

"Give this to your dryad friend," he said, dropping an extra into my palm.

"What about mine?" I tucked the charm into my pocket.

Dad shook his head. "Your kind is resistant to magic, especially that of illusion."

I tucked that thought away. "Am I seeing what everyone else is?"

"Not quite. You see Lugh for who he is." He gestured to Moira. "Ask her what he looks like."

Moira overheard. Her brow furrowed, but she answered. "Enormous. Built like a raiding Viking. Tall, at least six four. Black hair, blue eyes." She shivered. "Super hot. Big hands and unshaven."

I stared at her. "Umm. What?"

Dad snorted. "Now ask Tess."

Tess still had the blanket wrapped around her. The shell-shocked expression hadn't lifted from her face. "He kinda looked like Ash, but with swirling blue eyes."

He didn't look like that to me at all. "His eyes were violet and pink, and he was tanned and lean."

Dad nodded. "He looked like one of those ancient statues carved from marble, correct?"

"He did. That's what he really looks like?"

"Yes. Your kind is resistant to his kind of magic, but it doesn't mean you are immune. Smaller tricks might get past you, so be on your guard at all times."

"You don't think he's gone?"

"Not at all. Returning Tess was his way of throwing you off his trail." His eyes took on a faraway look. "He is clever but fickle. Be wary of his offers. He will give you what you want, but it will cost you everything."

All I wanted was a week-long nap and a memory wipe. But killing Lugh would work, too. "We should go hunting then." There was something I wanted to do first, and I didn't want to give her the chance to slip away before I got the chance to pay her back.

Caelan stepped outside. Everyone stopped talking.

"I'm going to find Rachel," I told him.

He blinked in surprise. "You cannot kill her. Doing so will cause war—"

I held up my hand and interrupted him. "I don't care."

Caelan sucked in a breath. "Evie—"

"Even after all this, you still care too much about toeing the line." My voice broke. "She *ruined* us. And still you urge me toward caution." I straightened and squared my shoulders. "She is an enemy and shall be treated as such."

His upper lip curled, those stormy eyes flashing with gold. "You'd kill someone for stealing a boyfriend?"

"A boyfriend." I'd said the words, but they sounded cold. Dead. Unfeeling. "If that's all you were to me, if that's what you think this was, then I don't regret what I'm about to do."

Caelan crossed his arms over his chest.

"My words from before stand. Once you step off my property, you will not be welcomed back. Whatever this is between us is finished. Right now."

His jaw tightened. "And if I say it's not?"

"You hold no power over me, Lord. I am no longer one of your subjects. And even if I was, you don't get to say when a relationship is over."

I softened my tone. "I loved you very much. What happened to you is not your fault, but you have to admit there were problems beforehand."

"Me asking you to marry me is not a *problem*."

"Oh man," Dad said under his breath. "It's like trying to teach a toddler not to touch a hot stove."

"It is when you repeatedly violate my boundaries and refuse to accept the answer."

"This is it then?" His voice was a low, deadly growl.

I nodded. "But this isn't the time to have this conversation. We have two common enemies."

"And yet, you're going after Rachel first. Who's done nothing to you except take me away."

"She's done far more than that." I gestured at Simone and Garrett. "You should be angrier than you are. I've gained from her betrayal, and you've lost more than you'll ever know. But even if I hadn't, she will soon learn she cannot insult the royal family. And if she does, she will pay the price."

Mom nodded. "We cannot intervene, but we can keep your family and friends safe."

"I'm within my rights to answer these insults even though I've accepted the crown?"

Dad grinned. "He started this before you'd taken your rightful place as heir."

I smiled back. "Good. Let's go find Rachel first."

I turned to go, but Caelan reached out and gripped my arm.

"Don't do this. You'll bring the wrath of Europe down around my head."

I jerked my arm away. "Your fight with her is your own. She insulted the fae. Our fight is not with the Lords."

"She insulted you," Caelan growled. "Are you so prideful you'd resort to this criminal behavior?"

"Watch it," Dad warned. "You've been in power far too long if your kind do not recognize us for what we are. We allow you all of this," he said, sweeping a hand out to encompass the land. "None of it belongs to you. Be careful not to remind us of how easy it would be to reclaim it all."

"Stop talking," Garrett muttered under his breath, his focus on Caelan.

The Lord shot him an incredulous look and opened his mouth to reprimand him only to blink as he undoubtedly remembered Garrett was no longer under his command.

I shot Caelan a look. "I'm happy to involve the Lords in a fight if they pursue their petty grudges. They should be glad I'm removing someone dangerous from your territory, since you've been unable to."

He took a step back as a crimson sheen rolled over my iris, the Chimera magic thrumming through my bloodstream, eager to come out and show everyone what we were made of.

"Come," I said to my people. "Let's go hunting."

We found Rachel in the town square, sitting in the covered area next to Sirena's gelato shop. Moira laughed under her breath.

"This woman either has balls of steel or she's so fucking stupid I almost feel sorry for her," she said under her breath.

"Maybe both," I agreed.

The night sky was clear, stars sparkling high above us. A gentle wind kept the temperatures lower than normal, but I was too boiling mad to feel the cold. People milled about the area, though Rachel was the only one enjoying a cold treat. Most walked around with coffees or hot cocoas, steam milling lazily from the tops of their drinks.

She hadn't seen us yet, and the wind did us a favor by blowing our scents away. Sirena stepped in front of us.

The owner of the gelato shop was stunningly beautiful, and she knew it. Her dark hair was long and loose, flowing in waist-length lazy curls. She wore an emerald-green sweater that brought out the bright color of her eyes and dark wash jeans that hugged every dangerous curve.

"Hello, Evie," she said in her low, husky voice.

"Sirena."

She smirked. "We all know about your stunt earlier. Seems congratulations are in order. You managed to pull the wool over our eyes for a long time, but now the secret is out. How does it feel being a queen?"

"I could use a nap and a few weeks' vacation, and this is only my first day on the job," I admitted.

Sirena smiled, genuinely this time. "I'm here with a warning and a boon to request."

"I'm listening."

Sirena's eyes flicked over my shoulder and lingered on the party with me. Moira, Garrett, Simone, and my mother and father. At our urging, Tess had chosen to go home, and Ash had swung by the house to grab her, giving me the opportunity to pass him his charm.

He'd asked no questions, only wished me good hunting. Then he brought me in for a tight hug before bundling Tess into his car and hurrying off into the night. Moments after Ash left, Caelan had shifted and disappeared into the night without another word.

"Your quarry is here somewhere, sowing chaos behind the scenes. Something is off in the air this evening. Be careful. Not everything is as it seems."

Nothing I hadn't already known or expected. "Thank you."

Sirena nodded. "Please lure her away from my shop before

you confront her. I can't afford one more insurance claim." She grimaced. "Living in a magical town is hard on my rates."

I blinked at her. "That's your boon?"

Sirena shrugged. "Making gelato isn't keeping me in jewels, but it's an honest day's work."

"I would have done that regardless."

"Good." She inclined her head in a small bow and started to turn when she halted and looked over her shoulder at me. "I can feel your broken heart."

I stilled.

"Sometimes the wrong people interrupt our path with necessary lessons before the road curves and leads you to the one who was there all along."

My throat clicked, and I couldn't find any words.

Sirena grinned then. "But even if this doesn't happen for you, the best way to get over someone is to get under someone else."

Moira barked a laugh.

"Goddammit, Sirena," I growled.

She wiggled her fingers at me and disappeared in a shower of blue sparkles.

Rachel looked up from her gelato at that moment and froze.

I walked up to her and smiled.

"Hello, bitch."

Thirty-Seven

Rachel went pale. "It wasn't my fault! He—he made me! I didn't want to do it."

"Lie, lie, lie," Mom sang.

The shifter shot her a hateful look. "I couldn't say no. He would have killed me."

"Lie," Mom sang again.

When Rachel fell silent, my brows lifted. "No more excuses?"

"You're a half breed fae bitch and don't deserve to be Lady," she snapped.

If she knew I was a Chimera, she would have used it against me by now. Even after everything, Caelan had not betrayed my origins. I wasn't sure how to feel about that.

"I'm a half breed fae bitch queen," I corrected. "An important distinction there." I smiled down at her. "And you're a shifter with no morals or loyalty to anyone."

Simone stepped forward. "I spoke to your father earlier today."

I glanced back at her, my eyebrows lifted.

"Sorry. We were a little busy," she said apologetically before refocusing her attention on Rachel. "He said you did not have his permission to leave his territory, and he had no idea where you were."

Rachel swallowed.

"He was very interested to know you were over here spilling lies."

"So," she snapped. "He's my father. There won't be any repercussions."

"On the contrary," Simone said, her lips curving in a satisfied smile. "He has stripped your title and has told us to bestow whatever punishment we see fit."

Rachel sucked in a sharp breath. "Caelan would never allow that."

"Caelan is no longer under your influence."

At the narrowing of her eyes, I added, "Nor is he under Lugh's."

Once it hit home that she was well and truly without allies, Rachel rose. "And what shall my punishment be?"

Simone lifted a shoulder in a careless shrug. "Caelan will have to decide."

The look of relief she wore was short lived.

"After Evie decides what to do with you first."

Rachel took a step backward. "You—you can't do that. This is Caelan's territory."

I smiled. "The fae do not fall under his rule. I am well within my rights to do whatever I want to you."

"You'd start a war over losing Caelan?" she demanded. "Over a *man*?"

The difference in our thought process was astounding. "No, Rachel. This is not about a man. Caelan is only a small factor. You insulted my bloodline and me. You inserted yourself into a relationship you had no business being in."

Rachel started backing away, heading closer to the forested area and away from the town square, no doubt to make a break for it as soon as she could. Hilarious that she thought she could lose a Floromancer and two wolves in the woods.

Garrett and Simone fanned out on either side of me as we herded her away from Sirena's business. Mom and Dad stayed some distance behind them, and Moira had disappeared.

A frisson of worry went through me, but Moira would be fine. She was powerful in her own right and had survived this wrong. Taking on a simple shifter would be like eating cake for her. Easy peasy.

Rachel held up her hands. "I'm sure we can talk about this. My father will make amends. Is it money you want? We have plenty. Recognition?"

When I stayed silent, her pleas grew desperate. "Do you have a brother? We could join our families together."

Simone barked a laugh at that. "Evie would rather open a vein and slide into a warm bath than join your house."

"And we don't allow filth like you into ours," Mom added from the back.

I nodded in agreement. "Sorry, Rachel. We don't need money. We don't want anything you're offering. Why don't you stand your ground and take your licks like a real shifter would. Are you a coward?"

We were almost away from the business area of town. Only a little more to go.

But my luck had never been amazing. A golden-skinned male appeared in the middle of the street.

"Hello, Evie," Lugh said.

Rachel stopped in her tracks, a slow, wicked smile curving her lips. She turned to face Lugh. "Took you long enough."

The look he gave her sent a chill rolling down my spine. That was not the look of an enamored man. In that instant, I knew who was a greater threat to Rachel.

It wasn't me.

But Rachel, a woman who'd gotten by on charm and her looks all these years, smiled at Lugh and shimmied up to him, settling by his side. "Should we get away from here?" she asked him.

Lugh looked at no one else but me. "No. Everyone should see this."

I planted my feet into the earth. He'd chosen a spot that would make using my Floromancy a little more difficult, but not impossible. The woods were several feet away, and we stood on concrete. I could tear up the roads if need be, but it would take more effort than I'd like.

"Are you going to dazzle everyone with your illusions?"

A crowd had started gathering around the edges of our party, far away enough to run if they needed to, but close enough to hear our conversations. Not good. Mom turned and walked over to them, but Lugh continued on.

"I might be a powerful illusionist, but you know what else I can do?"

"Talk your victims into unconsciousness?" I asked.

He chuckled. "So flippant for someone with so much to lose."

Moira's dark head came into view on a rooftop of one of the businesses. It took everything I had not to scream at her to get away. She sank into a crouch and watched us.

Safe for now. That's all I could ask.

Garrett and Simone remained by my side, both standing loose limbed but ready.

"I've always had a lot to lose," I responded. "Nothing new about that."

My arm started tingling. The tattoos hiding my true heritage had been repaired some time ago, tweaked to allow me access to my magic when I needed, but still functional enough to hide my true nature from those who could distinguish one's nature from their scent. In a way, those tattoos acted as a powerful glamour to—

Oh. Shit.

Fuck.

My fingers started trembling. I clenched them into fists at my side.

Lugh's amused chuckle slid off my skin like oil. "I love it when a puzzle piece clicks into place."

Shadows rolled from Lugh's skin, his eyes flashing that strange pink and violet light. The murmurs of the townspeople rose, but no one had started running yet.

"Evie?" Garrett asked quietly.

"I'll sever the oath if you're not prepared to deal with this fallout," I whispered, hoping he would understand what I was talking about.

A loaded silence fell before Garrett swore. He walked over to Simone and whispered in her ear.

"The thing about having powers over glamour," Lugh said, "is that not only can I create them, I can also strip them away."

My arm turned into a fiery hell. And if that wasn't bad enough, Caelan walked up behind Lugh and made no move to interrupt him.

Rachel's laugh rang out. I sank to my knees with a hiss of pain, clutching my arm. On the surface, there was nothing wrong, nothing to account for the hideous pain, but inside, I felt like I was being torn apart.

Lugh wasn't only stripping away my glamour, he was stripping away my self-control, the tight leash I kept on my power. My Floromancy roared to the surface, roots tearing through the concrete as they reached for Lugh.

But the dark shield the god erected was too powerful to pierce. Thorns and poison slapped ineffectually against its surface, and I fought to shove down my Chimera magic.

"Come on, Evie," Lugh chided. "Don't you want your friends to know what you really are? All these people you've lived and worked with for so many years assume you're a simple Floromancer when you've been hiding so much more from them. Right under their noses." He made a tsking noise. "Maybe they won't care. Maybe they'll see your true form and marvel at your strength."

They wouldn't. We all knew they wouldn't. They would run and scream and hide until they returned with pitchforks and death in their eyes. My kind would not be allowed to live.

A familiar power stepped into the square, someone who'd chosen to not hide behind their human visage.

Barrett came up beside Garrett. "I overheard the commotion."

He crouched down beside me. "How can I help?"

"Think you can kill him?" I hissed.

Barrett examined Lugh. "A god?" He chewed on the side of his lip, and I almost laughed. He seemed so nonchalant about the entire situation. "Probably not alone. I can give him a good run for his money."

He touched my arm. "This is what's been hiding you all these years?"

A scream tore from my throat as Lugh turned up his power. To my horror, the tattoo began to flake away, my skin burning from the inside.

"This isn't ideal for you," Barrett said. "But our kind have been wanting to come out for a while. Maybe it's time to stop fighting what's living inside you and embrace it."

A broken sob bubbled from my lips.

He scrubbed a comforting hand over my hair. "You're the fae queen, Evie. And you can be ours too. Stop being afraid. I will fight with you."

The power roared through my blood, its sinister call a siren's song.

Barrett peered into my eyes and held out a hand. "I'll show you mine if you show me yours."

A pained laugh broke from me.

I took his hand and allowed him to help me rise.

Lugh's low laugh sent my hackles up. "Will she do it?" he mused to himself. "Or will she continue to run and hide?"

"Why me?" I asked.

Lugh shrugged. "Why not you? My enemy's daughter. A town full of luscious new things to explore. Secrets, wounded hearts, shifting loyalties?" Lugh shivered. "It's all a delicious soap opera."

The Chimera roared to the surface, tearing through my skin. Barrett's savage smile was the last thing I saw before I was no longer Evie.

I became a beast of legend and launched myself at Lugh.

Thirty~Eight

The screaming began seconds later. I shoved those sounds of horror out of my mind, focusing solely on the two people who'd caused such heartbreaking havoc in my life.

Lugh's eyes widened, as if he were surprised I'd chosen to shift in public and quickly stepped out of the way. Rachel's scream was horror movie worthy. She took one look at me and turned on her heel, hauling ass for the forest.

I was enormous, but I wasn't slow. Catching up with her took seconds. I caught her at the edge of the woods, hooking one sharp, black-tipped claw through her belt. She continued running like she was on an invisible treadmill until I tossed her up in the air and let her crash onto the ground.

A keening wail tore from her throat as she stared up at me. "D —don't kill me," she breathed. "I'll do whatever you want."

I wanted to kill her so badly, but she was weak and helpless beneath me. Killing someone like her was too easy. It felt… unsporting. The voice that came out of my mouth made Rachel piss her pants, the acrid scent of urine filling the air as I loomed over her.

"You are banished from this country permanently. You will

have no contact with any other Lords, and if you do, I will send my people into your home to carry out the punishment you deserve. They'll drag your sorry ass in front of your family and slowly rip you apart. When I let you go, you will head straight to the airport. Do not take anything with you, do you understand?"

She blinked up at me in confusion. "You're letting me go?"

"You are a waste of space, and your father's eternal punishment will be dealing with you." I released her and stepped away, concrete cracking under my massive paws.

"Th—thank you." She scrambled to her feet and backed away.

I snorted, fire blowing from my nostrils. Rachel paled and spun on her feet. In a flash of light, she was a small wolf running away.

Barrett and Lugh circled around each other.

"Two Chimeras?" Lugh's eyes were lit with a wild purple light. "If there are two, there must be more. How delightful. My contact mentioned only Evie and how important she was."

I stopped in my tracks, my mind working furiously.

Realization hits me like a truck. The *swans*. Fucking birds.

They were next on the list. I was going swan hunting, and I didn't give a shit if they were out of season.

Caelan had disappeared. Moira was nowhere to be found, and Garrett and Simone circled around the god and Chimera, searching for a way to assist, but doing so could get them killed.

Mom and Dad were lingering somewhere close, the comforting tingle of their combined power in the air around us. They'd step in if Garrett and Simone endangered themselves, but other than that, their hands were tied.

A real bummer, that. Dad could snap his fingers and turn Lugh into dust.

I needed to get closer to Lugh. Taking him down in a physical fight wouldn't be easy, but I had no plans to go that route.

As if he sensed my thoughts, Lugh blinked away from Barrett. A moment later he stood before me, wearing a slight smile.

He snapped his fingers and the world fell away.

We stood in a field of heather, the sky lit by the stars. I was back in my human form dressed in clothes I had tossed long ago. A cool breeze lifted my hair from my neck and my clothing…

I took a step back. "No."

Lugh's soft laughter sent the hair on the back of my neck standing up. He hopped up on a fence post and balanced on one leg. The bastard knew his illusions wouldn't work all that well on me, so he'd sent me back into my memories. These were real. I knew this had happened—this moment that changed the entire trajectory of my life.

"What do you want from me?" I asked, my gaze scanning the field for the man who'd destroyed me.

"You are queen," Lugh said. "Maybe one day I'll require a favor."

I searched for a way out of this place.

"You can't leave. This is not an illusion. It's a memory. We aren't in the town square, and we aren't in Scotland. We're inside your head, Your Majesty. Everything here is real."

"What favor?" I asked, my heart a pounding thud in my chest. He would be here soon. I wasn't in the field for that long before he showed up.

Concentrate, Evie. Be the bridge.

I took in a deep breath even as hot tears burned my eyes.

"Open ended," Lugh said, hopping from foot to foot like we were two friends hanging out in a field on a quiet Friday night.

"No."

"Mmm. Finn is not far away. He's eager to attend you."

I bit my lip so hard, I tasted copper. "Why are you doing this? You could have asked my father for a favor, left me and my friends out of this."

"Your friends and your father do not have the influence you do."

I stared at him incredulously. "My father has more power than I could ever dream of!"

Lugh's brow furrowed. "You really believe that don't you?"

He laughed and hopped off the fence post. "No. He doesn't. Your father was made from…" His voice trailed off and he squinted at the sky. "Primordial ooze, I suppose. His powers are limited."

I'd never seen my father unable to do anything.

"I see your doubt," Lugh continued. "But he is. He's more powerful than anyone you've seen, of course. Especially your Lord. A Shifter Lord is usually a one-trick pony, though there are a few exceptions out there. Cernunnos can walk through worlds and perform many feats, but his bloodline does not have the glory yours does."

I frowned. "You've got the wrong droid."

Lugh blinked. "What?"

Not a Star Wars fan, then. I moved a few steps closer. "You're betting on the wrong horse. I'm just a girl with a messed-up bloodline who keeps rolling around in shit and somehow coming up clean."

Footsteps were coming up behind me.

Lugh looked over my shoulder and smiled. "You're about to have company."

My body shook, the memory of what was about to happen playing in my mind over and over again. "Even if I could help you, I wouldn't know how," I said hurriedly.

I took a few steps closer to Lugh. "Please," I begged. "Please don't make me relive this."

Lugh smiled. "You don't have to. I'll need help in the future, and it's the kind of help only someone of your ilk can help with."

That told me I wanted nothing to do with the favor at all.

The footsteps behind me came to a halt. I looked over my shoulder.

Finn stood there, tall and handsome, moonlight gleaming on his dark hair. "Hey."

He shoved his hands in his pocket and gave me a sheepish smile.

It had started out so innocently. The way he looked at me that night made me feel like everything was going to be okay, like maybe I was worthy of love, worthy of someone staying with me when things got hard.

I couldn't…

I couldn't go through it again. I wasn't sure I'd survive.

And when the wind shifted and a slight furrow appeared on Finn's brow, when he inhaled a deep breath and that crimson sheen rolled over his eyes, I knew I'd rather die than experience that night again, even if it was only inside my head.

I threw open all the doors in my mind, power such as I had never known flooding through my body and launched myself at Lugh with such speed the god had no time to react. Even as he blinked out of existence, my hand was locked tight around his wrist, and I thought of the darkest, most dangerous world I could imagine.

I had no idea if it would work, if the image in my head even existed, but that was the theory of the universe, wasn't it? The theory of the fae, too. Multiple worlds stacked on top of each other. I'd seen it firsthand with my mother.

The bridge opened in my mind, every fae realm and more realms I never could have imagined available to me. All I had to do was reach out and touch them. I could go anywhere, leave my life and start all over in a new world of flowers and forests.

But I had no desire to leave Moira or Ash or Tess or my mother and father. My life was here.

But Lugh's wasn't.

The god ripped and scratched and tore at me, trying to loosen himself from my grip. His teeth were pulled away from his lips in a rictus of effort, but I held on like a pitbull on a tire swing.

Magic boomed in my voice, in the air around us. "YOU ARE NOT POWERFUL ENOUGH TO BARGAIN WITH ME."

Lugh cringed. "I'll take you out. Just…don't. Don't do this." Real fear flickered over his face, his voice a plaintive whine.

"TOO LATE."

I chose the coldest, darkest realm, a place of barren stone and monsters, of shadows and hate, and held it in my mind.

"Evie. No. *Please*."

A swirling vortex appeared beside us. When Lugh saw the world I'd chosen, he went feral. The god kicked and screamed, tossing out image after image that bounced right off my power. We were no longer in my mind. Where we were, I had no idea, only that I was the one in charge here.

"I'll do anything," Lugh begged. "I'll disappear and never return. I'll—"

"You kidnapped my friend. You brought in a woman to tear Caelan and me apart. You manipulated people I loved, and then you tried to manipulate me. You signed your death warrant the second you took me back to that field in Scotland."

"We can talk this out. You don't have to do this."

But I did. With barely a thought, I moved the portal closer.

Lugh let out an unholy shriek and pulled with all his power.

It wasn't enough.

With a heave of effort, I tossed Lugh through the portal and watched him slam against jagged, jutting stones. And when he turned and tried to stand, I waved and slammed the door shut, mentally severing his link to the bridge. The sound of his agonized scream echoed in the nothingness.

All the power I'd summoned drained away in an instant, and I found myself plummeting through nothingness.

Thirty~Nine

I have no idea how long I fell. A minute, an hour, a week, a year, but eventually I fell back into my body or my body fell back to earth. I couldn't tell. Exhaustion leached into my bones, and I groaned as I tried and failed to stand. Strong, warm, familiar hands reached to steady me, and I rested against a leanly muscled back.

"Is it over?" I slurred.

Dad stood in front of me, pride shining in his eyes. "It's over. Lugh is…" He shook his head.

"Gone," Mom said. "Wherever you put him, he can't be found." She studied me. "Is he alive?"

I lifted a trembling shoulder. "He was when I left him."

"Interesting," Mom said, a second before her eyes widened in realization. "Holy gods. It worked! You severed his link."

I nodded.

"Good girl," Mom said, pride shimmering in her voice. "We'll discuss in more detail later."

"Moira," I wheezed. "Is she okay?"

"She's perfect. Moira had a feeling Caelan would show up and thought her best vantage point would be the rooftop. She's been following him all night." Dad chuckled. "I thought you should know Rachel never made it to the airport."

I blinked in surprise. "Did Moira kill her?"

Mom slowly shook her head. "No. Caelan did the honors."

I let out a low whistle. Pins and needles made my feet and hands numb, and I could barely focus on the conversation.

A sharp inhale of breath at my back. I patted Garrett's hand. "It's fine. We'll figure something out later. She deserved it."

But the voice spoke, and it wasn't Garrett. "I'm sure she did," Rowan drawled.

I jerked and craned my neck back to peer up at him.

"Hi." His hazel eyes held nothing but concern for me.

"Hi," I breathed.

"We should get you out of here soon."

At that moment, my eyes took in the massive crowd we had standing around us. Everyone was staring at me. Very few of those stares were friendly.

"Yes," Dad said. "About that. Word spread rapidly about your other form."

Barrett stepped up beside my father, clothed in a pair of sweatpants and a t-shirt. "If I were you, I'd lie low for a little while. It's going to take some time for people to get used to Chimeras being back."

I swayed again, the blood draining from my face. People I knew stood in that crowd, staring at me with hostility and distrust.

"What about my shop?" I whispered.

"Moira has already said she and Ash would step in."

"Where is she?"

"Caelan is wounded. She's taking him back to the Keep." Mom reached out and touched my face. "He's going to be okay. Moira said to tell you she loves you and she will see you soon."

"She knew," I breathed. Moira had known what would happen the moment I revealed myself.

"We all knew how badly it might go. But take heart. Word will soon pass of your fae identity as well, and they will know to harm you is to bring down the might of the fae upon their heads." Mom touched my chin with her thumb and smiled. "Rowan's arrival was fortuitous. He has agreed to allow you into his territory for an extended stay if need be."

Fortuitous might have been Moira giving him a heads up, but I held my tongue.

"I didn't have to allow anything," Rowan said. "Evie has always been welcome in my lands."

"You take my heart with you, Lord," Dad said. "I entrust you with her safety."

"I can obviously take care of myself," I grumbled, my cheeks heating at his words.

My vision was down to two pinpricks of light. Nausea roiled in my stomach.

"Evie?" Rowan's grip tightened.

"I'm fine," I whispered.

Mom fished in her pocket and held out two glowing bottles to him. That hellish portal formula to take us from here to wherever in a blink. "Take these," she said. "Courtesy of Moira. She swore me to secrecy, so maybe consume them away from the prying eyes of everyone."

Even Cliona's angry glare didn't phase the townspeople still watching me with preternatural intensity.

"Go now," Dad warned. "Danger stirs in the air."

Rowan scooped me into a bridal carry and shot through the town square. I wanted to protest, but I was so very tired.

I tried to stay awake, but exhaustion weighed my entire body down. My eyes finally drifted shut, safe in the circle of the Lord's arms.

Epilogue

I awoke in a green paradise, the soft scent of honeysuckle and jasmine gently nudging me from a deep, restful sleep. My eyes opened to a canopy of glossy leaves and vining flowers. The room, or wherever I was, felt warm and a touch humid. I shifted and flowers fell from my shoulders and hair.

A hand appeared in my vision holding a saucer and a mug of steaming coffee.

"You're finally awake." Rowan pulled a small stool over and settled onto it.

His shaggy brown hair was messier than usual. His hazel eyes were bright in the natural light, but dark circles made crescent moons under his lower lashes. A five o-clock shadow graced his cheeks and chin, and he was dressed more casually than I'd ever seen him in grey athletic pants and a black t-shirt.

"Hi." What else could I say?

A faint smile crossed his lips, and he waited for me to sit up before he handed me the mug. I inhaled and let out a little grunt of happiness.

"All I have is dark roast."

"It's perfect." I took a sip. "Oh." This was not Keurig coffee.

This was fresh-ground, real coffee that hadn't been stored in a hot warehouse for months at a time.

A faint, tired smile touched his lips. "This isn't Joy Springs, Evie. You're in the PNW. The coffee is good here. Better than good."

He was watching me with an intensity that made me uncomfortable. I sipped my coffee and watched him back.

"You're safe here," he said after a moment. "In case you were worried."

I was, but the worry wasn't for myself. "Are you sure it's not dangerous for me to be here?" The last thing I wanted was to endanger Rowan or his people.

"I might be the friendliest of Lords, but it does not mean I'm weak."

"Rowan, I didn't mean to imply anything of the sort."

An uncomfortable silence fell between us. "You know, don't you?" I might be safe, but for how long? With Rowan's knowledge, he could make life extremely difficult for me, no matter where I went. But who was I kidding? After my stunt in the town square, word had probably already spread like wildfire. It was only a matter of time before all the other Lords knew my secret, too.

"I've suspected for a while and waited for you to trust me enough to tell me yourself." This smile didn't reach his eyes. "I have to admit, I got the surprise of a lifetime when I pulled into downtown and saw a beast the size of a two-story house walking through town."

He snorted. "No. *Two* beasts. It looked like something from a Halloween movie marathon."

"I'm sorry," I whispered. "I didn't want you to think any differently about me."

"So, a Chimera." He scrubbed his hand over his jaw. "I assume there's a story there."

When I stayed silent, Rowan nodded. "Ah. Okay. For what it's worth, I'm sorry."

"I can leave. You don't have to—" I set the mug down on the small table and went to swing my feet over the edge of the bed when Rowan stood and put a warm hand on my thigh.

I stilled.

"Stay." His eyes beseeched me. "I won't promise to protect you because I know you don't need my help, but I will stand by your side for as long as you need."

I swallowed hard. "Things are different now. Everyone will know what I am. I wouldn't want any harm to come down onto you for harboring me."

Another faint smile. "I don't care."

My eyes squeezed shut as relief and worry roared through my veins. "You should. I'm a Chimera. My blood is tainted. I'll never—"

Rowan cut me off. "What did you say?"

I blinked. "I'm a Chimera—"

"No. Tainted? Who said that to you?"

Caelan. I'd forgotten about Caelan being wounded. I hadn't even thought about him when I'd woken up. Even though there was an ache inside me where his presence had rested, the thought didn't bother me as much as it should have. Something to think about later when I could make more sense of everything.

Rowan's jaw tightened. "That sonofabitch."

"No. It's okay. He's right." The words held a sound of defeat I'd never heard myself utter before.

Gold rolled over Rowan's eyes. "Evie," he breathed. "No one, no matter how powerful they perceive themselves to be, has the right to say that to you. You are perfect exactly as you are."

Tears burned the backs of my eyes. "But what about my children?"

Rowan lowered his head and took a deep breath. His frame trembled with rage. When he looked at me once more, his hazel irises burned with power. "They will be as wonderful as you are."

Rowan's hand still gripped my thigh. I laid my hand over his, soaking in his warmth and power. "Thank you."

We stared into each other's eyes for a long moment until he pulled away and stood. "You have free rein of my territory. The Keep rests on fifteen hundred acres."

I gaped at him.

"There are orchards and gardens all maintained by me and a small staff. You're in the greenhouse which is attached to my main residence. I do not keep a regular staff, but there is a chef who comes in three times a week, and a cleaner who comes once a week. The fridge is stocked, but if there's something specific you want, please tell me and I will make sure you have it."

He opened his mouth to continue.

I interrupted before he could say anything else. "Rowan."

The Lord stopped talking, a faint blush of color on his cheeks. "Yes?"

I touched my hand to my heart. "Thank you. I won't stay too long. Just enough for the furor to die down. Then I'll get out of your hair and figure out my next steps."

Gold rolled over his irises once more. "Evie, you are welcome to stay forever if you wish to."

Without waiting for a response, he turned and left me alone in his greenhouse. He didn't push for answers, didn't pepper me with questions. Rowan simply took me out of danger, put me in a safe place, let me rest, and brought me wonderful hot coffee when I woke up. I stared at the doorway for a long time before I let out a long, slow breath and tried to calm my panicked mind.

Oh man. I might be in *serious* trouble.

The Aftermath

"Lugh was our best option," the god said.

"Her magic is unpredictable," another said. "We should have better prepared for the eventualities."

"Few are immune to illusion," yet another pondered. "There is much we don't know about the Chimera."

"Brute force might be a better solution next time." The first rubbed his hand over his chin, a thoughtful expression on his face.

"Will there be a next time?" the second god asked.

"There is a reason the Chimera numbers were decimated almost to extinction all those years ago," the first mused. "They can be killed."

"They seek power," the third added. "That cannot be allowed to happen."

Another stepped into the room, a being of golden light. "Fools," she chided. "She is not merely a Chimera. You could have chosen any other place to begin your idiotic war, but you failed to do even the most basic homework."

"We can take on Cernunnos, too," the first said, fury in his eyes at the chiding tone in the last arrival's voice. "Now that his daughter has taken the crown, his power begins to wane."

"And Cliona?" the woman drawled. "The goddess who is not

only Queen of Banshees? She is perhaps even more dangerous than Cernunnos, and she is Evie's mother. None of you understand how fiercely a mother will fight to protect her young."

The third scoffed. "She hated the girl up until recently. The only reason Cliona is with her now is because of her crown."

The last god shook her head and let out a soft laugh. "If you believe that, you are far more foolish than I expected." She reached over and tapped a pale pink nail on the stone table the others sat around. "The new queen commands loyalty far easier than any of you wretches ever have. Be happy with the peace the fae and mortals have obtained and do not continue pushing to reclaim your former glory."

"And if we do not?" the second asked, a more thoughtful look on his face than before.

A wicked smile curved her lips. "Then you will find out exactly how far a furious woman will go to save those she loves."

Keep reading for a look at Book Seven
Shift of the Wild

Shift of the Wild

BOOK 7, SHIFTER LORDS

When Mother Earth comes calling, you'd better answer the door...

Evie has asked for sanctuary with Rowan, and he's accepted, allowing her into his territory to lick her wounds and heal. Things are good for a while, until strange occurrences start happening when Rowan and Evie are together.

With similar magic, Evie feels like she's found a kindred soul in the Shifter Lord, but other forces are about to shatter her rest and respite time and plunge them both into a type of danger they've never experienced before.

Someone is poisoning Rowan's land and attempting to wrest his territory away from him. This time, the Lord isn't powerful enough to win. But the enemy never counted on the fae heir and Floromancer's visit, and one thing Evie is very good at is fighting for her friends.

Complications arise when Caelan figures out where she is and attempts to bring her home. But Evie never abandons a friend, and certainly not for a man who wouldn't fight for her when she needed him to. Between fighting Caelan and fighting for Rowan, Evie is mentally and physically exhausted, something the enemy jumps on.

When the chips are down and the future looks grim, Evie will have to muster all her strength and power to fight back for Rowan, for herself, and to save Mother Earth from total annihilation.

Even if she loses herself in the process.

The Magical Soapmaker Mysteries

The Goddess Chronicles

Vikings of Virginia

The Deadicated Matchmaker

About the Author

Sheryl likes cake too much and can be found hoarding it while hiding from her children in the pantry closet.

Follow her on Amazon at: https://www.amazon.com/S-E-Babin/e/B00J1J236A

A small press bound by the belief that every voice matters.

Sign up for our newsletter to learn about new releases and more.
https://oliver-heberbooks.com/subscribe/

Follow us on social media:

facebook.com/oliverheberbooks
instagram.com/oliverheberbooks
amazon.com/oliverheberbooks
youtube.com/@OliverHeberBooksPublisher